ANNAH TORCH

THAT GUTSHOT SMILE

Jim DeFilippi

BROWN FEDORA BOOKS

ANNAH TORCH   Jim DeFilippi

ANNAH TORCH: THAT GUTSHOT SMILE is a work of fiction.

Copyright © MMXX by Jim DeFilippi and BROWN FEDORA BOOKS.

ALL RIGHTS RESERVED.

Published in the United States by BROWN FEDORA BOOKS.

See: www.brownfedorabooks.weebly.com

Photo credits: James DeFilippi III, K. L. Wallace, and Book Covers

ISBN: 9798566463612

First Edition

10 9 8 7 6 5 4 3 2 1

ANNAH TORCH   Jim DeFilippi

[X]

A Brown Fedora Book

ANNAH TORCH   Jim DeFilippi

To Shoshanah and Jack, double-barrel inspiration

ANNAH TORCH   Jim DeFilippi

"In ceremonies of the horseman, even the pawn must hold a grudge."
—*Bob Dylan*

ANNAH TORCH   Jim DeFilippi

Chapter One

The three men had arrived at the edge of these Woods before the sun, a sun that remained cold and weak through the morning, a sun that was now tracking them through the trees to their right, to the east, hanging a few degrees above the horizon and ten degrees below freezing.

Pushing their way through the brush as they moved forward, the three could have been mistaken from a distance for a children's story—the big papa bear, the momma bear, the little bear—and that was the order they were walking in. The burdock prickers and puncture-vine grabbed at their booted ankles as they moved. Scrub brush and bittersweet leaned in from each side of the trail, brushing across their Carhartt trousers as they went.

The air was mixed with the gray sight of their breath as they mouthed out whispered comments about trails and tracks, blazes and deer beddings, but mostly about the freezing tips of their ears and fingers.

"No gloves," the big man in the red and black checkered lumber jacket had commanded. "You don't want to see big daddy buck standing there, fifty yards off, and you got to pull your faggy little mittens off your fingers there, with him and his rack disappearing like a shot, his white ass a-bouncing, never to be heard from again. No, it's no faggy fucking mittens for us, boys. That ain't the way."

The two others had nodded, not looking at each other.

They were in a section of the forest that the locals called Topher's Woods, an area whose boundaries had never been delineated nor sketched out. The name wouldn't appear on any topographic maps or elevation surveys, surveys with their meandering circles holding numbers from 1500 to 1900 feet above sea level.

The surrounding and shadowing woods were backdropped and sketched with basswood and beech, quaking aspen, holding tandems of color—

ANNAH TORCH   Jim DeFilippi

gray and yellow birch, black and white ash, some black and pin cherry, scattered red and sugar maples. The red oak displayed pointed leaves, pointed like the arrows of the red man who had first settled this area, the white oak's leaves were rounded at their edges, like the bullets the white man had used to conquer.

Among the bigger trees, which were spaced out like the Pretorian Guard—each conceding space to another—were the thin saplings and second growth sprouting of the lesser flora.

A week ago, last weekend, a light tracking snow had covered the deer trails, which would have been perfect for the three men's purposes, but the big man had a weekend flooring job and Horn's daughter had hockey.

Both of the two smaller men were carrying Savage Trophy Hunter XP Bolt Action hunting rifles, slung over their right shoulders. Each had his right thumb hooked across the stud attached to the sling swivel.

The big man seemed to be carrying no weapon at all, just an African-mahogany box, the size and shape of a briefcase. It was tucked safely beneath his right arm, and was being cared for like a treasure.

A cold, late-season rainstorm had passed through during the night, and now they heard a far-off clap of thunder. The big man put his hands together and looked up to the sky, mimicking prayer. "Our Father, who fart in heaven." He looked at the two other men, who each gave him a forced laugh.

When they had reached a clearing—ten yards across, smooth and soft except for a few windblown tree branches, acorns and twigs, white birchbark on green moss—the big man silently held up his arm, like a squadron leader or a buffalo scout sniffing the presence of the enemy or a target.

The big man—Elton "Ruck" Ruckhouser—undid the top button on his lumber jacket. His two companions were wearing camouflage jackets atop their matching canvas pants, one a thirty-four length, the other a twenty-eight.

Ruck squatted down and laid the mahogany box upon the cool green moss. Both of his two buddies had pointed at the box with a smile as they had climbed into the six-pack Dodge that morning, but both times Ruck had grinned back at them and said, "I'll show you in the woods."

ANNAH TORCH　　　　　　　　　　　　　　　　　Jim DeFilippi

Now he was ready to display his prize. His thumbs flipped open the two copper clasps of the case and pushed up the monogamy lid. The three men leaned over the box in a tableau of adoration.

Ruck gently touched a large, pristine silver revolver, nestled in its form-fitted velvet indentation. He lifted the revolver from the wooden case and he moved it about in the air, displaying it for the congregation to admire. Sun rays bounced off the barrel and muzzle as the gun was twirled.

The small man, who seemed to be half the size of the other two, asked quietly, "That case come with it?"

"Got it special."

They were gathered around the weapon like it was the first child born to a proud father. The revolver was huge for a handgun, heavy but perfectly balanced, its body and barrel brushed silver, the rubber handgrip a deep black and formed into the shape of a shooter's grip. Attached to the gun's top was a black metal gunsight that looked like it belonged on a rifle rather than a handgun. The sight's eyepiece was directly above the edge of the grip, its front end ran half the length of the imposing barrel. The barrel was completely smooth and even, with no indentations to indicate where the cartridges were housed or how many there were. A tiny eight-digit serial number was stamped into the side of the weapon, just below the barrel, along with a tiny logo that appeared to be an incongruously smiling cartoon face.

A tiny splotch of paint speckled the front sight. Its color was orange, but somehow it hinted at blood red.

No introductions were needed. All three men knew the gun to be a .480 Ruger Super Redhawk. They gazed at the weapon. No one spoke for a while.

Finally, the smallest of the three whispered, "You got yourself one scary hand-cannon there, Chief. My God, that it is for sure."

Ruck nodded, trying not to grin.

The middle-sized man, only a bit shorter than Ruck and weighing about the same, added, "Most guys would be nervous just to carry this thing, much less to pull. Shitless. What'd you say it's chambered in again?"

ANNAH TORCH   Jim DeFilippi

Ruck whispered, "I got .454 Casull."

"You didn't go with another one?" the man asked. He was called Horn —although that wasn't his given name. "Why not? How come?"

Ruck kept his eyes on his gun. "Stronger this way. Dumps all the energy right into the target, right there where you want it to end up. With three-hundred fucking grains of spray. Couldn't get torque like that with some other chambering."

The little man, nicknamed Box, was showing agreement with a series of quick nods. When Ruck had finished speaking, Box added, "Could stop a bear, dead on, if we ever encountered one, huh?"

Ruck had let his smile creep across his face. "I hope we do. Bear would shit his pants he sees me holding this thing."

Horn was shaking his head, making sure he was doing it questioningly, not dismissively, as he asked, "I don't know there though, Chief, that .454 Casull must've cost you more by a lot, no? You could've gone cheaper, right, you think, and still be nothing short of dead? You're still going to stop anything comes your way, am I right? Either way, they're dead is dead."

Ruck shrugged. "Yeah, sure, I could've gone a lot of different ways —.44 Mag, this .454, 10 mil auto, and yeah, the .480 Ruger, but this one is better. The .454 gives it some oomph. Two thousand foot-pounds of energy. I need oomph, okay?"

Box was agreeing, "That's got a shitload of oomph right there, that's for sure."

Ruck said, "Listen, this'll be the only hand cannon I'm ever gonna carry. See? For life. Blanche, she don't know shit about what it cost, so, so what, right? You must a noticed, woman's got a mouth on her, but it's almost never my mouth. She knows everything else in the world, but she don't know this, okay?" He was grinning and massaging the barrel of the gun with his fingertips.

Box and Horn were kneeling on the damp moss. As the three men surrounded the case, gazing down at the weapon like it was the Christ Child and

ANNAH TORCH   Jim DeFilippi

they had just come in from the East, a woman appeared from the Woods behind them. Her voice was calm, natural, almost soothing. "Boys."

Her approach had been silent. Her voice startled them.

&&&

She had come onto them with the stealth of a hunter. The woman was tall, over six feet, exquisitely muscled. And preternaturally beautiful.

She moved with the power-laced confidence of a jungle creature. A while back, her only friend had started referring to her as "a white panther," until she had abruptly put an end to that foolishness. Yet she had moved through these woods as a jungle creature would–like a leopard, a panther.

These Adirondacks were no jungle, just a National Forest of 6.1 million untamed acres of old-growth forest, holding over 10,000 lakes, 30,000 miles of rivers and streams.

She lived there.

She stood looking at the three men. No one spoke.

Her black North Face wool cap was pulled down, grazing the top of her eyebrows, with a black scarf pulled up to cover her nose, so that only two inches of her face were visible. But even these few exposed inches showed her appearance to be remarkable.

Her auburn hair held streaks of ashen blonde, it was silklike and long, long enough to reach the mounds that her breasts were making beneath the black zippered parka.

Her eyes could be listed as hazel, which bespoke a bluish-green tint, but the flecks of blue and of green in these eyes never joined together or mixed, each color merely stood separate from the other, like proud trees against an untroubled sky.

A strand of white shirt was visible between the face scarf and the zipper of her parka. An orange piece of plastic–maybe a whistle or a lighter–was hanging from her right shoulder.

ANNAH TORCH   Jim DeFilippi

Ever since this woman was fourteen, and even before that, upon seeing her, men would begin entertaining impure thoughts, feeling mildly perverted, staving off hints of temptation, as they whispered to one another, "Stunning."

&&&

Finally she called out to the three startled and staring men. "Fellas, do you think you should be here? Have you checked the season, on the calendar? The manual? It's over. So I would have to say no. No, you should not."

As far as they could see, she was carrying no weapon.

Ruck looked at the others. He was the one required to speak. He let the Redhawk drop to his side as he attempted to dig up some bravado. A woman. Without a gun. And yet something about her...

"Hey there now, Goldilocks, who the hell did you come from? I mean where. The hell. You got lost in the woods here, baby girl? Where the hell you come from anyway?"

"I spring from the very earth itself," the woman called to them, grinning. "The earth is my mother. My father was from Bayonne, New Jersey."

"What? Whose mother? What? Who the fuck are you, out here all by yourself?" Ruck was looking around at the trees, then back to the woman. "Pardon my Cherokee tongue, but I guess I been hanging around with these jokers too long." Ruck was smiling toward his companions, but the smile seemed forced. "Makes me seem somehow crass, don't it? But you heard the word 'fuck' before, I bet, don't you? Sure you do. I bet you even been present a few times when that word was going on, huh? The fucking, I mean. What's your name then, Sweetie? Tell me."

"I am Smokey," she told him, and she waited. Then she added, by way of clarification, "the Bear."

Ruck was gaining a bit of confidence. She had startled them, that's all, coming up on them so quiet and sudden. "Okay then, well, Smokey the Bear, you don't look like no Smokey the Bear I ever seed. You the first Smokey managed to get me a bit hot under the collar. And all over too. Down there in my pants, a little bit."

ANNAH TORCH   Jim DeFilippi

Ruck was grinning at his two buddies, who were making sure to grin back, trying to make it look genuine. Ruck was tapping the muzzle of the Redhawk against his leg, in rhythm. Telling himself, "Just impatient. Not nervous."

The woman was shaking her head. "I have been on your track, not liking what I see here."

"Oh no, you don't, huh?" Ruck asked her. "What don't you like about it, about us? We get to know each other, I'm sure I could get to like you. You carrying a weapon? I don't see one."

The woman held up both hands in the symbol of being unarmed. "You men even leave the meat, you leave the carcass to rot, the poor thing. To rot. This cannot be, fellas. You are all finished doing that."

Ruck was still smiling, still tapping his new pistol against his pants leg. "We take the rack, Sweetheart, cause that's the best part. And talking about racks, and best part, what you got hiding there underneath your overcoat there? You got yourself a rack you want to show us all?"

Ruck turned and grinned proudly at his two cohorts, without saying anything but telling them, "Ain't I a card though? Ain't I something?"

He turned back to the woman. "Show us something you got, why don't you, dear?"

He brought the weapon up and began waving its muzzle, pointing it menacingly across the top of her thighs a few times. Then he aimed and held it directly at that spot where her legs met.

The little one, Box, started to say something, probably a tentative warning, but Ruck cut him off. "Shut up. She's all mine, this one."

The woman took her eyes off Ruck and his gun, to look over at Box. "Are these guys pals of yours?"

"Huh?" What?"

She asked, "You hang around with these two? Do you?"

ANNAH TORCH   Jim DeFilippi

Box looked confused. He asked, "Huh?" a few more times, and then told her, "Sure. Sure I do. What of it?" His voice sounded unsure, reedy.

The woman's voice changed. "You three should leave now, and not return. I will be watching."

Ruck's voice was getting louder. "Take off your jacket, missy. Stay awhile. We're not going nowhere. Get comfortable for us, why don't you? Take it off. We'll start with that." He was waving the pistol at her parka and smiling.

She stood without moving.

"I mean now, girl. Off. On the ground with it, missy. We want to see your rack."

"You can stop calling me that."
"Why not? You're a missy, aren't you? So why not?"

The woman stood for a moment—the only motion was in her eyes, which were sweeping across the three men, seeming to reconnoiter the scene. When she spoke again, her voice was softer, almost inviting. "Okay then, all right. You win. You could do things to me, sir. Anything at all. I guess I would not mind too much."

When Ruck was grinning, his yellow teeth stood out against the dark tan of his face. "I like that. Anything at all, huh? That's very lovey-dovey of you. Anything, you say, huh? Me likes the sound of that. So, what'd you got in mind? Show me something."

"There is one thing men do that I like it. This one certain thing."

The big man took a step closer to her. "Oh yeah, what's that called, missy? What'll you have?"

"I find it difficult to say. With the others so near. Step closer please." She was beckoning to him. "Step to me, sir."

The big man took a step toward her, lowered the revolver a bit, so that it was aiming at her feet. "What do you want to do to me, huh? Let's begin there."

"Closer. Lean your head to me. The others should not hear my words."

ANNAH TORCH　　　　　　　　　　　　　　　　Jim DeFilippi

The big man twisted his head a bit, his left eye just a foot away from the woman's lips. His smile was widening.

She said, "I would like it if you would..." and then she started mumbling gibberish, making nonsense sounds. "The donst is glaven, yiel da shot?"

Ruck's brow curled up in confusion, his head leaning more towards her, as he struggled with trying to decipher the woman's words. What was she saying to him?

While continuing to quietly whisper her mumbled, foolish sounds of gibberish, but simultaneously moving so quickly that none of the men could detect any movement, much less understand it or react to it, the woman's large left hand grabbed the Ruger Redhawk and gave it a violent twist that sent a cracking sound through the clearing and across the woods—maybe a wrist, an elbow, an entire arm had been snapped—as she formed her right hand into the shape of a metal spear and she drove the point of that spear at least an inch deep into the big man's left eye socket.

It took three seconds before any of the three men could process what had just happened.

Then the big man began squealing like a wounded pig, sinking to his knees, holding both hands to his face, blood leaking out through the fingers of his left hand.

The woman had stopped making her nonsense sounds as she watched him crumble. The big man was on the moist ground, writhing, whining, holding his hand up to where his eye had been. He tired to bring the wounded arm up with a cupped hand, but the dislocated limb could not be moved. He was crying loudly and kept repeating, "Jesus Christ, Jesus Christ."

The two other men stood paralyzed by the sudden and brief violence. It had been too unexpected for them to form any reaction.

"Lay your rifles on the ground, fellas. Box, I have a job for you. I want you and this other guy to pick up your pal, and drag him on out of here. Try to stuff his eyeball back in if it's still dangling. Go home and do not ever approach these Woods again. I will be on watch. In the future, my head will be on swivel."

ANNAH TORCH   Jim DeFilippi

The two men could not force themselves to move. They were not doing as they were told. The big man's eyeball indeed seemed to be dangling from the socket, but neither of his buddies could look at it, much less attempt stuff it back in.

The woman's voice had returned to a natural timber, but with a drone of command. She was looking from one to another. Ruck was still kneeling on the ground, crying, saying just "Jesus" now.

"Put your rifles on the ground." When they still didn't move, she barked the word, "Down!" at them. Each man leaned over and placed his rifle on the ground cover. The big man was using the sleeve of his lumber jacket as a compress.

The woman picked up the Ruger Redhawk, turned away from them, and threw the gun over a thirty-foot high white pine. It was a prodigious toss, almost un-human, but she did not impress herself with its might. She turned back to the two men, who were still standing, frozen. "Pick him up now. And carry him on out. First, push his eye back into the socket, if the thing is still attached."

The two men leaned over and picked up their friend, held him dangling, each on a shoulder. Ruck was still whimpering. Blood and pus were covering his face. The eyeball was hanging down by a tendon. Neither man would make an effort to touch it.

"Leave the Woods as they were found." Box steadied his wounded friend as Horn ran back to picked up the revolver case, not looking at the woman.

"Leave the case. It's a nice wood."

Horn dropped the case and ran back to his friends.

When they were fifteen yards away from the woman, they paused. The little one, Box, turned around to face her over his shoulder. "What...how did you learn to do something like that? My God."

The woman was leaving the clearing, heading back into the brush. She called back to them, "I studied under Moe Howard."

ANNAH TORCH   Jim DeFilippi

&&&

Chapter Two

One man was grinning, pointing, the other was looking down.

"Doesn't it get lonely, wearing a shirt like that?"

"My daughter bought it for me, all the way from Hawaii."

"Oh. And she's got eyesight, does she, she can see, she's not handicapped or anything at all?"

"I put on something quick, anything, just go, when I got this call."

"So Goofy's interested?"

"Oh, sure, she'd have to be, why not? So, what'd we got going...?"

"Take a look."

The two men stood staring at the body. Neither of them spoke for a while.

Finally, Protski sucked in a deep breath. "Oh, my, my God. Just what got done here? What are we looking at?"

Gumm answered him, "Yeah, it's grizzly and it's gruesome all right. Pretty bad, for all my years."

"Can you tell me about it?"

"Let's the both of us take a look around for a while first. Then we'll talk."

&&&

The two men had been meeting at crime scenes—not quite like this one —for many years. Their respect for each other had heft and depth and time going for it. Each man could be defined by the things he was carrying—with Sergeant Simon L. Gumm, it was a racing form and a stack of loser stubs. Leo Protski—a horny bitterness toward his ex-wife.

ANNAH TORCH Jim DeFilippi

Gumm was shaped like his name, round and sagging, a wad of chewed bubblegum.

Protski's shape was a giraffe's neck. When he wore a red necktie, Gumm would pretend to mistake him for an outdoor thermometer.

Protski was a special investigator for New York State District Attorney Sarah T. Guffleberg, a woman with burgeoning political aspirations—Albany or the Senate, maybe even beyond that.

Even though Protski's boss pronounced the "u" in her name as short—as was she herself, five-foot-two—her name had been facetiously mangled into "*Goofle*-berg," and she was referred to as "Goofy" by her staff and the police department, when she was not in the room.

Protski accepted the appellation for his boss. Her auspices gave him unchallenged entry into crime scenes like this one, as well as related festivities. It was all he lived for, his entire content of his current life—his wife was gone, his daughter out in Ohio, so it was just crime and crime scenes.

Boss-lady Goofy had politically intwined herself into being a sort of consortium coordinator for five neighboring upstate New York counties: Oswego, Onondoga, Oneida, Herkimer, and Cayuga. With Albany County as the home base. When anything interesting occurred, Goofy would send Protski to the scene with his nose for crime and eye for potential publicity. He liked working with the crime part, while Goofy hungered for the publicity.

The other man, Gumm, had no rabbi like Goofy shepherding his career. He was still just a sergeant, an old one, although acknowledged to be the most effective homicide investigator in the five-county area. His official title was Head of Major Crimes for the White Leunge New York Police Department. He was stubborn and sarcastic and ornery, he knew that he would never make any pay-grade above Sergeant. This didn't bother him, as long as he was given charge of any of the more "interesting" homicides within White Leunge's jurisdiction. Local crimes of the major variety had become an endangered species, but the weekly paycheck stretched far enough to cover his gambling debts. Sometimes.

ANNAH TORCH   Jim DeFilippi

Gumm was never without his tiny spiral notebook, tucked into his suit-jacket's breast pocket, even though the younger cops had told him a thousand times about apps like "Voice Memo."

"I don't want to hear my own squeaky voice talking back to me, acting like it knows a lot more than I ever will."

&&&

For ten minutes, these two men went silent, as they separately surveyed the crime scene before them. Each man kept looking, looking, studying, their eyes sweeping across the longview of the room, then moving in close to check the minutia from a few inches way. Looking at everything, touching nothing.

The blues, the photographer, the print and forensic boys, all stepped aside, stayed out of their way as the two men each focused and studied.

Finally, Gumm took hold of a young patrolman's uniform sleeve, guided him over to Protski, and said, "Inspector, this young man was first through the door. He and his partner did a nice job of preservation for us. They're both rainbows, but they seem to know what they're doing already. I give them credit."

The young patrolman's face creased into the start of a smile.

Protski looked at him and nodded. "I've never heard Sergeant Gumm compliment any officer in blue before. Or anyone else, except maybe for a tout, out at the track. You should feel honored."

The patrolman's smile widened and he said he was. Then he overstepped himself with, "It's like Agatha Christie a little bit in here, huh?"

Gumm gave him a stink-eyed look. "Who? What?"

The young patrolman swallowed and said, "You know, the mystery writer. This is a closed-door mystery, right? I mean, we took off the door, we came in, entry, there's no window, see, and the body's in the chair there, so..."

Gumm cut him off with, "Yeah, locked door mystery all right, I heard of that, books, but let me ask you this, patrolman, is it still much of a mystery involved if the percolator is locked in the same room too, along with the vic? Now there is that then, huh?"

ANNAH TORCH   Jim DeFilippi

The patrolman lapsed into an embarrassed silence. The two were staring at each other.

Gumm brought the tiny notepad up to his face.

Protski broke the silence. "Don't worry about his percolator gag, patrolman. Sergeant Gumm thinks he's cute, he always refers to them as 'percolators,' as a gag. Now that I think of it, Sergeant Gumm is kind of cute himself, isn't he though?"

They both looked at Gumm. The patrolman looked down at his shined brogans and said, "I guess so."

Gumm hiked his thumb in the air, indicating to the young cop that it was time to get lost, so the officer did. Gumm stepped in closer to Protski, made a concerned face.

Protski asked him, "So you got the killer already?"

Gumm nodded. "Yeah, Ponch and Jon over there found her asleep in the rocking chair, bad bruise on her forehead. Couldn't wake her up. Bruise was probably from the kick-back from the gun. The shotgun of malice was lying across her lap. It's been bagged and over to Evidence, where they'll probably lose it. Ugly gun."

"Yeah?"

"Sawed off at the handle and the barrel. Something a gangster would use, be found with. Scarface or somebody. But these two were college girls. Not even. Prep school girls. Where's she going to get a sawed-off from?"

"Over and under?"

"Single barrel."

Protski asked, "Where is she now?"

"The percolator, you mean?"

"Great gag, it never gets old. Yeah, her. The perp."

"Taken to be booked. Murder, I suppose. Probably M-One. That's Goofy's call. It gets a bit trickier when the perk is out of it, drunk or deranged,

ANNAH TORCH Jim DeFilippi

of course. She was lights-out when CHIPs came though the door. She hasn't come to yet, they'll call me. First, she got taken to St. Jeans, for emergency treatment. Then over to Leunge Memorial, where we'll keep her until we can get her caged up. Usually then it's usually in court for the next morning, of course, but this poor murderer-girl might not be awake yet for that. So I'll take out the complaint and get her arraigned right there, whether she's up or down, conscious and competent or sloshed and sleeping."

"Can I see her, talk to her?"

"Be my guest. But bring anything you might need for a seance, though."

"My crystal ball."

"Your balls are crystal now? You *have* been divorced a long time. I hear they got treatment for that, though. Medication. But anyway, we don't want to wait on the arraignment. She's already under arrest, so even if she wakes up, she's not going anywhere. That way we've got control of the hospital room, and we can delay the arraignment if we have to."

"She have a lawyer yet?"

"Don't know. How could she? She will though, soon enough, I heard already her family's pretty rich."

"And you Miranda'ed her, of course."

"Oh, yeah. But it's like reading your rights to a zombie. But that's the way it is with every arrest now. They don't listen to what the hell you're talking about. They see it all the time on television."

"A rich daddy, family? What's her name?"

"Amanda Silver. Twenty years old. Deceased is—was—twenty-one. Name...?" Gumm took a look at his note pad "...Dede Constaghulia, you want I should spell it out for you?"

"No, I'll get it later, from the booking."

"Must be Italian."

ANNAH TORCH   Jim DeFilippi

"Wow, Italian huh? That's why you've been proclaimed the McGruff of all Crime Dogs, Sergeant, it's observations like that. So the name's Italian, is it, Kojak?"

"Stop it, you're embarrassing me."

The two men walked over to the body, which was splayed out across an upright recliner. The midsection was gone, just a mass of bloody flesh and tissue. They stood looking at her for a while, their faces frozen in contemplation and amazement.

Finally Protski asked, "You ever seen anything this bad, all your years?"

Gumm answered, "Yeah, sure, but only if they been floating in the canals for two months. Or in the woods, chewed up by animals. Or run over by an Amtrak. But just shot, just an hour ago? She's been cut in half, almost."

Protski asked, "You think she'll come apart once the M.T.'s come to pick her up? I'm only being half-serious."

"M.T.'s? No, no M.T's needed, buddy, that ship has bailed. Out. It's our forensic pathology facility will come cart her off."

Protski leaned in to look closer at the body. "You can call it a morgue, Sergeant, that'd be okay."

Gumm was looking down at his notepad, a bit longer this time, distracted. "Yeah, they might need two body bags instead of just one to get her all collected and carted off. So I guess some jobs are even shittier than this one I got."

Protski leaned back away. "What do they say about that painting of Kramer, on *Seinfeld*. 'It's a loathsome sight, and yet I cannot look away.'"

"Yeah, something like that."

Protski pointed at the face. "And she's smiling, she really is. I swear. That's...that's...I don't know what that is."

"Yeah, she is. Everybody looks in and tries to see something else, tries putting a different spin on it, but she is, that dead girl is smiling at us. That's the only way you can see it."

ANNAH TORCH　　　　　　　　　　　　　　　　Jim DeFilippi

Protski leaned over the body again. "So she's sitting there, a couple seconds away from being shot to death, her assailant's five feet away..." He turned to Gumm, "Five feet?"

"That's what forensics was guessing, something like that, not much farther off than that."

"So someone she knows..."

"Her roommate. The landlord recognized them both."

"So her pal is standing right in front of her, she's pointing a sawed-off shotgun at her belly, the gun gets fired, it goes off, she's still smiling, grinning, her eyes wide open, well, open, not wide, kind off half closed-down and calm, aren't they, don't they look?"

Gumm leaned in to check the eyes. "Yeah, dreamy, what they used to call 'bedroom eyes,' didn't they? Lauren Bacall or somebody. Like she seems to be enjoying herself. Must take a lot to get this gal upset, huh?"

Protski was shaking his head. "So she was drunk then? Drugged up maybe?"

"Could be. Must be. We'll see."

"Crazy."

Gumm said, "Yeah, both. Maybe drunk, drugged, and crazy. So the gunner is standing right here, where I am now, she's an executioner, and she lets fly with the sawed-off–boom, boom, boom, gonna cut you right down–buckshot to the belly from a couple feet away. Cuts the poor thing in half. She's what, maybe a hundred-ten pounds to begin with? The buckshot she took in must weigh more than she does."

"And she's grinning, like she's watching Eddy Murphy, enjoying herself. The autopsy's gonna say drunk, or drugs."

"Even that wouldn't account for that smile. Maybe she didn't think her friend really meant it, wasn't really about to do it."

ANNAH TORCH   Jim DeFilippi

"Still though, to be smiling? No, not some twenty year old school girl, maybe never saw a gun before in her life. Grinning, looking down the barrel? No. Well, maybe the autopsy will tell us something."

Gumm said, "Don't count too much on that. More than likely be a sloppy job. Cobbler the Gobbler is halfway out the door to retirement. Some say he retired five years ago, they just haven't had the heart to tell him. But once a body like this has been blasted from the chest on down to the knees, by a .12 gauge shotgun, close range, the manner of death becomes fairly evident."

&&&

Two days later, the two old friends were again discussing the murder, this time each holding cold coffee and talking across the top of Gumm's desk. Gumm was holding his tiny notepad in one hand, flipping and checking it from time to time. In his other hand he was holding coffee in an Aqueduct mug.

Protski's coffee was in a cardboard cup, stained around its edges.

Gumm half-read, half-extemporized. "A locked bedroom of a condo in White Leunge, New York."

"White Leunge, White Leunge, the city of sin, on the bottom rung."

"No window. Exterior lock installed years ago by mistake. The girls didn't mind it, for privacy. Only two keys, fit both the regular lock and the deadbolt on the door. Both locked tight. Both keys were found in the room. One on the dead girl's dresser, it's her bedroom, the other key in the shooter's pocket. On a chain along with her car keys."

Protski asked, "Interviews?"

"Cursory. Friends and classmates got concerned, they weren't around, like they disappeared. Neither one answering their phones. Didn't think they might be bar-hopping. They call it 'clubbing,' I guess. Asked the landlord, who smelled trouble. I'll read you his quote." Gumm leaned in to study his notes. "Says, 'I smelled trouble. And this trouble smelled like a white sock you used to wipe your ass with when nothing else was handy.'" Gumm looked up from his pad. "Guy must be a poet. Should be writing crime novels. So he's troubled, he

ANNAH TORCH   Jim DeFilippi

calls the precinct. The two patrolmen popped off the door, the barrel of the pivot hinges, found the two girls, one dead, one unconscious, they called it in."

Protski said, "So Dede is gutshot while sitting in her brown, upright recliner, in her own bedroom, by her own roommate. And they get along?"

Gumm answered, "The friends say mostly they did. Could be. Couple of squabbles about guy friends and who's doing the laundry, and who's stealing food out of the fridge, but nothing serious. The classmates said they were maybe out at a party or friend's house or something. Then they must've come back here."

"To hold an execution. Her father's some rich guy, you said?"

"Yeah, the percolator's dad is. Something like eightieth richest dude in the whole world, it's been calculated. Right ahead of a couple sheiks. So that's why Goofy's so interested?"

Protski said, "Sure. Ink. Plenty of money and blood here, so sure she is."

"This one'll spill a lot of ink all right."

"Chelsea girls, right?"

"Chelsea. Yes, both vic and she. Roomies."

"Rummies?"

"Maybe that too, we haven't heard. Maybe somewhat. Probably just at a school girl level, nothing more significant."

"School girl, but she comes armed with a sawed-off shotgun."

"I don't know. Seems excessive."

"How about what the pathologists are saying?"

"Not much. Not much to add. Dead girl's blood was still partially liquid, but that's not surprising. Recently done it. Shelf life."

Protski asked, "Anything interesting with hair? Blood? Stomach contents?"

"Stomach contents? We got no stomach contents, pal, because we got no stomach. Maybe we better call in an upholsterer, instead of an M.E. There was more blood and stomach contents on the upholstery than in her. For Christ sake."

"Yeah. Jesus."

"Daddy's rich. He could get it dry-cleaned I suppose." Gumm checked his notes. "Murder weapon was a Filipino-Blitzer .12 gauge shotgun, been sawed off."

"You ever hear of it?"

"No. Filipino. Must've come from the Philippines."

Protski gave a phony impressed nod. "Filipino, from the Philippines. Your mind sometimes, Sergeant Gumm, a steel trap, it works so fast, sometimes I can't even keep up with your thought process."

"Try."

&&&

Gumm's packet—made up of his own report, plus forensics, plus related reports, all prior to the complete formal autopsy—gave a formalized structure to the bloodbath with no attempt to stem the bleeding.

The decedent had been identified as twenty-one year old Dede Marie Constaghulia.

Over one-hundred pellets of .12 gauge shot were removed from the decedent's body. These pellets had done extensive, nearly completely destructive damage to all major internal organs. Any significant portions of the heart, lungs, liver, bladder, kidneys (right only), stomach and non-lower interments, were categorized and filed. The brain was intact, as were lengths of the lower intestinal tract.

The utilized weapon was identified as a Filipino-Blitzer .12 gauge shotgun, break open, single-action, single shot. This long gun's original barrel length, according to the manufacturer's published dimensions, was 28 inches, but the barrel had been reduced, probably by means of a handheld hack saw, to a length of 10.2 inches. Handle, six inches.

Three clearly delineated finger prints were lifted from the muzzle of the weapon, along with numerous matching prints on the stock, muzzle, trigger and finger guard. All of these belonging to the assumed assailant, Amanda May Silver.

Very minor discolorations were found on the decedent's facial area (mouth, jaw, cheeks, and neck), as well as on both elbows, right forearm, small of the back, thigh and lower leg. In all likelihood, these were incidental ramifications of the shotgun wound.

Due to the severity of the wounds, no vaginal trauma nor indications of sexual activity could be ascertained.

Absolutely no defensive wounds were found on any of the decedent's extremities. Arms, hands, legs and feet all were in healthy, non-traumatized condition, commensurate with a twenty-one year old female in good health and physical condition.

All blood splatters and traces were commensurate with the victim's O-Positive sample. No other blood types were discovered on the body.

The decedent's body did not appear to be moved subsequent to the lethal assault.

Matching blood samples were found on the decedent's blouse, bra, panties, as well as on her left sock. The right sock was missing, but was probably inadvertently overlooked by investigators at the scene.

Very small pieces of what were probably a cellphone and wallet were collected and preserved for future examination.

The other individual discovered at the scene was twenty-year old Amanda May Silver.

As previously mentioned, this individual's fingerprints were prominent and multiple. A gunshot residue test was performed and showed that the individual had recently discharged a firearm.

ANNAH TORCH — Jim DeFilippi

Bruise on forehead. Comatose.

The scene of the crime was a twenty-two foot by fifteen foot bedroom, containing only one single portal for entry or egress. The room was discovered as being highly secured at the time of law enforcement's entry. Both the normal lock and a deadbolt lock (highly unusual for an interior passageway door) were fastened, necessarily from the inside of the room.

What remained of the body was discovered in a semi-sitting position in a large recliner. The chair was in an upright position and the original faux leather had been covered by a brown, corduroy-like slipcover. Skid marks on the carpet and flooring indicated the force of the shot had driven the chair back a distance of six to ten inches.

No footprints were found on the carpet or on any wooden sections of the flooring.

Two-hundred and twenty-seven evidence items were sampled or bagged. Only thirty of these were turned over for further examination.

Over four-hundred and eighty DNA and Y-haplotype tests were performed, but only seven of these yielded DNA which was deemed useful for comparison.

Eleven tests are being run from samples taken from the interior of the room. Early indications have the samples being commensurate with either the victim or with Ms. Silver.

&&&

ANNAH TORCH   Jim DeFilippi

Chapter Three

As Head of Major Crimes, Detective Sergeant Simon Gumm was reviewing his notes and the case study reports detailing the murder of Dede Constaghulia, while seated in the windowless and hopelessly dank interview room of the White Leunge New York Police Station.

At the same time, twenty-two miles and minutes to the north-northeast, the parents of the all-but-charged-and-convicted suspect, Amanda Silver—Johnnie and Grace Silver—were enjoying a crustless Quiche Lorraine for brunch. The dish had been prepared for them by Andre Andreescu, a chef that Johnnie had stolen from the *LeCing* restaurant in Paris the year before, where Andreescu was know as "King of the Caramelized Onion."

The couple was enjoying a tasty *Alsace Riesling* along with the quiche, a wine which they agreed was a perfectly concentrated and fruity complement. As they munched and kibitzed, they were working on drawing up a list of where their daughter might submit her college applications for next year.

Her grades at the Chelsea Two-Year Preparatory Academy for Young Women—both the website and the letterhead always used the school's full traditional title—coupled with the cachet of the Silver name and the cash in the Silver pockets, would be sufficient to assure their little girl's entry into any university in the country. Or overseas. Germany and Rome, and of course Britain, had some magnificent schools.

When the quiche had been devoured down to a single slice, and the bottle of *Riesling* nearly to its dregs, both parents agreed that a domestic school would be best. Keep their little girl within this hemisphere. Brown? One of the Ivy's? Stanford?

As they were trying to decide if even the West Coast was too distant, a phone call from an anonymous source within New York State District Attorney

ANNAH TORCH   Jim DeFilippi

Sarah Guffleberg's office informed Johnnie that their daughter had been arrested for murder and was being held at the White Leunge General Hospital, in a comatose, perhaps even catatonic state.

After clicking off his phone without a parting, Johnnie grabbed his wife by her arm and rushed her out to the five-car garage, where Johnnie fired the chauffeur on the spot for being drunk, and then drove his BMW-X7 luxury SUV away from their 3.5 million dollar A-frame, glass-front chalet, to the White Leunge Memorial Hospital, where their daughter was being held by the authorities until she could manage to regain her consciousness and would be booked.

After being told at the reception desk that they would not be allowed to see their daughter, Johnnie bolted up the staircase two steps at a time to the third floor of the hospital, where its CEO, a middle-aged woman wearing a turban from her cancer treatment, reiterated the denial, with apologies, and asked them to please be patient.

Johnnie Silver was not a patient man. As Grace was Googling the area's top legal counselors, and his corporate staff was tossing out suggestions and names over the phone, Johnnie drove well beyond the legal speed to the law offices of Howard "The Weasel" Wyzell, where they were told that Counselor Wyzell was unavailable, not on the premises at this time. With no plans to return for the day.

Silver's cellphone quickly reached the lawyer at his home, which became the couple's next destination. It had been less than forty-five minutes since they had received the powerfully disturbing phone call, with most of that period of time spent in travel.

As the SUV sped up the American elm-lined, half-mile driveway of Wyzell's white colonial house, in the upscale town of Langley, New York, Grace Silver's eyes fixed on an incongruous sight in the side yard, pressed up against the tree line. She silently wondered about the only eyesore on the three groomed acres of property—an abandoned Herkimer School District bus, flaking its yellow paint and standing on eight mud-sunk cider blocks, wobbling in the wind like it was levitating.

ANNAH TORCH   Jim DeFilippi

The frantic couple was met at the door by the somewhat disquieted lawyer, who graciously led them into his living room and offered them either coffee or a drink. They both declined both.

Even when in a flustered state, which was rare, Johnnie Silver made sure to let everyone in the room know that they were in the presence of greatness. Wyzell had seen this attitude before—maybe not to this extent—so he accepted it, and the three sat.

Johnnie told the lawyer the story of the phone call, and of their morning thus far, and how the whole thing was completely absurd—their daughter would burst into tears if her car hit a squirrel.

Grace Silver's job apparently was to offer sidebars and footnotes to her husband's narrative, without interrupting its flow. She managed to squeeze in the fact that they had purchased their chalet in Watervliet—"Is that how you say it, with that cute little V in the middle? We live there, I'm not even sure"—in order to be close to Amanda while she attended Chelsea Prep. "We're both sort of a couple of helicopters, I suppose," Grace explained with a teary smile. "Amanda doesn't seem to mind us though. At least she never says anything about it." With a raised finger, her husband cut off her brief soliloquy.

When Johnnie's retelling of the entire *pasticcio* reached its end—or at least was on Pause—Wyzell asked a few brief questions, leading off with the most innocuous one.

"So you live in Watervliet?—yes, you said it right, Mrs. Silver."

"Not really," Grace explained, "Just to visit. I mean, we have a house there. For homecoming, parents weekends, some field-hockey games, things of that sort. We love being just a few towns over from Amanda's schooling. That way we get to see her. We like it here. People seem nice." Grace's husband again raised a halt-demanding finger.

"Mr. Silver, you're a high profile personality, of course. But I never read about your getting a place around here. I didn't know."

"No, right, it's all New York City and Vegas and the Vatican in the papers, on the news, right? We keep it quiet. Our day-to-day whereabouts.

ANNAH TORCH Jim DeFilippi

Almost all of our domestic holdings we keep quiet."

Grace said, "Our homes."

Johnnie said, "Houses. So as not to be bothered. We do that quite a bit. The anonymity you have to pay for, but it pays off in the long run."

"Sure," Wyzell agreed. "And your daughter, she's a second-year student at Chelsea? Was? Is."

"Yes, that's right. The Chelsea Two-Year Academy–blah, blah, fuck all that. But we're clued in enough to know that the Chelsea Deuce would help get her accepted to any college we chose. That she wants."

Grace forced a wet smile and said, "We wanted to do things the right way. We didn't want to end up like those movie stars on TV, you know?"

Wyzell nodded. "That college admission scandal stuff."

Grace started to respond, but her husband cut in. "We just want to get this nonsense dispensed with, over with, so that our little girl can get on with her life. I of course have a teeming army of lawyers to help me out on this, all of them frothing to get their hands on the project, many of them criminal—I mean criminal law experts, not actually criminals—well, some of them might be that too." Silver allowed himself a sardonic smile.

Wyzell asked, "And now you want me to join the team?"

"Exactly. The people I've talked to say you would be our best choice. Plus, it never hurts to have someone local involved. You know the territory, the jury pool, God forbid it comes to that, the prosecutors, the judges, which ones will—well, never mind—you know the lay of this land, I'm sure."

"Yes, I do."

"Your first job, naturally, is to get us in to see Amanda. The hospital staff over there is all Nazis and Fascists. Ridiculous. So you would be on the team. Actually, the project manager, something like that. I was told this morning that the local District Attorney can be a barracuda bitch, excuse me."

"Sarah Guffleberg. Well, she can take quite a bite out of things."

"So I've heard. Well, I don't want her getting her pit-bull teeth into this. Not into my little daughter. Amanda's a pussy cat, Counselor, a doll, she's an innocent little Barbie Doll. She could never have done anything remotely like what they've been accusing her of. So, Counselor, Mister—I can call you Howard —are you in, or not? Money of course plays no part in your decision. Whatever."

Johnnie waved a dismissive hand. Then he mentioned a few more particulars he had gotten from his Albany mole, the one with a planted ear in Guffleberg's office. The names "Gumm" and "Protski" were mentioned.

Wyzell told Johnnie that he knew Sergeant Gumm and had met Protski a few times. Both pro's, as far as he could tell.

In her nervousness, as the two men were talking, Grace Silver had risen and wandered over to the louvered windows. She was staring at the bizarre skeleton of the yellow school bus out there, across the lawn.

Wyzell was studying Johnnie, and told him, "You should know, Mr. Silver, that I don't, won't, subvert the truth for my client. Ever."

Johnnie: "That's fine, I wouldn't want you to. The truth will always out."

Wyzell assured Silver that he would take Amanda's case, and he would move it right to the top of the firm's priority list. Almost before he could get out the words of acceptance, Silver had thanked him, started to shake his hand before he remembered the distancing, had bowed slightly instead, and left the house with Grace in tow.

Silver often instructed his underlings, "When you got what you want, leave the room."

&&&

As he watched the BMW's taillights disappearing down his driveway, the lawyer thought about how the wife had stood for a while just staring at the abandoned school bus in the side yard. She had wanted to ask about it, he was sure, but she had not. Visitors rarely came right out and mentioned the eyesore, and Wyzell never explained that the bus contained a kerosine radiant heater,

ANNAH TORCH   Jim DeFilippi

plus one parka-wrapped occupant on the coldest Adirondack nights of the winter.

That evening, through a series of short and laser-focused phone calls to friends and associates, coupled with a storm of Google searches, Wyzell created a portrait of his new client.

This billionaire was usually referred to not simply as Johnnie, but as Baby Johnnie.

In the 1950's, his father—the original Johnnie Silver—along with a puppet named "Li'l Gloopy," was a moderately popular television and stage performer. Before that, the two had hosted a local radio show for a while, with Johnnie Senior resenting the fact that the radio audience couldn't appreciate the delicacy of a good ventriloquism act. "If I move my lips, who the hell is going to see it, who the hell cares, you know?"

With the help of a theatrical agent who was fairly aggressive when not dead drunk, the older Johnnie and Li'l Gloopy managed to get on Ed Sullivan a few times, back when it was still called "The Toast of the Town." The two even made a few movies with Mickey Rooney. Mickey would joke that he and Gloopy were a pair of "pint-sized partners."

But the original Johnnie's talents as a ventriloquist were dwarfed by his talent as a businessman. He bought and flipped his agent's agency, then took out a partially subsidized business loan to gain partial ownership of a local Los Angelas radio station, then another, then more and more stations, three newspapers, a string of movie houses, along with a collection of businesses that were completely unrelated to show business.

Eventually the original Johnnie made a tidy fortune for himself, and became a respected figure in the business world, although he never lost his love of the stage, and was said to have been performing the original act with Li'l Gloopy for his loved ones in his bedroom at the age of eighty-seven when he died of complications from pneumonia.

His son, to be known henceforth and forever as Baby Johnnie, along with Li'l Gloopy II, temporarily tried to follow the Dad's show business career, but this Silver was more interested in business than in ventriloquism, explaining that both professions involved deceit, misdirection, and dummies.

With no misgivings or self doubts, at the age of thirty-three, he retired from "the stage" and concentrated on his business holdings. He eventually became something like the eightieth richest man in American, even silently owning the majority share of an NFL club which he didn't root for. Most years his earnings were increased by at least a million dollars from his tournament winnings in *Pai Gow* poker, his sole recreational passion.

Recently, he had been ingratiating himself and his businesses into some sort of secretive negotiations with the Vatican in Rome. People suspected it had something to do with using his business acumen to help the Church crawl out of the financial hole that the priest-altar boy scandals had drowned it in. No one knew for sure.

Along the way, Baby Johnnie had married the former Grace Esterhorn, who at the age of eighteen was already presenting herself as a scion of the prominent and opulent Esterhorn clan, which had made its money in cattle, oil, and facial cream.

Their union had produced one offspring, a daughter named Amanda, who at one time was blessed with riches and beauty, but now lay hospitalized and catatonic, and was being arraigned for murder.

&&&

That evening, Baby Johnnie Silver conducted a lengthy Zoom meeting with his corporate legal team, discussing bringing Wyzell on for the criminal defense. Each of the lawyers agreed that bringing "the Weasel" on-board was a smart move, not only because he was the best locally at what he did, but was nationally considered "one alligator of a litigator."

Johnnie recontacted his mole in D. A. Sarah Guffleberg's office. His money allowed him to keep permanent "eyes and ears" in legal and financial institutions throughout the world. He called this one his "A to B Mole," delivering information across the top of New York State, from Albany to Buffalo.

ANNAH TORCH　　　　　　　　　　　　　　　　　　　Jim DeFilippi

Not his most important or prominent insider, but a competent and dependable one nevertheless.

What Johnnie was told indicated that the Weasel was the perfect choice for this hornet's nest. In the courtroom, he never resorted to lying to the jury, never tried to convince the "magnificent twelve" that his client was innocent when he was not. Despite what is seen on television and in the movies, this defense usually backfired and resulted in the defendant being dealt with more harshly. Instead, the Weasel would admit upfront to his client's commission of the crime, but then would go about avoiding or decreasing jail time by using a pulsating combination of references to things like: extenuating circumstances; diminished mental capacity—which could range from unbridled but justifiable emotion to deep seated or temporary insanity; self defense; and one of the most overlooked exculpatory elements in any jury trial—sympathy.

Although aurally related, the term "Weasel" was somewhat of a misnomer for Howard Wyzell, Esq. In fact, he was one of the few high-profile defense attorneys who had the respect of both prosecutors and the bench. His practice had grown into a hugely successful endeavor, with satellite offices both down in New York City and over in Boston.

As Wyzell often reminded people, the subset of the entire firm was its recognition that neither the Constitution of the United States nor any state or local statutes allowed the defense attorney to lie or prevaricate for his client, guilty or innocent.

Honor above all. A defense attorney's only goal was to get his client the best possible deal from the State.

From what Baby Johnnie had learned thus far about his daughter's case —her roommate's body, the locked room, the shotgun—this could be Amanda's best legal stratagem.

&&&

ANNAH TORCH   Jim DeFilippi

Chapter Four

Howard "The Weasel" Wyzell's burgeoning practice committed him to a forty-five to fifty hour workweek, but his level of success allowed him to choose when those hours would occur. So he generally drove into his office very early in the day, in the dark, by doing so avoiding the clog-ups on the New York State Thruway. He returned home with a bit of sunlight still hovering in the sky, even in the winter. His house was in Langley, New York, fifteen minutes from downtown Albany, if he could fly there on a crow.

A few mornings each month on his way in, he would pull off the Thruway and park in a commuter lot where the exit ramp bumped into State Route Twenty. He would lean over and take his Trailblazer flashlight from the glove compartment. From there he would walk about thirty yards down a deer path, sweeping the light-beam before him. He would arrive at the rotted stump of a mountain maple, which was standing in the center of a copse of younger, healthier birch saplings. He would bend down, reach into a carved-out small cubbyhole behind the peeling bark of the dead tree, and he would pull out a beautiful black hematite stone.

Heart-shaped, the stone was the size of a baseball, but looking like it had been reshaped by the bat of some baseball player from the juiced-up era, Barry Bonds or Sammy Sosa. The stone had been highly polished, its black surface so shiny it appeared to be wet, with a streak of red running diagonally across its slightly convex front, like the heart had been pierced by Cupid's arrow. The shade of black approached the darkest found in nature. The red was the vibrant red of a pileated woodpecker.

Wyzell would place the stone on the flat top of the stump, like a busboy setting a dinner table, and then head back out of the woods and into his day's work.

ANNAH TORCH   Jim DeFilippi

The stone's placement was a red-embossed invitation. On his ride home in the evening, if the rock had been replaced back into the crevasse of the stump, he would know that she would be there, and so he would head into the woods to the Smoking Boulder, walking more quickly in the colder months in order to preserve sunlight.

This particular evening, the rock had been put back behind the bark, so he knew. He headed down the deer path into the deeper woods, this time carrying a wooden cigar box in his left hand.

As arranged, he found her there, sitting on her Smoking Boulder, looking out at Robert's Pond. They greeted each other with just nods and eyes, as friends, without artificial pomp or unnecessary decorum. Wyzell sat beside her, and they remained silent for a time, staring out across the water and the weeds of the Pond. Two Canadian geese were having a loud vocal argument, as a third floated away peacefully, just looking for something to do. The water was still and dark, catching a few rays of the retreating sun.

Eventually, she asked him about the current Fever numbers. He called her a pussy for asking, then told her she should get herself a TV. Offering a very slight grin, she told him, "Hey listen, pal, I came into the Woods a couple years before the Fever hit—had nothing to do with it—although it worked out well. For me at least, I suppose."

"Well, I guess it did, if you don't mind eating roots everyday and wiping your ass with maple leaves."

"Beech leaves. Maple is too pointy. So, Weaz, why the visit? It was not on the schedule, no need for groceries or supplies."

Wyzell smiled and placed the wooden cigar box on the Boulder between them. He said, "Look what Timmy Thompson just sent me, up from Florida." He opened the lid and revealed twenty box-pressed *Hosienda Vintage Reserva* cigars.

The Hacienda Cigar Rolling Company was originally a Cuban enterprise, but since the embargo in the Sixties had successfully relocated its operation to the Dominican Republic. Its cigars, especially these *Vintage*

ANNAH TORCH — Jim DeFilippi

Reservas, were consistently ranked in the high nineties by *Cigar Aficionado Magazine*.

When the woman reached across the top of the Boulder to grab one from the box, Wyzell slammed the box closed and said her name, almost apologetically. "Annah."

"Yes, I knew. I knew what was coming."

He began slowly. "So I was at home, early afternoon yesterday, I get a knock at my door, there's a guy standing there trying to look like Ricardo Montalbán. With his wife, a wrung-dry cheerleader. I let them both in. Turns out their daughter..." and from there Wyzell told her everything about the Silvers, their daughter, the murder, the room, the shotgun, and the smile.

When he had finished his report, Annah pursed her lips and looked down at her hand, which was pressed across the face of the Boulder. "So, you need me for something this linear?"

Wyzell sat looking out at the meadow. "But there's something screwy involved here, pal, something compellingly screwy."

Annah smiled. "So you thought of me."

"Name anyone screwier."

Annah shook her head. "This sounds so straight-up. Guilty as charged. You know that I am never going to trip up the truth, pal. On any packet. Do the crime, yonder comes your blues, your punishment."

Wyzell asked, "How many years you were my Snoop Dog?"

"Too many, as it turns out." Now Annah was also looking out across the water.

"In all that time, Annah, did I ever have you do anything except that which should be done? Did I ever say to you, 'Annah girl, find me something that gets this guy off the hook, even though he shouldn't be let off? If you can't, then make it up.' Did I ever ask you anything like that?"

"No."

ANNAH TORCH   Jim DeFilippi

"Did I ever do that myself even? Let the guilty go free, did I?"

"No, I don't think so. You are a black swan, Mr. Wyzell, an honorable defense attorney."

"Yeah, well, then not this time either. Promise. So, what do you say? You come into the Fever for a short time, you grab your big girl clothes from the bus for a couple weeks, you find out what's going on with this girl. What happened. She's a kid, Annah, not even gone to college yet. So she goes gunning down her roommate with a sawed-off shotgun? It's peculiar, there's something wrong. She's not Mad Dog Coll, for Christ sake. What's it all about?"

"God only knows, God has a plan."

"Maybe you can find out for me, pal. For us, for me, for her rich parents even. Mostly for the girl herself. Let her look forward to having a life. Come on, you've done this for me before. More than once. So I'm here asking you."

Annah twisted so that she was facing him. "Look, Weaz, I always respected you as a lawyer, as a mouthpiece for the defense, because you never tried to get an innocent client set free. No O. J. Simpson, 'the glove doesn't fit, you must acquit,' under your auspices. Yes, I have helped you out before, both before I came into the Woods and since that time, but only to defend someone who deserved defending. This one..."

"Everyone deserves a defense, Annah, this girl does too."

"Pal, if you are going to start up with that lawyer bullshit, I will head back to my hut."

"Annah, you've helped me out with clients when the powers-that-be were coming after them for all the wrong reasons. Just to prove they can do it. Just because they will look bad if they end up changing their mind now. So they can grab onto any shit-stained junk science to try to put someone away. Just so their reputation will not get stained. Just so they can pay big money to some asshole who claims to be an expert in blood splatter, or bite marks, or handwriting. It's all garbage, Annah. Tire tracks, shoe prints. We know that."

"Defense uses it too, Weaz."

ANNAH TORCH — Jim DeFilippi

"Of course, both sides do. I have looked at that crapola from both sides now, up and down, and still somehow...that's Joni Mitchell."

Annah smirked. "I know."

Wyzell gave her a proud little nod, but his rant wasn't finished. "Profiling experts. Psychologists. Bite mark weasels—no, not weasels, that's me—bite mark phonies. As if everyone's mouth doesn't have incisors and canines and molars."

"Jesus, pal, how long does this speech go on? I came to the Woods for some quiet."

"You are correct, ma'am, I have been too long without smart ears within bending distance, so I'm tugging on your coat right now. So humor me. Some poor and powerless black slobs like Levon Brooks and Kennedy Brewer get to spend half their lives in a six-by-nine cell so that some bloody hemorrhoid of a human being can steal a bit of puffed-up prestige and money by pretending there is such a thing, a real science named 'Bite Marks'? Chemistry, physics...and bite marks? A science? What a frolicking load of Ferdinand shit."

Annah said, "But this sounds different. It is not teeth marks, rather it is her sitting there with a gun in a room....this does not need Barry Schenck trying to..."

He cut her off. "Oh, that Schenck, he's another one. Does good work, but I get the feeling he's trying to atone for getting O. J. Simpson set free. Some football hero hacks his wife's head off, along with some waiter who was just returning her sunglasses for her, and Schenck takes a job getting him off Scott free."

"Weaz, you are a defense attorney who has no use for defense attorneys."

"For some I do, a few, but for those polliwog colleagues? No, I don't. I hold my nose at both sides now, like Joni says. And psychics, mind-readers. 'Let's use psychic readings from another world. By all means, let's bring in a person with bugaboo psychic abilities to help convict this poor schmoe, or else

ANNAH TORCH   Jim DeFilippi

to get him set free.' Whichever side is paying more. The high bidder gets his testimony. It is all so ludicrous, Annah, so sad and silly."

He seemed to be done speaking, so Annah said, "That silliness is precisely what drove me off the job."

"And out of the world."

"Hey, pal, I was never driven out of the world." She swept her arm across the vista below them. "This is the world. Always greening, even now, in this season of sticks. This is the real world. Yours is nothing but a fever."

Wyzell held up his hands in surrender. "Okay, okay, so welcome to my world—you see, I can quote songs and books and movies like a madman, go on all day. Welcome to my world, Annah, but you've helped me stem the bullshit in the past, I'm asking you to do this one more time. Will you help out this little girl? No, not get her off, not if she's guilty, but just to get to the heart of what's right."

"Shotgun, dead body, locked door, that is what is right. I simply do not see anything beyond that, Weaz."

"I don't know either, but let's take a look."

Annah sat silent for a while. Then: "Maybe. Maybe one quick look. For you, my pal. If it appears to me that some cop, or someone in Goofy's office, or maybe even Goofy herself, has developed macular degeneration to such an extent that they are crucifying this girl, then I will help out. Maybe." She pointed at the cigar box. "But only for that box of *Haciendas*."

"Thank you, my dear. One at a time, though. Only one a week. I leave one now as a retainer. Oh, and did I mention polygraphs before?"

"Please stop, Weaz, I haven't had a headache since I came to the Woods, but now..."

"That bunk. Some bozo lifer cop goes to school for a week, becomes an expert in strapping a cord across some poor guy's chest, and they can tell if he's lying? I've watched them slip the cable across the subject when they don't even have him take off his corduroy sports-jacket. Such unadulterated malarkey."

ANNAH TORCH Jim DeFilippi

"Malarkey? I've never heard you say 'malarkey' before. How old *are* you?"

"I run out of names for it. But you and I are the antidote to all that *bullchitna*, Annah, all that *menzogna*. Help me clear away the misdirection. There's only one reputable lie-detector that I know of, and she's sitting here beside me, thinking about blowing smoke rings with the cigars I'm about to give her."

"My detection is different. I do it correctly, and it works."

"Yes, you do. I know it does. You are the only poli-*wanna-cracker*-graph machine that I trust."

"But from what I see, Weaz, you have a perfectly guilty client on your caseload, no?"

"Yes, it does seem it. But it doesn't go against that moral code of yours to get her justice, right? Her father made it clear to me he's made a boatload of powerful enemies in his struggle to the top of the dung pile. And Annah, you and I both know that the penal system is based on two parts revenge, one part deterrent and rehabilitation. We don't want to see this little girl put to sleep. She's just a kid."

"Hey, Counselor, you know the last New Yorker to ride the lightening was Eddie Mays, and that was back in 1963. There is no death penalty any more."

"Annah, the legislature and the courts have gone back and forth so many times, trying to please everybody, trying to keep their poll numbers up, that we don't know what tomorrow will bring for death row. But you're right, kid, there's no chance this kid, even if she wakes up, will be executed. Can't happen, even with everything Goofy has on her. But life? Life without? That's a definite possibility, pal, you know it. So help her out. Have her get only what she deserves, nothing more, but nothing less too. She's a kid, for Christ sake, a baby. Come on out of the wilderness for a few weeks and help her out. Help me out. Be my main snoop again for a little while. Just like the old times, before.

ANNAH TORCH　　　　　　　　　　　　　　　　Jim DeFilippi

Back when you were actually working for me. And like the times you've done it since you've come out here, locked yourself off the grid."

"To help this billionaire out."

"Sure, him too. Billionaires are people too. They breathe. They bleed. They bleed, do they not?"

"Shakespeare? Shylock?"

Wyzell gave an embarrassed grin. "Sort off. That's what I was shooting for anyway."

"Do they expect her to wake up? Catatonic?"

"They don't know. They think so. They hope so."

"But she did the killing."

"Sure looks like it."

Annah pointed at the cigar box. "Do they sell these in different *vitola?*"

"I think so. But I got you the Churchills, big smokes for my big girl. They're box-pressed."

"I love that."

"You know the deal, Annah, same as always. One stick a week, for your Friday smoke, till they all run out."

"It won't take the whole box. It better not." Annah raised her separated thumb and four fingers up to her mouth, drew in a breath, as if she were already enjoying one of the *Haciendas.* "You know, pal, the only packets I ever enjoyed, the only time I got something out of the work I did for the Weasel Corporation..."

"Excuse me, ma'am, only you call it that. It's 'Harold Wyzell and Associates at Law.'"

"... for the Corporation of the Almighty Weasel, were the cases when they actually tried to put an innocent man away. I mean, that happens, and it never should."

ANNAH TORCH   Jim DeFilippi

"But it does." Wyzell pushed up off the rock to leave.

Annah watched him go and called, "Weaz, just don't pull a Rickles on me, pal."

Wyzell turned back to her. "A what?"

"Don't screw me."

"What?"

"When Don Rickles was young, he was opening for Frank Sinatra and dating this girl. He says to Frank, 'It would really impress her if you dropped by the table, said hello.' 'Jeez, I don't know, Don, I'm awful busy.' 'Please, Frank, just do me this one favor, please.' He is asking Frank for a sprout, just like you are asking me."

"So?"

"So Frank drops by the table. 'Hey, Don, I just came over to say Hi.'"

"And?"

"Rickels tells him, 'Get lost, Frank, can't you see I'm busy?'"

Wyzell was grinning. "Good story."

As he started back to his car, Wyzell stopped, turned, and called, "Annah."

She looked at him.

"Just don't bring your Daddy's Hammer."

&&&

After her visitor had left, Annah sat and watched the sun go down over Robert's Pond, as she licked down the single *Hacienda* he had left her.

Her Smoking Boulder was set into the hillside one-hundred feet above the water. The steep cliff led down to a narrow hiking trail along the shoreline. Each spring snapping turtles would somehow make the climb up that cliff to lay their eggs in the sand at the top, right behind her Boulder.

ANNAH TORCH — Jim DeFilippi

It wasn't a Friday, but the *Hacienda* Wyzell had left her was too tempting. She fired it up.

She sat and blew smoke rings out across the water. The wooden bones of a town pump-house peaked out from above the reeds of a shallow, marshy corner of the pond. In the 1930's, the WPA had planned to pump water from the Pond all the way to a holding tank above the town of White Leunge, but the distance proved to be too long and circuitous, and the water too metallic.

Annah sat and puffed, and blew her rings. She would miss this serenity. The cigar smoke and the cool temperature were keeping any bugs away, so she stayed long after sundown.

She had no sense of the time, but finally she sighed and shrugged, as she did when facing an unpleasant task. She pushed up from cool surface of her Boulder. She headed west, into the Woods.

Tomorrow she would hike to Wyzell's bus, then climb into her big girl clothes. From there she would head back into the Fever for a while.

&&&

ANNAH TORCH

Jim DeFilippi

Chapter Five

For her whole life, Blanche *nee* Leunge Ruckhouser's parents had been telling her what a shitty little town they were named for and lived in. They later added that if she married this Elton "Ruck" Ruckhouser, it would just be more of the same, warmed over and served again, like refried beans, but worse.

Now, driving home with three doped-up men in her brown Pontiac, she had to admit that there was some validity in their critiques and warnings.

Ruck had instructed his crew—Horn and Box—to come along with her when she picked him up after the surgery. She could smell the booze on both their breaths when they hopped into the back seat, reserving the passenger seat upfront for their leader, of course. Then, when her husband had climbed in and added to the mix, she could tell that he was still brain-clouded by the fumes of anesthesia. She was resigned that these three would be making little to no sense during the ride.

Ruck was ignoring her, twisting around to the back seat to tell his buddies that he could never get the doctor to tell him whether he was a plastic surgeon or an ocular specialist, but Ruck did finally get the fucker to admit that the procedure would be more cosmetic than reconstructive. The other doctor, the real one, told Ruck that his right arm would stay in the sling for a few more days, then maybe some x-rays.

In the hospital, Ruck had gone after the eye doctor, until some nurses, a security guard, and a hospital administrator had managed to subdue him.

The three men had obviously coauthored a story for their wives and for the general public about what exactly had happened to Ruck's twisted right arm and his M.I.A. left eye, back there in the woods. According to the narrative which all three insisted was their story and they were sticking to it, Horn had just stepped over a large rotted-out log with his rifle slung over his shoulder. When

ANNAH TORCH   Jim DeFilippi

Ruck went to follow, he had slipped on some wet leaves or grass and had fallen forward, his eye meeting the muzzle-poke of Horn's rifle. The slip had also dislocated Ruck's right arm, at first they thought it might be broken. He had stoically refused any treatment for either wound until the hunting day had ended.

Blanche knew it was all foolishness, a fable reeking of incongruity, uncertainty, and contradiction. Nobody would believe that the accidental log-slip story was what had really happened, but it didn't matter to either the doubters or the prevaricators. Just leave it lie.

She drove on, intent on keeping her mouth shut. She allowed the babbling three to babble on, as she drove them through their town and for the thousandth time revisited her parents' version of the place, the town—a version which might have been apocryphal in spots, but she had to admit, probably for the most part held validity and substance.

&&&

Blanche's maiden name had been Leunge, just like the town itself, and the family could trace its DNA as far back as the town could. Instead of saying the name as "Lung," like everyone else, she and her family had always pronounced the name as "Long Jeans," like the five-thousand dollar wristwatch. Her dad would tell her, "Leave it to the Frogs to be sticking on extra syllables and letters that nobody needed or wanted to begin with, but still."

Although the "White Lung" pronunciation was generally accepted, townspeople were incorrect when they related the appellation to the pulmonary disease suffered by the talc miners of Blight, New York, one-hundred and fifty miles to the west and one-hundred and fifty years in the past.

White Leunge was more a product of illicit activity than of the talc industry.

According to Blanche's parents, whether by design or exaggeration, the town was situated at the bullethead of a few centuries filled with a saturating sense of disrespect for the law. The history of the town reverberated with stories of renegades and scofflaws, along with more than a few weak-minded rapscallions.

ANNAH TORCH   Jim DeFilippi

In either 1710 or 1712, the town of White Leunge was settled by seventeen bottom-feeders who had recently been exiled from the town of *Nonfleu-Falaise* in the north of France. Even though this French town was known as a hotbed of corruption, coupled with a deep-seated disregard for authority, these seventeen *loups maléfiques* were so much worse than the city average that they were driven out of town, out of country, and off the continent, driven by a cadre of fed-up citizens, supported by the Board of Selectmen holding pitchforks, and a pack of snarling street dogs.

Upon their arrival in northern New York State, these European refugees immediately set about stealing pelts from the native population, and then abusing the Indians both physically and economically, a practice which escalated into capturing and selling their women into sex slavery, centuries before the phrase had even been coined.

During both the French and Indian War and the American Revolutionary War, the descendants of these first seventeen would hire themselves out as mercenaries to either side of the conflict, with no loyalty except to personal gain. They often managed to "fight" for both sides simultaneously.

When raids led by Joseph Brant and his band of Iroquois warriors completely destroyed the town, it was rebuilt with an even deeper commitment to fucking over all honest people, along with the authority they rode in on.

In the years before the Civil War, the less-than-savory citizens of White Leunge were to assist the noble cause of Abolitionism, by hiding and caring for the runaway slaves of the Underground Railroad, but only for a price, and if a better price was being offered by the trackers and bounty hunters, that was obviously the way to go.

In 1903, Tony Capo opened the Landlock Hotel, where temperance was held in such low esteem the place was refereed to as "the cesspool of iniquity."

During Prohibition, the town was the major producer and distributor of alcohol for the Albany area, and although never proven, it was rumored that

ANNAH TORCH   Jim DeFilippi

Depression era gangster Dutch Schultz had a summer house in White Leunge, where he would entertain and torture his business partners and friends.

In the 1960's, as recreational drug use was infesting the mainstream of American life, the town became a rest-stop for the illegal drug traffickers traveling the "Ho Chi Horse Trail," running heroine from the mafia dons of Montreal down to the street dealers of New York City.

Throughout its history, the town and its residents showed little or no regard for tax or hunting laws. Statistics showed that the town had the highest percentage of draft-dodgers per capita during both the First and Second World Wars.

In this town, gambling and poaching were not considered harmless vices, nor as victimless crimes, but rather not as a vice or a crime at all. And White Leunge might well be the only town of any size in the United States to never have registered a single arrest for prostitution.

How many of these accusations could be proven in a court of law, or on the pages of a history book, was suspect, but the overall impression of the town held by surrounding communities was concrete. The bordering towns liked to refer to it as "White Leunge on the bottom rung." That didn't quite rhyme on paper, but in the air it did.

Blanche's husband's family had arrived in town in the 1940's, when his grandfather, Boyd Ruckhouser, found employment in a small, local shoe factory. When the factory burned to the ground in a suspected case of arson for insurance, Boyd absconded with a cache of stolen leather goods and tools, which he used to set himself up in business as a shoemaker, a business which paid little or no heed to tax laws or to the Sunday Blue Blues of the time.

As far as Blanche knew, Box and Horn's families came a bit later, in the 1950's, and each generation since then had passed on the traditions of early school truancy and illegal hunting.

Blanche often admitted to herself that her mind was a vast and useless encyclopedia. She could tell you that the town's population of 3,205 consisted of 98.3% white, .36% black or African, .48% Native American, .12% Asian, .97% Hispanic or Latino, with mixed races accounting for the remainder. It had

ANNAH TORCH   Jim DeFilippi

a sizable but unmeasurable number of citizens who tended to keep alive their historical inhabitants' preference for out-of-season hunting, alcohol abuse, and a less than strong commitment to following the letter of the law.

She could recite the town's total land mass as 29.96 square miles, of which over 99.5 percent was dry land, and the rest water. Crime seemed to be evenly distributed across both.

She could explain how the town was now considered a bedroom community for the Albany area, and tended to vote Republican in local, state and national elections, or not vote at all.

The town's solitary slice of status came from its hosting the Chelsea Academy, but that bejewelment was now tainted, since one of its students had been accused of murdering her roommate.

Yes, Blanche Leunge Ruckhouser could tell you everything there was to know about the town of White Leunge, New York.

Except how to get out.

&&&

Ruck instructed Blanche to drop them off at Horn's place, they were going to hang out for the afternoon. He didn't want to sit around the house all day, his eye still hurt.

Before the Fever, Blanche would have been dropping them at the White Leunge Fishing and Hunting Casino, which they called their "Lodge." The Lodge had been their go-to spot for years, but the Fever had drained all the life out of the place, so today it would be Horn's back yard instead.

When Blanche had pulled her Pontiac to the curb, she leaned over from the driver's seat and gave her husband a soft peck on the lips. Then, before he could pull away from her, she added two gentle taps on the side of his head, right next to the white, puffy bandage that would be covering his eye for the next couple days. She tapped him like you would tap a little baby. As he was getting out, he said to the back seat that she was always trying to turn him into something he wasn't.

ANNAH TORCH   Jim DeFilippi

She called out, "Watch your step, darling, remember, you don't have any perception left at all."

As she drove away, Blanche added to herself, "As if he ever did."

While Horn was cutting through his house to get some beers from the fridge, Ruck called, "Meet you in the back," and he and Box went around through the side yard.

Horn came out the back door carrying two six-packs and pointing out that none of the wives, and no one around the town, was going to fall for that accidental poke-in-the-eye story.

Ruck asked him, "What, getting your eye poked out by a sucker-punch throwed by some bad-ass, sweet-ass, bimbo Bigfoot babe in the woods is gonna be any better?"

Ruck knew that his immediate future would be filled with snickering comments about the Hathaway Shirt man and Sammy Davis Junior. Some guy in the waiting room with him must have read a book at one time, because he made a reference to a Cyclops.

The three men seated themselves in aluminum folding chairs, five feet apart, and they started drinking their Yuengling Black and Tans. Bottle, no glasses.

For a while they reminisced about how they all missed being at The Lodge, which was club-housed in a shaky, carpenter-ant infested building just off the main drag of town, between Sonny's Ice Cream Parlor and Su Yee's Hair and Nail salon. Despite the lofty name of White Leunge Fishing and Hunting Casino, which hinted at felt-covered gaming tables and semi-clad waitresses dispensing free cocktails to gambling patrons with gold horns dangling down onto suntanned chests, the place was nothing more than a den of impropriety, saturated by the smell of stale beer and overly ripe meat products. Along with bar tabs, rather large sums of money would be changing hands in various gambling activities within—on shaky legged poker tables and wobbly roulette wheels, and floor-mat crap games—but all of this activity was kept "off the books," so to speak, as were the three unsanctioned bookies circulating about the crowd who would take your wager either in person or by telephone.

ANNAH TORCH   Jim DeFilippi

The boys missed all that. Now the place was little more than a ghost house, which made the three men nostalgic and mad.

Horn said he thought of something that could cheer them up. He told Box to go into the garage and bring out this cage he had in there. It was right by the rolls of Tyvek.

"Why I gotta do it for, it's your garage?" Box complained.

"Cause I'm going in the house to get a pellet gun. You'll see. Just go get it. By the Tyvek."

Box looked at Ruck for direction. Ruck told him, "Go get it," so he did.

A minute later, the three men were sitting around a three-by-two wire-mesh cage that held a small weasel that Horn had trapped underneath his porch. The animal was no bigger than a squirrel. It had quick movements and terrified eyes, and it kept running from one corner of the cage to another. The three men were passing the pellet gun around and firing at it.

Box called out, "Careful, careful now, those things can squirt. They can squirt you like a skunk if you give them reason."

Horn's second shot hit the animal in its face. It was spun around by the impact, and when it was again facing them, they could see a patch of blood above its nose. The three men were laughing.

Box said, "Look, you shot its eye out, now it looks just like Ruck."

They both looked at Ruck to make sure he was still laughing. He was smiling, but then he announced, "Enough of this shit. Put the gun back. Let's get serious. I want my Redhawk. I want my eye back too, and my arm, but mostly it's the gun."

Box shook his head and told Ruck quietly, "She gone and threw it in the pond, Chief."

Ruck yelled loud enough to wake up the neighbors, "I know she threw it in the God-damn lake—the pond, I'm not blind, for Christ sake."

Horn held up his thumb and index finger. "A little bit. Little bit."

ANNAH TORCH   Jim DeFilippi

Ruck looked at the two of them. "So what are we gonna do about it? That's the thing all right, right now it is."

Box carried the metal cage with the wounded weasel back into the garage. He came back to join the conversation about recovering Ruck's stolen Redhawk sidearm.

Box asked, "Sure, but how, but how, huh? We're not frogmen, are we? That's a deep lake, that pond is."

Ruck said, "We should go find that jungle slut, she's somewheres out in Topher's Woods, then we keep raping her until she offers to dive in, bare ass, muck around down there, find me my Redhawk."

Box was shaking his head. "No. I'm not in with any of that, Chief. Maybe we should just be like frogmen, get some scuba gear and flashlights and go down, get your gun ourselves."

"Do they work underwater?"

"Frogmen? Of course they do, that's what they're hired for."

"No, flashlights."

"Some of them do. Get the good kind, the Navy kind, the kind the Seals use. But what kind do frogmen use, that's the question."

"Ain't none of us any frogman to begin with."

"Jill's brother was almost a Ranger once, a Green Beret or something, but he's old now."

"No, instead, so we take out my dingy, we reach in over the side, we grab the revolver off the bottom."

"How deep is Robert's Pond? It's over your head, you think? Just how deep is it?"

"Box, you little midget, everything's over your head, including most of my jokes." Ruck and Horn liked that line.

Horn began explaining, "No, so now we take the dingy out, but we bring along some rakes with us, we fish with them over the side, we skim the bottom till we hit it. Scoop it up."

"Long rakes?"

"Yeah, but really, really long."

"How deep is Robert's Pond anyhow? Nobody ever knows."

"We got scuba gear? Who we know got that equipment, is willing to lend it? Something like that?"

"It's cold...dark..."

"So we hire somebody. There's guys who do that for you. Scuba guys."

At that point Ruck interrupted the train of thought—such as it was—to pound his fist into his palm, which hurt his injured arm, and to yell out, "No, God damn it, I want *her* to get it, bring it on back to me. It's my gun. I want to strip that bitch naked, find out what's underneath that body of hers, throw her ass in the water, have her come back out with my Redhawk hanging in her mouth like a retriever bringing in his duck. That's what I want."

"His dick?"

"I said, 'His *duck*.'"

"Underneath the body of hers?"

"What?"

"What?"

"What?"

"You said underneath that body of hers. Where's that?"

"I meant underneath her clothes. Her clothing, I was talking about."

"Oh then, her body, you mean."

"Yeah, sure, her body, what else?"

ANNAH TORCH   Jim DeFilippi

Alcohol usually has the effect of making any communal thought process less and less realistic, less logical. But in this case, as the Black and Tans continued to flow, logic seemed to actually start prevailing, gaining the upper hand.

Finally, Box said apologetically, "Boys, guys, fellas, boys, you know what? If we do anything like that, rape her or anything, Jill'd kill me. If I get sent off to jail, my married life is done for."

Horn told Box he was always such a candy-ass, but maybe he was right this time. He turned to Ruck. "So maybe we just play the game, Chief, what do you think? Do it the right way, the legal way, you sue her ass all to bits."

Ruck thought about it. "No, this here is criminal, what she did, so we don't have to be civil, no suing involved, we get the law to arrest her ass, throw her in jail. For what she did to me."

"Okay."

"For what she did to my eye, to my face, to my arm, to my gun, to my future."

"Okay."

Ruck said, "We make her pay for that. But we do it legal. With lawyers and cops, cops and lawyers. Okay, but you guys have to back me up. With your testimony though. In court, down at the police station. Everybody agree?"

Box said, "Agreed."

Horn said, "I'm in, we agree to that. All in. Make her pay. Time served, to be served. Let's toast to that concept."

Which they did, with clinking bottles.

This decision of pursuing a legal path from which to punish this hated woman of the woods, as opposed to using brute force—illegal but effective—had not been an easy one for this band of three. None of them had ever bothered much with moral or legal decision making. Or with ethical choices. Or even practical ones. Box always did what he was told, Horn simply did what he thought would look good, and Ruck did whatever he felt like. Or whatever he thought Blanche would let him get away with. All three men were in their late forties now, and this method had been working okay for them so far.

Horn pointed out that if they crossed over to this other pathway—lawsuits and arrest warrants instead of assaults and batteries—then they would have to come up with a new truth, the old "accidental rifle poke to the eye" story wouldn't work any more.

After a few mores rounds, they agreed upon a new truth, something about a wild-eyed giant of a woman who had jumped out from behind a mulberry bush and attacked them all with something that looked like a fireplace poker.

Box asked if those woods had any mulberry bushes.

Later that night, as the three were splitting up, Horn dropping off Ruck at his house, Box asked, "How about that weasel in the cage, you gonna keep it?"

Horn told him it was probably dead by now anyway.

&&&

Chapter Six

It was too early in the day for a Mare's Leg, or for anything this expensive, but Grace Silver needed it, needed something to soothe her spirit, as well as the excruciating pain, something to hide away her thoughts like—dare she say it?—like the thoughts buried within the mind of her poor, unconscious daughter, lying there corpselike in a hospital cell with an armed guard sitting outside the doorway.

Who could blame Grace? Who could deny her this glass of *Chilcot Veuve Blue*?

Baby Johnnie was sitting on the couch across the living room from her, jabbering into his cell, trying to get some paperwork delivered so that they could get in to see Amanda. He hated being called that—Baby Johnnie—although that's what the papers and magazines and TV shows always used. She did too, but only in her mind and to friends.

He was seated in front of the huge triangular window, twenty feet high, of maple framed double-insulated glass that made up nearly the entire front wall of the chalet. The roadway was forty yards down at the end of the drive, but still, anyone driving by could catch a glimpse of him sitting there, his back in a velvet robe, barking orders into his iPhone. He pretended that he hated being seen, being studied, being exhibited and diagnosed, but of course he loved the all of it —the attention, the admiration, the respect, the awe. Along with the envy, and even the hatred.

Grace took another sip from the wine glass as she read the description that had come tucked in the corrugated Amazon box. They had received the bottle from the two-hour delivery service when they were down in the city. She sipped now and took a look across the room at her husband. Sip, read, look. Sip, read, look.

ANNAH TORCH   Jim DeFilippi

This horrible crisis with Amanda had not changed her husband, it had only brought more of his dominant features to the surface. Like the wine, he was beautifully complex—tender one moment, inflexible the next. At first sip—sweet, bright, ripe. Sparkling. Then—deeper, subtle, restrained. With hidden layers of guilty pleasure. That was her baby. That was her Baby John.

And like the wine, he was "medium bodied," no more than five foot seven, but presenting himself much, much larger, with pectoral muscles and abs and biceps being groomed daily—but still not quite as impressive as his high-priced trainer would lead him to believe.

Johnnie had never acknowledged that he was half an inch shorter and half a year younger than his wife.

He was looking away from the phone now, in anger, then shouting back into it, obviously at some underling, or somebody at the District Attorney's office, something about his rights and privileges and entitlements. He said, "God damn it to hell and back," and took the cell down from his ear. He mashed his finger into the screen, turning on the speaker. He was too young to be losing his hearing, but there it was. He refused to wear any hearing devices, but had his personal physician looking into the cutting edges of Cochlear implants.

Her husband was proud, confident, conceited—Grace wondered if any of those adjectives could be applied to a wine. Of course they could. Read the labels. Check the wine connoisseur magazines. Her husband was a good man in so many ways, his generosity overdubbing his flaws. His generosity toward his staff, his workers, mostly to his family. Grace need not drop even a hint at something she wanted that it wouldn't be delivered, usually within the forty-eight hour Amazon time frame. And there was absolutely nothing he wouldn't do for their daughter, even before this mess had started up.

He was prepared to take any action, to spend any amount of money, to call in any number of favors, to twist or break any number of arms, or balls, to skirt any amount of laws, to get this daughter of theirs set free.

He clicked off the phone and called across the room to Grace, "Let's go, I got us in."

&&&

ANNAH TORCH   Jim DeFilippi

Their daughter had been formally charged, and a cop named Gumm had told the doctors and staff to alert him the moment she awoke, so that he could come over and re-recite the Miranda warning to her. "If you cannot afford a lawyer, one will be appointed for you." The lawyers on Johnnie's staff and on retainer cost him roughly two million dollars a year, and the Weasel was charging him nine hundred dollars an hour on top of that. The family could afford a lawyer.

Johnnie and Grace were rubbing their hands with alcohol gel and he was calling his name into the small speaker box on the wall. The two electronic doors swept open and he and Grace walked down a long sterile corridor to a second set of similar doors, where they repeated the procedure—alcohol gel for the hands, identifying himself, trying to sound patient, but failing.

Johnnie leaned over the counter at the nurses' station and again pronounced his name and the patient's name. The nurse seated at the console seemed a bit flustered, a bit wary. "She's confined, sir."

"We know she's confined, where is she?"

The nurse made a phone call, then gave them the directions to Amanda's room. A blue line down the center of the corridor showed them the way.

A metal cage which they had to pass through instructed them to remove any outer garments. Hooks were provided for their clothing. Johnnie ignored the command and told Grace to do the same.

"Johnnie Silver," he called to the cop when they were about thirty feet away from Amanda's door. Johnnie took a legal sized white envelope from the inside pocket of his suit jacket and held it out to the cop.

"Officer, paperwork here from Sarah Guffleberg. It grants us access to see our daughter." He pointed at the closed door of Room 418. "That's our Amanda in there."

They were standing in front of a bullish, previously bored cop who had stood up from his stool and was brushing some lint from the front of the blue baggy pants of his uniform.

ANNAH TORCH   Jim DeFilippi

Johnnie began waving the paper in front of him. "Here, take a look at it, take hold, you'll find it in order, with the proper…"

The cop interrupted, something Johnnie wasn't used to. "No, that's fine, sir, they called me, you can go right in. There's no lock. Fifteen minutes though, okay?"

"Fifteen," Johnnie repeated, as if he didn't believe it. Then, "Fifteen's fine though, okay, Officer."

The couple started to squeeze by when the cop said, "Oh, wait a minute, sir, I'll have to wand you both first."

"You'll have to do what?"

"Magic wand."

"What?"

The cop bent over and reached down to the linoleum floor. He picked up a black metal-detector the shape and size of an old-fashioned police Billy Club. Johnnie and Grace both raised their hands in the air and spread their feet a bit apart as the officer waved the wand across and over their bodies as if he were disinfecting them. He nodded and put the wand back onto the floor as they entered their daughter's room.

Inside the room, the air smelled like Lysol and disinfectant and urine. In the bed lay a person that neither parent could recognize. For a moment, Johnnie considered going back and checking the name on the door, but of course there was none.

The face was as white as the sheets that had been pulled up to her shoulders, with an inch of bare flesh exposed. The white sheets were decorated with tiny blue crests or shields that at first Johnie mistook for pictures of cockroaches or ticks.

The center portion of the sheet had been tucked beneath a puffy length of white gauze that surrounded the patient's neck like a garrote.

Amanda's face resembled that of a crudely wrapped mummy. Lengths of white tape with yellow splotches were spread across her upper forehead, below her nose, and over her chin. The bruise ran across her forehead and beneath the tape like a black thunderbolt.

Johnnie turned back to Grace. "Jesus Christ, what have they done to her? What are they doing? They didn't say she was injured, did they? Psychogenic coma, what the hell is that? Did they tell us she was injured? Did she have a stroke or something? My god."

Grace shook her head. "It's just to...it's to make sure she stays alive." Grace had started crying.

Johnnie told her, "Don't let her see that. Dry it up."

Grace shook her head as if to ask, "See? All right? She won't notice me?"

Yard upon yard of blue and white tubing encircled their daughter, some of it crawling over her body like a bundle of snakes, the end of tube finally entering her mouth, where a clear plastic mouthpiece was held in place by a crisscross of adhesive tape.

Her thin, dried-out lips seemed to be sucking at the plastic.

Johnnie said, "That hose is too God-damn big for her mouth, it's choking her, for Christ sake. What are these people thinking?"

Grace said her husband's name.

Amanda's hair was pulled back tightly from her face and held by what looked like a white headband. Her eyes were closed, the muscles of her face were loose and motionless, lifeless. Both of her arms were under the material that seemed more like a straitjacket than sheets.

Johnnie looked for restraints, but didn't see any. He wanted to press the call-button that was hanging uselessly from the bed railing. He wanted to get every doctor and nurse into that room and demand immediate treatment, demand change, demand...demand...he didn't know what.

He stepped back from the bed and surveyed the room in an effort to calm himself down. It didn't help. The room was a crowded jumble of wire and tubes and machines and screens with blinking blue lights. The place made

ANNAH TORCH   Jim DeFilippi

Johnnie think of a Rob Gonsalves painting that he had hung in their Florida living room. An abstract of a bad dream. This room was like that.

Two cardiac monitors seemed to be contradicting each other with blue glowing numbers showing heart rate and blood pressure and oxygen saturation. Beeping. Every surface in the room was crowded with bottles and jars and tubes of medication and fluid, and gastric feeds.

Something that looked like a Star Wars character was standing guard by the bedside. Its face was a television screen, with blue tubes for arms and small blue plastic wheels for its feet. The thing seemed to be alive, it was buzzing and humming and clicking and ticking. Johnnie wondered how his daughter could sleep with all that. Then he remembered sleeping wasn't the problem, that was the opposite of the problem.

Johnnie steadied himself by holding onto a tower of five box-shaped machines that looked like old DVD players, stacked to the left of Amanda's bed. On top of the tower hung a clear plastic bag that was feeding a clear liquid into Amanda's arm.

Johnnie told his wife, "All of this shit is so useless. It's all for show."

Grace sighed. She was looking down at her daughter's face.

Johnnie pushed Grace out of the way and stepped in close to Amanda. He leaned over the bed so that he was an inch away from her left ear. "Baby... baby...Mandy...it's Daddy...let's us two..." He sobbed and stood back up, and said, "Grace, you talk to her first. Go talk."

He went over to the lone plastic chair, sat down in it, and buried his face in his hands and sat sobbing. When he managed to get himself to stop, he wiped his face with his sleeve, stood up, and watched his wife talking quietly to his daughter. He went over, pushed Grace out of the way, told her, "All right, let me," and leaned over once again, to whisper to his daughter.

"Baby-girl, you can hear me. It's Daddy. You're just napping, that's all, like when you were a kid. You used to nap all the time." He turned back to his wife. "Didn't she, Grace, remember what a good baby, napping all the time, she was?"

Grace said, "She was golden."

He turned back to Amanda. "You can hear me, Mandy. When you wake up, we'll get you out of here and out of this mess. You hear? Daddy's got many good, smart, good people working for you. There's been a possible mistake, this is bad times, but it will all be over with, sweetheart. We'll get you out of this bed and back into your bed back home, okay? We'll all have a good summer, do all the things, and we'll see what college you want to go to, okay? Maybe be a vet? Do you still think about being a veterinarian? Remember old Buzzy, how you loved him, took care of him when he got sick? I don't want you worrying about things, okay, dear? About what happened. Don't kill yourself over it." Johnnie winced at his choice of the word.

He turned back to Grace. "I have to talk alone to Amanda for a minute now. Go wait in the hall. I'll meet you out there. Go wait now."

Grace left the hospital room as Johnnie turned back to his daughter.

&&&

Back out in the hall, they thanked the Officer and then walked ten yards away from him so they could talk.

Johnnie said to Grace, "She'll be okay. She'll be fine. Keep me up on things. You can come everyday, if you can stand it. Then give me a call."

"You're still going?"

"I have to, Grace, it's the Pope. You don't reschedule things like that. I told you, this is the biggest thing I might ever do. I have to go. It'll be a couple days, most."

"Then home. Back here."

"Of course."

"Not Vegas. You were going to..."

"Of course not, don't be foolish. That's been cancelled already. No tournament, nothing for me, for a while, till all this is taken care of. It's Rome, then right back here. She'll be fine. Call me when she wakes up."

Grace looked back at the door of her daughter's room. "I hope she wakes up."

&&&

ANNAH TORCH   Jim DeFilippi

Chapter Seven

Each time Annah came out of the Woods to take on an assignment, in addition to the cigars, Wyzell would get her a new set of big girl clothes. This time it was a black Italian Stretch Wool Harvey Blazer with a single button closure and peak lapels. Matching pants and a white silk blouse complemented. The black leather Birdies were left from her last assignment, when she had helped three rape victims realize that the hunchbacked black man they had accused was innocent.

Before having her climb into her professional uniform, Wyzell had talked Annah into a shower and shampoo inside his house—"For just about everybody's sake."

Now, in the side yard school-bus, he had swung the squeaking, creaking driver's seat around on its swiveling pedestal and he was sitting, watching her drop her woods clothes onto the floor of the bus's aisle. First a pair of Solomon Gor-Tex boots and woolen socks. Then the deep-snow gaiters that she used to keep the legs warm, as well as for protection against ticks and scratches. The Turtle Fur vest and North Face zip-up fleece both hit the floor. Then the Snoopy Mad Bomber hat, with its fur earflaps and visor. Finally, one layer of North Face leggings, then a second.

She had left most of her fashion accoutrements back at the hut. The extreme cold weather military black gloves with the fingers cut off, the double-insul mittens, the pink bandana that she would tie around one arm as a warning, a hunters-orange vest. A few knives of various sizes, cans of bug-spray, a summer hat, and the one article that held any emotional commitment for her—her Daddy's Hammer.

She was reaching for the new Harvey pants as Wyzell grinned and called back, "I tried to order them with a little cloth hammer sling on the side of the leg, for your Hammer, like the carpenters use, but they don't come with that."

ANNAH TORCH   Jim DeFilippi

With one leg in, she looked up to the front of the bus. "You know, pal, if you can swing the seat around forward again, and just use the mirror to ogle me, maybe we could both pretend you are not such a slovenly pig."

Wyzell twirled around as ordered and said up to the mirror, "Ogle. Is that how to say it, with the 'o' sound? I always thought it hymned with goggles. I just see it written out all the time."

"No. It's ogle. The 'o' is long, just like your dick would be if you keep staring at me in the rearview, so eyes down."

"Rearview. Rear view. In this case, that's a good name for it. Rear view. Nice ass you have working for you there. It brings to mind the word, 'Scrumptious.'"

"Along with the phrase, 'Sexual intimidation.'"

"Ah, I'm not planning to run for President anyway, not that that stuff matters anymore. But 'ogle,' it's one of those words that mostly lives its life on the printed page, not out in the open air, people don't say it out loud that much."

"Ogle."

"It's sort of like you, living out there in the Woods, instead of back here, with all the normal people."

"Normal? Hey, pal, remember, if people were normal, you would be out of a job. All those rapists and murderers and felonious creeps pretty much bought you that big house of yours over there. Not the normal people."

"You don't care much for normal people, Annah, do you now?"

"Sure I do."

"No, you don't. Oh, that blouse looks good. It fits nice. No, m'lady, you are not a big fan of the normal."

"Of course I am." She was pushing her arms through the blazer. "My dad got drunk once and told me he didn't like my Mom. Never had, from the beginning. They'd been married forty years. He said it was all right, though, because there were plenty of other people he did like. He liked people. I like lots of people."

ANNAH TORCH   Jim DeFilippi

"Name two."

Annah shrugged and kept getting dressed. The shoes. She dangled a facemark, waved it a bit, asking. He lifted his shoulders, raised his palms upward —judgment call, game-time decision.

During the three and a half years that Annah had been in the Woods, Wyzell had talked her into helping out on one of his packets three different times. Each job would last from a single day up to maybe a fortnight. At first she would turn down the assignment, then he would play her, and ply her, she would know she was being played but would accept it, he would understand that she knew, and on and on it went, like two full-length mirrors facing each other.

"So, tell me, Tarzan, when you're out there in the Woods, are you and Bigfoot actually dating, or are you just good friends? Does he read? Does he chat? What are his friends like? Do you like them, or do you just put up with them because they're his friends?"

Annah was making sure to ignore him, so he asked how she was planning to proceed on this one. He added, "But we both know, you do what you will, I never guide you. You know what to do."

She gave him a list of people she planned to talk to—the cops, prosecutors, the girl's parents, friends, the girl herself. She asked him, "Can I get in? To talk to her?"

"There won't be much conversation. She's still catatonic."

"I still want to see her, can you get me in?"

"What for? So you can use your glorious lie-detector skills on her? Does it work when someone can't talk, can't tell lies, can't tell the truth, can't say anything, you can still tell them apart?"

"Yes. I think I can."

"Annah Torch, the human lie-detector. That's what all the people say."

"I hate that, being put in the same category as a contraption. It's just that...it's just that...everyone has a tell. Sometimes it takes me three or four sentences to spot it, but usually pretty fast."

ANNAH TORCH   Jim DeFilippi

"Even if it's true? Even if that first sentence the subject says, it's a true one?"

"Yeah, most of the time."

"How about when the subject is lights out, unconscious, not saying a word? It works for you then too?"

"I do not know. We shall see. Can you get me in?"

"Annah Torch, the gobbling piranha of lies."

"That I am."

"Oh, I believe it, I believe in the skill, I believe you can do it, I *know* you can do it, I've seen you do it too many times. I'm a believer."

"The Monkees."

"Right."

"So avoid placing me in categories like that—junk science, a sham upon man."

"Yes, garbage always rises to the top. Look at politics."

"So, boss, can I get in to see the accused girl or not? You were working on it."

"It's fixed. Finally, your Columbia Law has done you some good. I got you listed as co-counsel, so you can go in, see her. Are you still a member of the New York Bar?"

"Beats me."

"Doesn't matter, as long as they think you are. I've seen you separate the chaff from the wheat a hundred times over. You did it back when you were still out working for a living, and now, when you've decided to live your life as a savage—no offense. And you've never been wrong. I've never seen you miss, never misspoke about somebody. You can tell. It's just that, I don't know, you're always spouting off about 'use science,' *real* science, none of that ersatz shit. But then here you go, about some magical insight you have into human nature."

ANNAH TORCH   Jim DeFilippi

"No, Weaz, no, you have it all wrong. It is not that at all. It is simply a method of observation, microscopic attention to detail. As I said, everybody had a tell. Maybe a twitch, a move, a tick, does not even have to be around the face. It might be the way he is sitting on the couch, crossing his ankles, his legs. It might be how he pets his dog, touches his balls when he speaks. Sometimes there is even a smell he gives off..."

"Yeah, you sniff it out, my girl."

"...or how he pulls his socks up. Or how he allows them to flop down on his ankles."

"He? Always it's a 'he'?"

"Women are harder, they lie much better. It becomes a bit more difficult to spot, to tell the tell."

"How about an unconscious woman? How's that going to work?"

"We are about to find out."

"Okay, let's go."

"Ready."

"Wow, you look great. But, Annah, listen, as you work this thing with me, just remember, you have to dress nice and leave Daddy's Hammer at home."

&&&

Wyzell drove them over to the White Leunge Memorial Hospital, where they went through the same procedure that the Silvers had the day before.

Pumping the alcohol gel dispenser on the wall, Wyzell pronouncing their names into the small speaker—"We're her attorneys, our names are on the list you've been provided"—then the sweep of the electronic doors opening, like the Wizard of Oz was behind a curtain pushing buttons, the long walk down the corridor with its mixture of well and sick smells, side glances into rooms for quick peeks at the varying degrees of human disintegration, then a second set of doors, more hand gel, again—"We're her attorneys, our names are on the list you've been provided"—the nurses' station—"We're her attorneys, our names on are the list you've been provided"—the blue line leading to Room 418, the cop at

ANNAH TORCH   Jim DeFilippi

the door, half asleep and paging through a *People* magazine, checking for breast tops.

As the cop was scanning them for metal, Annah could tell that this doorman desperately wanted to stroke his wand over the breast of her Harvey Blazer, just to make a little contact, but one quick look dissuaded him.

Annah asked Wyzell to wait outside as she entered Amanda Silver's room. Once inside, she was not affected nor impressed by anything, neither the furnishings nor the patient. She had seen all of it, as bad or worse, many times before.

She pulled the wooden plastic chair up close to the bedside, and she studied the patient for a long time. The sallow face, the closed eyes, the stillness, the rate of her breathing. Annah decided most of the breaths were being controlled by the patient, not by the ventilator. She studied each of the numbers on each of the screens. She spent a long time doing that. Then she did it again, swiveling her eyes around the room and its monitors.

She pulled the chair even closer to the bed. She leaned over, so that her mouth was just an inch from Amanda's right ear. She reached down under Amanda's sheet and took out the girl's lifeless right arm. Annah placed the index and center fingers of her own hand into Amanda's palm and then gently enclosed Amanda's hand around her own two fingers. She squeezed the girl's immobile fingers a bit, looked around to check the monitors again, with their beeping, with the clicking, with their flashing, jumping numbers. She leaned in so close that her lips were almost grazing Amanda's right ear.

"Amanda, I think maybe you can hear me. Can you hear my words? Is it there?" Annah made her voice soft and soothing, hypnotically steady. "Amanda, I am a friend. A friend of yours. I am a friend of your Mom and Dad's. My name is Annah. Amanda, I know you are sleeping, and I seem far off, far away from where you are, but I want to ask you a question. It that okay? Just one. Can you feel what I have done? I have put my two fingers in your hand, Amanda, into your palm. Amanda, one question, if yes, squeeze my fingers one time, if that is the answer, a yes. If you want to say no, then squeeze my fingers two times. All right? One squeeze means yes, two means no. If you do not want to squeeze at all, that is fine too, okay, then just do not squeeze. If you do not want to. That would be fine. You can just go back to sleep. Should we practice? No?"

Annah looked up to check the numbers on the screens again. She leaned back in. "Okay then, Amanda, here is the question. Just one. Then you can rest again."

Without moving her head, Annah checked the screens again, just the ones she could see from the corner of her eyes.

"Amanda, did you kill Didi?"

&&&

A few minutes later, back out in the hallway, Wyzell was staring hard at Annah. With a nod, she indicated that they should walk down the hall a bit. They did. They waited until a nurse and two orderlies had walked by. One of the orderlies was pushing a tray that had a blue sheet dropped over it.

Annah and Wyzell looked at each other.

He asked her, "Well?"

She told him, "Not her. She did not perform the killing."

&&&

ANNAH TORCH   Jim DeFilippi

Chapter Eight

A nnah had changed back into her woods clothes, she was in her hut, studying the packet Wyzell had given her.

She had built the hut when she first came into the Woods. A ten-foot by twelve-foot rectangle with a northern red oak at each of its corners to provide some stability and permanence. Crossbeams of gray birch and striped maple had been nailed around three walls of the perimeter and across the top. Every nail used was a nineteenth century square-head, each having been driven into the wood by Daddy's Hammer.

One sidewall and the lower back-wall were vertical seven or three-foot lengths of gray birch, pressed together side by side with lengths of twine and vine, then stuffed with various chunks of grass and mud for insulation. The other sidewall was made of horizontal logs, each one-to-three inches in diameter, nailed from one corner red oak to the other, with the same materials used for insulation. The front was open.

The roof was five crossbeams of American elm and black ash, with strands of white pine woven between them for shade and protection. The white pine branches were thin and wispy, tending to be lifted by a strong wind or collapsed by snow, so they had to be replaced and rearranged periodically. The roof was pitched to the three-foot lower back end.

The front of the hut was open most of the time, but laid across the front elm beam were three thick woolen blankets that could be lowered like an awning.

Two thin gray pines, each two inches thick, stood before the opening like svelte sentries.

Large, immovable gray and green granite boulders extended out from each front corner of the hut before gradually tampering off into the dirt. This natural rock wall, combined with some gray birches that had been limbed and placed across the top, gave the appearance of the dwelling having a front yard, or a corral, or a garden.

ANNAH TORCH　　　　　　　　　　　　　　　　Jim DeFilippi

Leaves, twigs and moss carpeted the front yard and interior.

Inside, close to the front, large boulders had been stacked to construct a three-foot-across campfire. Its fuel was five cord of maple, cherrywood, and beech, stacked with the precision of a suburban wood-stove owner, between two white oak trees in the "back yard."

On the ground inside the hut was a mustard colored Marmot Col sleeping bag, effective for temperatures ranging down to minus-twenty degrees Fahrenheit. The bag was rolled up and stored in a large green garbage bag, with the plastic cord pulled tight. A similar green garbage bag held a bulging cache of books.

Stored very neatly and precisely around the inside of the hut were pieces of clothing and tools—three saws of various shapes and sizes, knives, clippers, pliers, and assorted twists of metal. In one corner leaned both a trenching shovel and a hacksaw. Annah appreciated tools that had tough names.

Hanging from a side wall were two identical Cordura backpacks—an empty one, used when moving around, and another one left hanging, more permanently, stuffed full of supplies.

Two large military canisters holding water sat beside cans of food, dry goods, and army surplus K-rations. A plastic first aid kit leaned against a Fushigi Glass Gravity Ball. Two toothbrushes and three juggling sacks.

And propped against the wall in the back right corner—stored in the mahogany box requisitioned from Ruck Ruckhouser—was the brutal and effective Daddy's Hammer.

The hammer had a cherry handle and an ugly, black tempered steel head. It was sixteen inches long, the head five inches across. The peen and face were both pimpled with red rust that had been smashed into the metal by a force that would keep the spots there permanently. Two metal wedges had been driven through the eye to keep the handle permanently in place whenever the tool was pounded into something with great force.

Wyzell always equated her Daddy's Hammer with her tendency to create violence, but in truth, Annah used this tool for mostly peaceful functions.

ANNAH TORCH   Jim DeFilippi

She used it to pound in the square-head nails that held the logs of the hut together. She had used it to flatten a copper medallion into a fire plate. She had used it to pulverize acorns into a cooking powder.

But the Weasel's concern was not without merit. In the past, Annah had used the hammer to kill men.

&&&

The sun was warm for the season, and steady, so Annah was sitting on a rock in the front corral, studying Wyzell's packet. As she paged through legal paper after paper, she found very little to encourage her. When he had handed her the packet, Wyzell told her, "I didn't waste money on an envelope for exculpatory evidence. There is none."

Annah sat studying each word and picture and diagram with the focus and strength of a laser beam, looking for anything that could indicate that Amanda Silver had not murdered Dede Constaghulia.

Most of the contents of the packet had been shoddily prepared and were unhelpful.

These papers were not like the ones talked about on television shows or movie screens.

These official papers of the court were generally poorly written, misspelled, slanted to one side or the other, confusing, disemboweled, truncated of any potentially vital information, incomplete, and stupid. They tended to be faked, phonied up, slanted, misleading, misguided, misdirected, misdirecting, contradictory, purposely twisted, manipulated, and spurious. Even in their best forms.

The victim's postmortem was even shoddier than the other reports, written by Dr. Franz Cobbler, a medical examiner obviously more interested in putting the final touches on his speech for the retirement banquet.

Autopsies are performed using one of four general methods.

The Letulle method starts with a bisection of the abdomen and then proceeds in a retroperitoneal "*en bloc*" direction, removing the various organs, beginning with the peritoneum, and moving backwards. This procedure would prove difficult, if not impossible, since the subject no longer had an abdomen, and few of the remaining organs were where they should have been.

The Virchow technique removes the organs starting up at the cranium and proceeds down to the thoracic, abdominal and cervical organs. This subject was intact from the shoulders up, but there was very little below that remained, except for twisting crumps of bloody tissue.

The Rokitansky technique is locally directed, starting at the neck and head, proceeding down from there to the larynx, esophagus, pharynx, and then the chest organs to get to the abdomen. Same problems.

The Ghon technique, is similar, but will instead opt for an "*en bloc*" removal of the organs. In this case, the organs had been removed pre-op, by shotgun pellets.

Dede's autopsy seemed to have been a cluster-fuck of all four methods, no doubt due to the fact that many of her organs had been nearly or totally destroyed by the buckshot.

The subject had trace amounts of alcohol and possibly various unidentified recreational drugs in her system at the time of her death, but none of the amounts approached the lethal level, certainly nothing as significant as a shotgun blast to the belly. Age, weight, sex and tolerance, all determine the amount of time it takes for alcohol to leave the body's blood, kidneys, bladder, liver, lungs, and skin.

The trace amounts of alcohol did not approach the level of legal intoxication. A slightly elevated level of insulin, a natural element found in the body, also did not seem to elicit any concern, since blood sugar and electrolyte levels seemed normal. A few additional chemicals of unspecific origin were also present.

Dr. Cobbler's notes were peppered with the label of "UND," which stood for "Undetermined." The cadaver obviously provided significant amounts of blood sampling, both interior and exterior, but the contents of the blood was again pockmarked by UND's.

ANNAH TORCH
Jim DeFilippi

The most fascinating and confusing condition of the body was never mentioned in the medical report. That of course was the incongruous smile on the face of the corpse, frozen for all time, or at least until burial and disintegration.

A glass of beer in her system wouldn't cause a smile that wouldn't be erased by looking down the muzzle of a sawed-off shotgun.

The smile. Always the question of that smile. Annah kept flipping back to the crime scene photograph of the smile. It was a closeup, side-lit, framed like a Hollywood headshot. The face looked so serene, so accepting, perhaps even enjoying that moment—the moment of her death.

That smile was frustrating Annah, even haunting her. She looked up at the quaking aspens above her, rolling their leaves against the blue sky to the west, and she thought about that smile. No answers came to her.

She looked back at the photo again. For too many minutes.

&&&

The report on the medical condition of the accused was nearly as perplexing and unclear.

The medical team at the White Leunge Memorial Hospital was now in agreement that the unconscious state of the patient was due to a "Psychogenic coma accompanied by intermittent organ system disfunction caused by either emotional or physical trauma or a combination of the two."

This of course was doctor-speak for, "We don't know what the hell is going on with this poor kid—a stroke, maybe?"

The large bruise across her forehead was credited as being at least a partial explanation for the patient's condition. When a hundred and ten pound female pulls the trigger of a weapon as powerful as a sawed-off shotgun, the kickback from the discharge could easily cause the weapon to be bolted back, causing the barrel to crash into the front of the shooter's face.

ANNAH TORCH Jim DeFilippi

The doctors were certain that a concussion had resulted, but they disagreed as to the extent the concussion was causing the patient's state of unconsciousness.

Alcohol and trace amounts of some recreational drugs in Amanda's bloodstream were discovered by a physical examination ordered by her father and his legal team.

As was the case with the victim, the trace amounts of alcohol could not be accurately measured, having been dissipated by time, but in Amanda's case, also present was a small amount of a recreational drug named Ketamine. Ketamine began its life as a horse tranquilizer and was still being used in the horse-racing and show-horse world. As many of these time-bombs do, the drug had managed to morph its way into the world of powerful recreational drugs. The street name for Ketamine was "Special K." The drug gives its user a sense of detachment, as well as a freedom from pain, pain of both the physical and emotional variety. The stuff is so fast-acting, some cops carry it illegally to subdue the other criminals.

Annah went back and searched for any sentence mentioning traces of Ketamine in Dede's system—could that have been the cause of that angelic death smile of hers?—but there was no mention of the drug in the autopsy report. Could Ketamine have been one of the "few additional chemicals of unspecific origin were also present"?

The drug also was the cause for temporary amnesia, the kids on the street referred to this state as the "K-Hole," which could blot out periods of time, usually for no longer than one hour.

But the Johnnie-directed physical exam also revealed the presence of some wine in Amanda's stomach. Maybe a lengthy "K-Hole," caused by Ketamine, wine, and a crime scene involving a shotgun and a lead-bisected room mate?

Annah had heard of Ketamine, although she had never encountered it in any of her investigations. The closest she could remember was the use of a related drug, another horse tranquilizer called Acepromazine, or simply "Ace," that a jockey had been distributing at Saratoga during its August racing season.

ANNAH TORCH   Jim DeFilippi

A fellow jockey had died from an overdose of the drug. Acepromazine was considered lethal for human beings, even when present in fairly small amounts.

&&&

The murder weapon that her client was holding in her grasp when the police broke down the door to the room was identified as a Filipino-Blitzer, break action, .12 gage shotgun. The weapon had been sawed off at its stock and its barrel so that it now measured only eighteen inches long, just a fraction of its original length. Its stock had a red and white plaid cloth wrapped around it, probably to ease the powerful kickback that would be caused by firing a weapon designed for two-handed use but with the gunman now compelled to use only a single hand.

This cloth wraparound looked like something that might have been stolen off the tabletop of a red-sauce Italian restaurant. One could imagine it holding drops of melted candle wax from the Chianti bottle candleholder. The White Leunge P.D.'s photos of the wrapping showed red stains that might have been blood, but looked more like red wine and gravy. The hacksaw cuts on both the barrel and the stock of the shotgun were crude and uneven. Both cuts showed a change of direction by a couple of degrees halfway through, probably from when the hacker's arm was tired or got cramped up.

This procedure of cutting a standard shotgun down into a sawed-off model was definitely an amateur job. As if there were professional shotgun hacksaw craftsmen to be found.

How would a billionaire's daughter, barely out of her teens, a student at an elite Northeastern prep school, lay her hands on a sawed-off shotgun? *Why* would a billionaire's daughter, barely out of her teens, lay her hands on a sawed-off shotgun?

Why was she holding a weapon like this as the police broke in? Why did the gunpowder residue prove that she had just fired the weapon?

And why was the victim smiling at the weapon, and at her roommate?

&&&

ANNAH TORCH　　　　　　　　　　　　　　　　　Jim DeFilippi

  Annah would find out. She would begin by interviewing policemen, prosecutors, family and friends of both the victim and the accused, as well as anyone else in the path of where her investigation would lead her.
  In the next few days, she would be meeting new people, never a favorite activity of hers. New faces, new personalities, new motivations, new moral codes, new secrets to hide. Despite what Howard Wyzell had said to her, Annah liked people, she really did. She simply didn't need their support or assistance or approval. She tried not to categorize, but she knew that in any group of people, 4.6% knew and understood things—complex things, important things. Then, 66% were in the blurry middle, ranging from insightful to oblivious.
  And the remaining 29.4% had nothing but sputum for brains.

&&&

ANNAH TORCH   Jim DeFilippi

Chapter Nine

Sergeant Simon Gumm was explaining to Annah Torch how his life's dream had always been to walk a tightrope over Niagara Falls, and then later go over the Falls in a barrel. "My body's sort of barrel-shaped anyway, don't you think? It'd fit right in like a glove. I have no immediate plans you understand, but it's something to keep an eye on. For me it is, anyway. I'd take a little action on the side that I would come out alive."

Annah had just told him that Amanda Silver was innocent and that Annah was working toward proving that.

Gumm kept nodding, then said, "Originally my plan was to do it the same day, but that of course is unrealistic. We all have our dreams. Innocent? So you think Amanda Silver is *innocent*? Ms. Torch, not to be a contrarian here, but have you looked at this case at all? Innocent?"

"I know she is, Sergeant.   I have yet to find out how, how what happened really happened."

"Instead of that, why don't you just come with me out to the Falls? Beautiful woman like you, we would get some fine press coverage. I could take you across in a wheelbarrow, me pushing, if you're not afraid of heights. Or of water. Or of tipping and falling into fast-moving, jagged-rocked bodies of water. You're not, are you?"

Annah shook her head. "No."

"So what d'you say? Give up that 'Miss Silver is innocent' dream of yours, you're no Don Quixote anyway. You're in much better shape than any windmill."

"She is, Sergeant. Amanda Silver is not guilty."

"Okay, if you give it the say-so, but." He started counting on his fingers. "Method...opportunity...motive. She's got a shotgun, all you have to do is pull the trigger. She's locked in the room with the victim. There's two."

81

ANNAH TORCH   Jim DeFilippi

"Motive?"

"Two out of three, those are pretty good odds. So you're working for the Weasel on this, huh?"

"Yes."

"Well, he's a good man, Ms. Torch, he really is. We're on opposite sides all the time, but I respect the man. He never tries to make any slime-dripping slug out to be Mother Teresa. With your guy it's more straight-on. He's more like, 'Here's what my client did, Your Honor, here are the facts, here is why his sentence should be this and that and no more.' But in this case, if he thinks the Silver kid is innocent, he's not only barking up the wrong tree, girl, he's out there in the wrong damn forrest. Maybe should be in the Black Forest somewheres, or some forest out on Mars. If he thinks this kid is innocent."

"He does not, but I do."

"Okay." Gumm gave a resigned sigh. "Okay. You do."

Annah said, "I have gone over the court documents, the police reports, your report, the autopsy. I have a handle on our client, a bit of a grasp at least. But let me ask you, do you know much about the victim? Anything you can tell me in good conscience?"

"Sure. Fair enough. I can help you with some Discovery, won't hurt."

Gumm reached into the inside pocket of his ratty sports jacket and took out his omnipresent spiral notepad. He flipped a few pages, studying the notes. "We're most interested in the killer, of course—what remains to be done to her—instead of the victim—what's done is done—but I've interviewed her parents, for example. The murdered girl's parents. Dad's a hot head, Mom's an oven mitt. Let me tell you a little bit of what I've found. Discovery, it legally belongs to you anyway. But don't go getting your hopes high here, there's nothing involved that'll help Amanda Silver in a court of law."

He began alternating between looking down, checking his notes, and looking up at Annah, reciting the facts...

&&&

ANNAH TORCH   Jim DeFilippi

Dede Ann Constaghulia was born and raised in Beverly, Massachusetts, to an upper-middle class family.

One brother—younger—no sisters.

Her parents' Christian names were, oddly enough, Carmine and Carmen, apparently a source of countless jokes and wordplay within the family. "Dede" was the name on the birth certificate, not a nickname. Both parents agreed her name could be "anything but Carmelita."

She was an outgoing, sharp, friendly child with a bit of a wild side to her. When she was eight years of age, the fire department had to be called to take her down from the garage roof. She told her rescuers that she was up there, "Talking to the satellites."

Her childhood qualities remained with her into her teenage years. She played field hockey at Beverley High School, and was a member of the Future Entrepreneurs of America. Her father had made a good living with his company, Mr. C's Complete Home Service, which met homeowners' needs in plumbing, heating, cooling, electrical, and unclogging drains. Started with one truck, built it up to one of the premier type businesses of that type on the North Shore. His selling point was the homeowner could just call one number for any of the household repairs or upgrades. People seemed to like that.

His daughter's interest in business, and her membership in the FEA, pleased him.

She remained very bright and restless, right through her teens.

Gumm checked his notes.

She became pregnant in junior year, but the pregnancy was "taken care of." After that little problem was solved, her parents wished to remove her from the boyfriend and from the other "bad influences" at the school, so for her senior year, they enrolled her at the Chelsea Academy here in White Leunge in something called the ASSPP, the Advanced Secondary School Placement Program. This was a program instituted by the school in which exceptional high school students lived on the Chelsea campus for their senior year in high school.

ANNAH TORCH   Jim DeFilippi

They got their high school diploma there, and then went on to the standard two-year Chelsea curriculum.

So, Dede was actually a third year student at two-year Chelsea when she was murdered.

A housing crunch at the Academy led it to allow off-campus housing for exceptional senior year students. The two-year Program of Studies at Chelsea was referred to as junior and senior year.

Dede and fellow Chelsea senior Amanda Silver shared their off-campus rooming at an apartment house situated at 314 1/2 Rantoule Street in White Leunge. The two girls had known each other for over a year by then, and they seemed to get along quite well. They were friendly, although not close. The two often were seen together at various social functions—games, mixers, parties—but it seemed to be more a matter of convenience than closeness.

Their domestic situation on Rantoule Street was peaceful, with only minor disagreements that never rose to the level of being called arguments. For example, they both preferred loading the dishwasher to unloading it, and any marriage counselor will tell you this—the secret of a lasting domestic partnership is teaming up a loader with an unloader.

Here Sgt. Gumm looked up from his notes and grinned at Annah. She nodded for him to go on.

There were also minor disagreements concerning the ownership of certain food items in the refrigerator, especially pudding, and concerning the standards of cleanliness that the rooms should be held to. They were a bit of an odd couple in the sense that Amanda was much closer to the "neat freak" category and Dede to the "slob" classification.

No problem between them with any boyfriends, that anybody could remember or mentioned.

&&&

Gumm flipped closed his notebook with another grin, but then his face grew serious as he told Annah, "We found nothing, absolutely nothing, that would indicate that anything that looked like it happened didn't happen. Did I say that right?"

The cop looked disconsolate at the thought of the murder, as if he were still seeing the crime scene in his mind. "The girl's remains are housed in a mausoleum in the Swampscott Cemetery, that's close by to where she grew up. The mother's name was..." he checked his notes, "...Stegler, and the Stegler family has had a mausoleum there for generations."

Annah thanked the policeman for the information as she rose to leave.

He said, "See, I told you there'd be nothing there to help you."

She said, "Well, it is all grist for the mill. Thank you, Sergeant."

"Grist for the mill, I suppose so. I feel bad, Ms. Torch, the poor kid never had a chance at much of a life. Twenty years old, you know?"

Annah shook her head. "Sad, Sergeant, very sad."

He said, "And I can't help comparing her to our esteemed former Governor, Nelson Aldrich Rockefeller."

Annah looked at him. "I do not...what?"

The cop was nodding at her. "Yeah, old Rocky died, in his seventies, of a heart attack. The newspapers and the doctors referred to the event as a 'myocardial infarction,' but rumor had it he was visiting one of his mistresses when it hit. I guess they were in the midst of *in flagrant delicto* when Rocky's old ticker gave out. Could be labeled as 'overly zealous whoopie-making for a guy his age.'"

"And that reminds you of this death here? Explain?"

"Well, they both of them died with a smile on their face."

&&&

The same morning, Annah drove to the Empire State Plaza in downtown Albany. The construction of that array of buildings had lasted from 1965 to 1976 at a cost of $2 billion. The complex included the New York State Capitol

ANNAH TORCH   Jim DeFilippi

and a number of state office buildings, and had been the pet project of Governor Rockefeller for decades before his possibly exuberant demise.

Annah drove to this area in a 2017 white Subaru Outback on loan from Howard Wyzell. If a cop had pulled her over, the driver's license in her wallet would have been three years expired, except she wasn't carrying the unexpired license, and she didn't carry a wallet. If stopped, she would have to rely on the impressive elan of Howard Wyzell's name on the registration, and the impressive length of her eyelashes.

Annah eventually found parking and later found the tiny corner office of Leo Protski, the special investigator for regional D. A. Sarah T. Guffleberg.

Annah hadn't gotten stopped by a cop on her way over.

She had met Protski a few times before—crossing paths on one or two of Howard Wyzell's cases. Protski was wearing a broad smile and a Hawaiian shirt that displayed an incongruous mix of palm trees and different World War II bombers, as he escorted her into his office and asked her to "Sit, sit, sit down, please sit."

He offered her coffee or anything else that she might want, but she refused. When she was seated, he looked at her a while and then said, "I'm trying to come up with a good torch and burn line here, with me being the burn, but it won't quite come. I'll be working on it as we talk."

All men flirted with Annah, is was as natural and annoying as black-flies buzzing at your ears. Annah said, "No need. We can move on from that."

"Okay, if we must."

"I know, sir, that we are opponents on this Silver murder case, at least on paper we are, but I wonder if you could fill me in just a bit on Guffleberg's plans for the trial, just in general terms of the expected course of action that the State plans to pursue. Nothing classified. Just things that will come out in Discovery eventually. It would be appreciated."

"Of course, of course I will. Glad to help out. I'll tell you everything I'm legally allowed to. Maybe I shouldn't, but I'm recently divorced—well, not so recently—and you're really good-looking."

ANNAH TORCH Jim DeFilippi

Annah said nothing, and Protski shifted around in a desk chair that seemed too small for the length of his body. "Well, let's see, the guilt, the conviction, that's all preordained. Locked room—shotgun blast—end of story. The District Attorney is mostly interested in the sentencing phase at this point. She'd love to get the death penalty reinstated. No chance, of course, maybe just the rack or some Chinese water torture. See, Baby Johnnie Silver's little girl on a platter, that would be a trophy to hang on the wall, for Goofy, for D. A. Guffleberg. Well, I guess you can't hang trophies on a wall. What I just do there, trophy-wall, mix my metaphor?"

"I think you crossed that bridge at platter and trophy. But Guffleberg is planning to shoot for a high-end sentence? This is personal then, with her, you feel? It sounds as if it is."

"Sort of. Not really, but in a way, it is. I don't know if you saw the press conference, with the parents of the accused, but Baby Johnnie referred to our regional District Attorney as 'Goofy.' Not once, but twice. Two times. Out loud. In a public forum. Probably a slip, but maybe just a purposeful tweak. That type thing's not to be done around here. It's to be 'Sarah T. Guffleberg, District Attorney,' at all times. Calling her, 'Goofy'? On the news? On television? No, no. Goofy doesn't forgive and forget things like that."

"You just called her Goofy, a few times."

"I checked the doorway and the intercom first. You're not wired up, are you?"

Annah smiled and held her jacket open.

Protski grinned and went on. "Plus, you know, it's a public figure's kid. Baby Johnnie's a very public guy, almost a celebrity. Well, he *is* a celebrity, I guess. That spices everything up to a whole other level. We're being told to red-ball this case, pick it up and run with it. Goofy of course won't be in court, she never is, but she'll be at the microphone after every session. She'll be there on the news when the kid is sent away, for a long stretch. Goofy will prevail."

"Well, she might. She's not worried about going into court with no motive for the crime?"

"Nah, not at all. This case isn't only open and shut, it's locked tight shut by that deadbolt on the door of the room."

As she steered the Subaru back to Wyzell's house, Annah tried to steer her mind to thoughts of Governor Rockefeller—dying in another woman's bed with his wife back at home—but the vision that kept reappearing was the smiling death-mask of Dede Constaghulia.

&&&

ANNAH TORCH   Jim DeFilippi

Chapter Ten

Women also flirted with Annah Torch. During her morning visit to the chalet home of Johnnie and Grace Silver, the billionaire's wife alternated between states of being devastated by murder, invigorated by lust, and cauterized by booze.

The chalet in Watervliet, New York, was a palace-like dwelling that seemed to be surrounded by drifts of soft, white snow, even though at this point in the year the ground was brown. If a building can be both quietly modest and boldly ostentatious at the same time, this one was. The inverted V of its front was made entirely of glass held in place by wide wooden frames, except for a small entryway in the lower right corner. The top of the V seemed to be pointing up to heaven, with no hint of modesty or supplication. The light wood paneling of both side walls ran vertically into portions of stone that seemed to be splaying out into the earth. The fourth wall, in the back, was nestled into the curve of the hillside that the place was built on. Annah didn't walk around to this back wall, which was facing north, but she knew it would hold no large windows, and if there were a door back there, it would be practical in size and well insulated.

Inside, Grace Silver, holding onto a midmorning, heavy tumbler of brown booze, insisted on showing Annah around the place before they sat down to talk about Amanda. "I always give the tour to everybody who comes, forgive me, you have to see the bedrooms." This from a woman whose daughter was being charged with murder.

As the tour progressed, the guide told Annah that her "toddy" was called a Mare's Leg, and would be accompanying them for the tour. Upstairs, with Grace heading back down to the kitchen to refuel, Annah waited in the main hall and studied pictures of various Silver houses around the world. As she had headed down the stairs, Grace called back to Annah, "Can I come back with two?"

Annah answered with a, "No, fine, thank you."

ANNAH TORCH   Jim DeFilippi

When Grace got back from her refueling stop, even though Annah didn't ask, Grace carefully explained the drink's recipe: three fingers of any cheap bourbon, a splash of soda, ice, a tumble of maple syrup, and many vigorous shakes of Frank's Hot Sauce. Tabasco could be substituted, "But you'd be sacrificing flavor." She added, "It's something I need, I admit, in these times of ours."

Annah silently followed Grace through the seven rooms, peeking into the three baths. They eventually returned to the Grand Room downstairs, which had a ten-foot polar bear pelt spread out across an upper level wall. The thing seems to be performing a high dive into the room's sprawling couch, which held six pillows, none of which matched any other. Hanging near each of the front paws of the beast were two large wooden Crucifixes, with a Jesus nailed onto each one, looking stoic but apparently not suffering.

Grace sat Annah down on the couch and, even though she had three upholstered chairs, two black Boston rockers, and a recliner to choose from, she sat on the couch next to Annah. The cherrywood coffee table at the women's feet held four large books of photographs, side by side—books of the great bridges of America, the great mountains of the world, and the great meals of Europe. The fourth book had a plain white cover with no printing. The only photograph in the room was a wood-framed shot of Amanda. She looked about fifteen, was wearing sunglasses, smiling, and holding up a glass of something that looked like a Mare's Leg to the camera. A chandelier of eight soft lights, each with a white shade that looked to Annah like a Chef's hat, hung from the upper level of the house, a good twenty-five feet above the silk-wool rug and the bamboo flooring.

"In some ways, this one is one of my favorite homes," Grace told Annah. "It's important for me to have a sanctum in a time like this. I sit here and think about our daughter in that horrible, smelly hospital room. Or a jail cell, even worse. It's driving us both crazy." She took a sip and held the tumbler up toward Annah. "You sure?"

Annah shook her head. "Your husband, not at home?"

"No, it's just me. All alone. Drinking a bit and seeking solace, seeking some comfort. Can I offer you something else then, anything?" Grace pointed

ANNAH TORCH   Jim DeFilippi

her tumbler at a six-foot high wooden cabinet on the other side of the room. "We have everything in there. I plan to have it emptied by the winter solstice. Johnnie doesn't drink. Maybe we could share something, a drink, you could help me..."

"No."

Grace suddenly looked around, like she had just been transported into the room from another universe. "Johnnie won't allow any servants in this house. Our chef stays in town, comes in just when we need him. Gardeners are okay, they're allowed, landscapers, outside, and of course they plow the snow when it comes. But inside it's just me. I do the cleaning and cook mostly. Andre tells me what to do over the phone, when I'm flummoxed. Laundry. We have so much money to be doing this myself, but I don't mind, I like it. Isn't that odd? Johnnie teases me, says I'll make someone a good little homemaker someday. Isn't that funny?"

"Yes."

"Isn't that strange?"

"Yes, it is."

"I don't mind though."

"Mrs. Silver, may I ask, where is your husband? I had hoped to talk to the both of you."

"Grace. Like in the church. I'm Actual and Sanctifying Grace. There's two kinds, you know. I'm Grace. I'm both types. So you can call me that. I hope you will. I hope...I hope...I hope for many things."

"Grace, where is your husband, may I ask you that?"

"He's over with the Pope. The Vatican. No, he really is, although that would be the ultimate name-drop, wouldn't it? No, he's gone to Rome all right. He had to. He'll be back Sunday—is today—what day, Sunday? I lose track. He'll be back soon and he'll make this mess with Amanda all right again. My husband loves my daughter, our daughter."

"I'm sure he does. Grace, does your husband go to Rome a lot? On business?"

"He's been over a few times, maybe once, before all this happened."

"I see."

"Las Vegas."

"What?"

Grace kept taking sips between sentences. "Originally he was scheduled to go to Las Vegas, after he left Rome. I was going to meet him out there. He plays this type poker, he loves it. He's very good at it. He wins all the tournaments. But he cancelled, of course. With all of this now going on."

"Of course. Grace, I have come here to do some questioning of you. Is that okay? Of your husband too, if he were here."

"Rome."

"Yes. Grace, I want to prove to the authorities that Amanda did not commit this murder."

"Of course she didn't...she didn't?"

"No, she did not."

"Well, Johnnie will prove it then. After he gets back. Money brings clout along with it as it goes."

"Yes, it does. Grace, does Amanda..."

"Did I offer you a drink already?"

"Yes, you did."

"May I?"

"No, I said no."

"May I slide over, lay my head on you shoulders? For a little while?"

"No."

"May I kiss you?"

"No."

"Of course not. What was I thinking?"

"Grace, was your daughter ever a violent person?"

"No, of course not. Never. She would let the butterflies out of the jar, even though we punched holes in the top, for them to breathe with."

"Does she, or you, or anyone in the family, have access to guns?"

"No. Of course not. Johnnie would go hunting, when he had time. But I think that was with a bow and arrow thing. Or one of those things Ivanhoe uses. Or Mel Gibson with his face all painted up."

"There are no guns in the house here? Or in her place at school? That you saw?"

"No, of course not."

"Do you have any idea where Amanda would have gotten access to a shotgun? The shotgun that she used?"

Grace began waving her hands in the air. "It's two different universes, dear. Amanda and shotguns. These cannot live together on the same plane. No."

"Did Amanda have a boyfriend, anyone special? That she talked about?"

"No."

"Do you know if Dede, her roommate, was seeing anyone?"

"No. Neither girl was anything. They were unattached at the hip."

"And they got along."

"Like blood sisters."

"Grace, I want to talk to some of Amanda's friends, at the school. Maybe they can help me figure out about the shotgun. Do you have the names of some friends she was close to, that I could talk to?"

"Besides Didi?"

"Yes, other than her."

"You've never met my Amanda, have you, you two?"

"Just since after it happened. In the hospital."

"She wasn't always like that."

"And she will not be forever. She will come back. But her friends' names?"

"Well, we didn't know them too well. One was Hanna, or Samatha, I remember. I don't know the last name. You could ask the school."

"I will."

"We had her for Thanksgiving, she couldn't go home. And her friend was Sandra. I can remember because the two names hymned, like in a song. Samantha and Sandra. Like a banana. They seemed nice."

"I will talk to them both."

"That's your name too, isn't it. Ann."

"Annah. Yes, with an H."

"They called her Samantha Banana, I think, just for a joke. Just like you do."

"Right."

"I want her back here, Annie, and well, and awake."

"I hope that she will be."

"I don't know how she could have done such a thing." Grace took another shallow of the Mare's Leg. "I'm sorry, sorry, sorry." She lowered her head and cried for a while. "I am so sorry for what my daughter has done."

"I hope that I will be able to prove that she is innocent."

Grace looked up. "Really? Do you believe that? That's wonderful. But I suppose lawyers have to say that, to act like that, so that they can act it out in their heads. To really believe it. For their performance in court." Grace kept drinking.

ANNAH TORCH　　　　　　　　　　　　　　　　Jim DeFilippi

Annah said, "Not a performance," but Grace didn't hear her.

Grace leaned forward, placed her drink on the coffee table. "I was an actor too, you know. They called us 'actresses' back then. I studied with Olga Raskolnikov. Like in the Bible. You've heard of her."

"Probably."

"East Village. Right by the Bowery, but better. Madame Raskolnikov showed us that all great acting must come from within." Grace picked up the tumbler and tapped her chest with it. "One must tap into one's deepest feeling– your emotions."

"Oh."

Grace leaned forward and put the tumbler back on the coffee table, on one of the books. "Johnnie put an end to all that. Made me quit. He said it's all bullshit anyhow. He said he's talked to the greatest actors in the world. On his travels. For his business. He's met all of them. Daniel Day-Lewis, Monty Python, all of them."

Annah was nodding.

Grace said, "Johnnie said to me, you get any of them drunk enough, they're tell you, it's all on the surface. Nothing within. It's all sight and sound. Just what the audience sees and hears, that's all. That's all that matters. It's technical. Technique. Window dressing. No artistry involved. That's what Johnnie said."

"That seems to be a different view. I have always heard…"

"Johnnie said he could act like John Barrymore, if he wanted to. Even better."

"Really."

"Johnnie told me that people go to the Louvre, they're not looking into the Mona Lisa's soul, they're just looking at her face." Grace stopped talking, picked the tumbler back up, took a swallow, and said, "For a drunk, I can be quite erudite, am I not?"

"Yes, you are."

Grace said, "Well, it comes and goes."

Annah stood up from the couch. "Samantha and Sandra. I will go talk to them. Thank you for the names, Grace. Thank you for the time. Stay strong, Grace, please. We will protect your daughter as well as we can, and that is a good legal protection to have. Howard Wyzell..."

"He's a weasel, I heard, but a good one."

"And Grace, again, you cannot come up with any reason, anything at all, why Amanda would want to do harm to her roommate?"

Grace shook her head, took a sip.

As Annah began to step away from the couch, Grace grabbed hold of the sleeve of her black jacket. "As long as you don't ask, I'm going to tell you. My Johnnie takes his lovers from all over the world, mostly right here at home. I have too. Somewhat."

"I'm sorry."

"Oh no, it's fine. Johnnie is not ashamed of anything he's ever done. And neither am I."

Grace Silver was drunk, but she was lying.

&&&

ANNAH TORCH   Jim DeFilippi

Chapter Eleven

    Samantha Gafton was telling Annah, "Oh, sure, we Chelsea Prep girls give the best hand-jobs in the state. Haven't you ever heard of the Chelsea Handlers? Well, that's us."

Samantha was a chunky, unsure coed at the Chelsea Two-Year Academy for Young Women, and Annah was trying to get her to talk about Amanda Silver, or maybe about Dede Constaghulia, but Samantha insisted that they wait for a second coed, Sandra McGwen, to get there before they discussed their friends. Sandra had Bio until eleven.

They were sitting on a green park bench in a central area of the Chelsea campus that the students and staff called "The Tri," a triangle of browning grass and stately elm trees bordered by bumpy, root-lifted concrete sidewalks on all three sides. Clumps of two and three students dressed in skirts and jeans, clutching schoolbooks and iPads to their chests, strolled by as Annah and Samantha waited for Sandra.

Annah wasn't sure if these kids could still be called co-eds, especially in an all-girl prep school, but this art student formally known as coed was explaining how in general Chelsea girls were the coolest and most sought-after girls on the planet. She seemed to be trying to convince herself. She often touched her hair as she spoke and gave out nervous quick bumps of laughter at nothing in particular.

Annah had started the morning with the Coordinating Dean of Chelsea, who at first refused to reveal any student names or information, but she had opened up once convinced that Annah was there on behalf of senior student Amanda Silver and her family. After getting the surnames of Amanda's two friends mentioned by the drunken Grace Silver, and arranging to meet the two girls, Annah had spent an hour strolling the campus and talking informally with passing students.

ANNAH TORCH   Jim DeFilippi

When any of the students would ask about her beauty secrets—and they all did—she would answer, "Deep Woods Off," and they would write it down or punch the name into their phone.

"They told Sandy to meet us here, just like me," Samantha was explaining. "She'll be here, then we can talk, okie-doke?"

&&&

The Chelsea Academy had been founded in 1880 and for nearly a century and a half had remained among the list of prestigious preparatory institutions for young females. The two-hundred and sixty-five acre campus had been designed by Frederic Olmsted, the greatest American landscape architect, the genius who had designed New York City's Central Park and the 1893 Chicago Worlds Fair, both considered high points of landscape architecture. It had been Olmsted who suggested that no walkways be pressed onto the Chelsea campus until a year of student foot-traffic would stamp out a blueprint. Thus the triangle that Annah and Samantha were now within had been laid out.

Although open to all religious denominations, the school had been founded by a devout Catholic, and until recently, its history had basically been a rosary bead string of high points, despite being in a town known for being on the "bottom rung," a sort of venial sin of towns. The school had survived a minor scandal in the 1930's when a faculty member had incorrectly named Zelda Fitzgerald as an alumnae. Accurately listed among its graduates were an Olympic diving champion and a popular cookbook author.

The scions of American industry had through the years fallen prey to the school's "Gateway to the Ivys" motto. This spin had even spun its way through the 1960's, when many private schools had been wounded by the anti-establishment emotions of youth.

The school being situated in a town of such dubious distinction as White Lounge cut both ways. Parents had to be convinced that the sinister reputation of the town had not leaked over onto the school, while the applicants themselves were quietly excited by a potential exposure to a subculture underbelly.

ANNAH TORCH   Jim DeFilippi

With the arrival of the Twenty-first Century—when everyone from Madonna to various B-List celebrities was keeping busy "re-inventing themselves"—a portion of the administration suggested a plan to "reinvent" Chelsea as a sports school. Private high schools dedicated solely to producing future tennis players, and even future female hockey players, were becoming popular and profitable, but the more traditional administrators won out and the movement was squashed.

The current yearly tuition at the school was $32,000, with room and board raising the total cost to $61,621. The full-color, shiny pamphlets which the school sent out as a recruiting tool somehow made these figures seem like a positive.

The last decade had been a difficult one for the Chelsea Two-Year Academy for Young Women. Expenses and salaries, along with insurance and tax increases, had the school running in the red for the last seven years. The endowment fund was still substantial, but it was shrinking. Faculty and administrative salaries had been frozen, some programs of study and special events had been done away with. The title of the position held by Christina Bausch, the woman from whom Annah had gotten Sandra and Samantha's names, was changed from "Headmistress," which seemed dated, to "Coordinating Dean," a longer title with a shorter salary.

The ASSPP, the Advanced Secondary School Placement Program, in which high school students like Dede Constaghulia became students, was a facade used to increase admissions and student numbers.

The Dean of Advancement and Recruiting Services—basically a salesperson—tried to spin the off-campus housing choice—the one that got Amanda and Dede into their apartment— as the result of an increase in qualified applicants. In reality, it was a response to a major portion of one of the housing dorms having to be renovated due to rodent infestation and a carpenter ant invasion.

The addition of Johnnie Silver's daughter was a huge publicity coup for the school, which was more than eliminated of course by her current status as a murder suspect.

ANNAH TORCH   Jim DeFilippi

As Annah was leaving Dean Bausch's office to go question Amanda's two friends, the Dean had jokingly said, "Chelsea will always survive, and if it does not, we hope to die with a smile on our face."

Annah couldn't decide if the comment was a reference to senior student Dede Constaghulia.

&&&

Samantha Gafton was chewing open a packet of granola bars and telling Annah about Halloween, when Sandra McGwen saw them from across the Tri, waved, jogged over, and sat on the bench between them.

Annah was barely through a brief introduction of herself and her purpose when Sandra asked her for her "beauty regimen." Annah mentioned the Deep Woods Off and both girls pronounced the name into their phones' Voice Memo.

"Girls, I am here to find out what happened between your two friends, Didi and Amanda. I have heard the adults' take on everything, but no one knows young people your age like young people your age do, so could I ask you some questions?"

Both girls smiled and agreed how horrible the whole thing was. Just terrible.

Sandra did most of the answering, with Samantha nodding her approval and agreement. Most of the information that Annah managed to elicit from the pair was little more than a teenage-slanted rehash of what was already known.

She did learn that Dede's nickname was "Dede the Dead." "And that was even before she was dead for real," Sandra explained. "It was the mean boys' idea of a joke, I guess, about how she was just a sack of potatoes in the sack. Wait, does that make sense?"

"Sure it does. So calling her Dede the Dead was just a cruel reference to her lack of sexual intercourse skills?"

Sandra asked, "What's that supposed to mean?"

Samantha asked, "What kind of skills?"

Annah shook it off. "Can either one of you give me any names of guys Dede was dating? These guys who called her dead in the sack."

The girls looked at each other and both shook their heads. Sandra said, "It was just guys, I guess."

"Town guys? Townies? Or maybe guys from other schools around here? Any ideas?"

Two blank stares. Samantha agreed with Sandra that, "Townies are gross though."

"How about Amanda? Do either of you know of any guys she was dating?"

Sandra said, "You mean hooking up with? No. But what guys would look at her now, you know? Anyway."

Samantha added, "It's too bad."

Annah asked, "Girls, did either of your friends ever show any violence? Toward each other? Toward anyone?"

Sandra said, "God, no."

Samantha said, "God, no."

"Did you ever see either of them with a weapon? A gun? Either in their room or anywhere?"

Sandra said, "God, no."

Samantha said, "I hate guns."

"So you can come up with no reason that Amanda would want to harm Dede?"

"No."

"They meshed."

"Dede used to tease her about she had a sugar daddy, but Amanda didn't."

"A sugar daddy? Do you know who?"

"No, it might have been a real one. She'd go to the bank and get some cash when she needed it."

Annah asked, "From her family? Maybe her real daddy was her sugar daddy?"

"Probably."

"Now girls, be honest now, I want you to tell me the truth—were the girls, one or both of them, into things that their parents did not know about?"

"No."

"No."

"No? No drugs? Drinking?"

Sandra perked up. "Oh, sure, that for sure, but nothing special."

"What sort of drugs, do you know?"

Sandra said, "I never did anything with them."

Samantha said, "I never did anything with them," and then added, by way of clarification, "Neither one of us did."

Annah told them, "So, okay, nobody is going to get into any trouble or anything like that. I just have to know. Have you ever heard anyone ever say that maybe, one or the both or them, they might be using something called 'Ketamine'?"

Both girls shook their heads.

Annah said, "It's a horse tranquilizer. Some people call it, 'Special K.'"

Sandra said, "I've heard of a cereal like that."

Samantha asked, "They use it to kill horses with?"

Annah asked, "How about Acepromazine? Horses again. Or any other drug you think either of the girls might have been using?"

Sandra said, "Amanda called me 'Sandy,' once, so I thought she might have been smoking on something."

Samantha said, "'Sandy' is cute for you, but those poor horses."

Annah was fighting an urge to head back into the Woods, but she felt compelled to ask, "So the two girls were getting along well, right up until now, that you saw?"

Samantha took the lead on this one and shook her head. "Not anymore they're not."

Sandra looked around the Tri, then leaned toward Annah and said, "There was only that one time, well, this one thing."

Annah asked, "What time?"

The two girls looked at each other, each one trying to decide.

Annah told them, "Girls, this is to help your friend. You both know, we all know, Amanda could not have murdered Dede. They might have her executed unless we can help her out."

Both girls seemed startled by the concept. Samantha asked, "You mean like on Netflix?"

Annah said, "No, for real. Unless all of us can help her out. Girls, I don't think Amanda did anything wrong. You both want to tell me something. I will not use it to get you in trouble. Nobody will ever know who told me."

Sandra swallowed hard a few times, then squeezed her eyes shut, then opened them wide and said, "There's this bus, see?"

Samantha said her friend's name.

Sandra looked at her. "We have to, all right?"

Annah put a hand on Sandra's shoulder. "Go ahead. The one time the girls didn't get along. Tell me."

Sandra swallowed hard again. "No, it's not that, but there's this bus. It goes by campus. You catch it down on Center Street. Walk right down. They call it the 'Dust Bus.'"

"Why is that?"

"Because years ago, kids used to take Angel Dust on the ride in. This was before the carnivore virus."

"Go on."

"It's a party bus. Dede and 'manda used to sneak in on it, into Albany. To go drinking. Kids do it all the time. Please don't tell anyone."

"No, do not worry."

"I rode it a few times, until I threw up."

Samantha went all in. "I did too. But not the throw-up part. I let some guy I didn't know feel me up on it one time. He was in the Navy, I think."

"But Amanda and Dede."

"Well," Sandra said, "They used to take it in together. To the Combat Zone. To this bar. A real bad bar. Then, all of a sudden, Dede's telling everyone there's something bad going on with Amanda. So someday, if they're drinking, she might come out and tell her she knows."

"Knows what?"

"I don't know."

Annah asked, "What was the name of this place?"

The two girls looked at each other.

Sandra said, "Thunder and Stumpy's. It's a bar."

Samantha said, "Thunder and Stumpy's. It's a bar."

Chapter Twelve

With concern over possibly ruining her big girl clothes, which were dry-clean only, Annah wore her woods outfit to Thunder and Stumpy's Bar in Albany, New York—that meant her heavy Solomon Gor-Tex boots, one layer of white North Face leggings, and a gray, long-sleeved thermal undershirt on top.

Since the Fever, a new, suspect group of bars and suspected dopehouses had sprung up on the fringe of downtown Albany. Locals christened the area "the Combat Zone," after the notorious section of 1960's Boston, once infamous for its decadence, now extinct. His constituency gave Boston Mayor Thomas "Mumbles" Menino credit for the area's re-emergence from sin, due to his efforts as a member of Boston's City Council and then President of the Council. The Mayor would mumble his appreciation.

D. A. Sarah Guffleberg was planning to follow in Mumbles' footsteps and become Albany's Combat Zone Eliminator, but this political stepping stone was still on her back burner.

Albany's local version of an urban rats-nest was small and centralized, although it still offered a hardy sense of intimidation and despair. At its center and heart was a block of rundown bars, frequented by renegades, mafia wannabes, out of work strong-arm men, and adventurous college kids.

Very few beyond the most foolish and reckless students would venture into a place like Thunder and Stumpy's. Upon entry, most of the naive youngsters would take a glance around, realize that they had made a wrong turn, and quickly head for the red Exit sign. "Toto, I don't think we're on campus anymore."

It was hard for Annah to place a couple of rosy-cheeked, barely nubile students like Amanda and Dede in such a place, an eyesore packed with thugs and bruisers, three-time losers—a cross between a Scarface speakeasy from the

ANNAH TORCH　　　　　　　　　　　　　　　　　Jim DeFilippi

1920's and a WWF wrestling crowd from the 1980's, except that at this here-and-now, every customer felt that he possessed keen political insight.

The innocent daughter of one of the richest men on earth—sucking down a beer—here? With her equally innocent and naive roommate? Why?

Annah checked the blinking neon sign outside, with its burned-out capital T and its dimming S, and she stepped inside.

The place was small and dark and smokey, crowded with maybe thirty to thirty-five customers intent on defying the maximum occupancy ordinance. Over the P.A., Merle Haggard was explaining to the clientele how his Mama had tried, but she just couldn't make him into anything more than what he was. Kegged beer was still being served in pre-Fever pitchers. Two matching front doors were set into the gray wooden front wall. Chairs and tables were crowded together throughout most of the room. The bar itself ran the length of the back wall, stopping short of the corner by a few feet to allow for a door that led back to the kitchen and storeroom. A small window behind the bar exposed a square of the overcrowded, apparently unoccupied and unused kitchen.

Health and law enforcement authorities had obviously given up trying to enforce any regulations on the place, which was stubbornly remaining ass-to-crotch crowded, packed with more facial hair than facemarks.

High-def, flat-screen television sets were dangling from each sidewall and above the bar, soundless, and giving the impression that the place wished to present itself as a sports bar. Adding to this impression was a glass trophy case set between the two front doors. The case displayed and labeled some second-tier memorabilia of various New York sports teams: Joe Pepitone's bat, a pair of Mookie Wilson's socks, an autographed picture of Kenny "Sky" Walker winning the 1989 Slam Dunk competition, a crotch cup supposedly worn by Thurman Munson with its scratch marks still visible.

The bartender was a big, pulpy guy wearing yellow aviator sunglasses and a stained white apron over his New York Rangers jersey. The jersey's right sleeve had been cut off to reveal a muscular, tattooed arm and a cheap wristwatch.

ANNAH TORCH   Jim DeFilippi

Annah ordered a beer—any beer would do, in a bottle or loose, didn't matter. She took a short sip that would be her only one, then slipped out of her backpack, laid it on the bar, and removed three photographs from the side pocket. She slapped each one on the bar, one by one, pointed at the bartender, then pointed at each photo.

The first was a high school graduation picture of Amanda Silver. A pretty girl with blond flipped hair, wearing a white graduation gown and mortar board. The bartender leaned over, pretended to study the picture, then shook his head.

The second was a yearbook picture from Beverley High School of Dede Constaghulia, alive, but showing that death-mask smile. Same reaction from the barkeeper.

The third photograph was of the Filipino-Blitzer .12 gage shotgun that had been fired into the Beverley High grad. The bartender looked at the picture for a while, then raised his eyes to give a nervous glance over at and across the crowd, like he was searching for someone.

Annah followed his glance and asked, "Who?"

The bartender yelled out a "Hey!" across the room toward a big, square-faced thug who was sitting with three friends in a back corner. The square-face waved a hand, pushed up from the table, leaned back in to take a swig from his beer, and shuffled over to the bar. He was followed by his three table-mates. Square-Face stood close in to Annah, making sure she would notice his appraising top-to-bottom look. His three mates stood close behind him, making noises of appreciation and glancing first at Annah, then at each other, then back to Annah.

The bartender slid the picture of the sawed-off across the bar, so that Square-Face could study it. The bartender nodded toward Annah.

Square-Face picked up the picture, held it close to his face, looked up at the dim overhead lighting, then back at the picture. He said to Annah, "You interested in this gun?"

Annah nodded.

"What for?"

"I want to know about it."

"You want to know, Miss Long-johns? Huh. Okay. Guy we know used to come in here, asking about things. He told us his name was Lenny Piper. You ever hear of him?"

"No."

"No, you won't. He come in here drinking all the time, asking questions. We thought he was just some drunk. We got to calling him the Fried Piper."

One of Square-Face's boys gave a short, sarcastic snort at the name.

Annah tapped the picture. "Does he have something to do with this shotgun?"

Square-Face said, "No, nothing at all."

"Then why are we talking about him?"

"Because he came in here asking a lot of questions. Just like you are. Turns out he was working for somebody."

"And?"

"And so...he disappeared."

Square-Face grinned, turned around and looked at the room. Everyone's eyes were following this bar-front summit meeting. There seemed to be some sort of a prearranged signal in place, because even though he gave nothing but a glance—no words, no gestures—people suddenly were getting up from their tables and walking toward the front doors. Guys with dates quickly dropped some bills on the table and hustled the women toward one of the two front doors. Everyone seemed to be in a rush. No one was looking back. Single guys were gulping a last sip of beer and leaving. One woman started to ask her date a question, but he just tugged her by the arm and out the door. No one else spoke a word.

ANNAH TORCH   Jim DeFilippi

When they were gone, someone pushed a button on the P. A., and Merle went quiet. With his expanded chest still facing Annah and her photographs, Square-Face called back over his right shoulder, "Roscoe." One of the men standing behind him went to the set of front doors. Each door held an old fashioned bolt and barrel lock. Roscoe slid each bolt across into its hasp, and flipped it down. Then he pulled the shades on each of the peep-hole windows, and he turned back to Square-Face.

Everyone stood silent, no one moving or talking.

Annah's eyes swept around the room. She took a rag off the bar, went behind the bar and stuffed the rag between the doorframe and the swinging door that led back to the kitchen. She pressed the door tightly closed, and then jiggled it a bit to see if the door was jammed solidly shut. She seemed satisfied.

This confused the men.

Annah came back around to the front of the bar. She sighed and shrugged, as if facing an unpleasant task. She surveyed the crowd. Twelve men, including the bartender. She calculated each one's physical conditioning and his preparedness to do battle. She was not impressed. Most of them were big and soft and slow, like third-string linebackers gone to seed. A few she classified as "tiny," maybe five-nine to five-ten, under two-hundred pounds.

Square-Face had turned and was numbering his army, pointing a finger at each one as he counted. He turned back to Annah. "I got twelve men here."

Annah agreed. "That was my total, yes."

"Twelve."

Annah said, "Counting you. Like the twelve Apostles." Her comment got no reaction from the men. "I think of the Last Supper. Have you guys eaten yet? Does this place serve food?" She looked back at the window to the kitchen.

The men were smiling, but they seemed somewhat confused, and a bit intimidated.

Annah told them, "I am sorry, I should not have gone Biblical. I apologize for that."

ANNAH TORCH Jim DeFilippi

Square-Face smirked, but didn't seem to know what he was smirking at. He wasn't taking his eyes off Annah. He told her, "I'm just wondering, you're a big girl, I'm just wondering here if...what's your name again?"

Annah didn't answer.

Square-Face said, "Doesn't matter. I'm just wondering if that snatch of yours can handle all twelve of us. You think so?"

The men behind giggled.

Square-Face went on. "Cause, girl, we're about to unflower you now. Poke you up your ass. One by one, nothing kinky, nothing front-door-back-door, same time. Except maybe if Roscoe there gets carried away, can't wait his turn." Roscoe grinned sheepishly and looked down. Someone punched his shoulder. "And so, Miss Long-johns, I have to ask, where would you like to have it done? On the floor? We get it done down there? On top of the bar? Everybody can see better up there. But it's your call. We aim to be gentlemen about this. I wish Stumpy hadn't got rid of the pool-table. I like girls on top a pool table. Something about the feel of felt on my bare ass."

"And hard balls," one of the guys called from the back.

During Square-Face's monologue, Annah seemed to be following the spots in the bar he was pointing at, but she was checking the crowd for weapons.

Square-Face asked, "Do them long-johns you're wearing have a trapdoor in the back, for your ass? Let me see." Square-Face pretended to look around behind Annah.

Annah said, "Twelve men. Of course, I must resist you all. You outnumber me, but I have something working in my favor."

Square-Face's grin broadened. "I'm looking around the place, I just don't see it. What you got going for yourself in this situation, Long-johns, huh?"

Twelve men.

Annah reached across for her backpack on the bar, took out a pair of leather gloves with the fingers cut off, and she began slipping them on.

ANNAH TORCH　　　　　　　　　　　　　　　Jim DeFilippi

Pulling the left glove tighter, she said, "This isn't for you, it's for me."

She stepped closer in to Square-Face and—pulling the right glove tighter—she said, "I have the element of sur..."—Annah's arm was a three-hundred horsepower piston—the steel fist at the top of that piston crushed and flattened Square-Face's nose. Blood squirted out to all four corners of his face as he crumbled to his knees, whimpering in pain, looking like he was hoping to go unconscious. His hands cupped his face, blood leaking from between his fingers. Two buddies were trying to lift him back onto his feet, but he was pushing them away as he whimpered. The center of his face was already turning a solid black.

Eleven.

Annah checked the others, they were yet to come forward, hesitating, their movements incredibly slow. She turned around to the barkeeper, who was foolishly trying to untie his apron strings behind his back. His arms were busy. Annah took hold of both his ears and slammed his face down onto the bar with a popping sound. His body went limp and he slowly slid down and out of sight behind the bar. Annah leaned over to take a look down at him. His aviator glasses had shattered, the glass had exploded from both lenses across his face. He was crying, holding the back of his wrist up to his forehead, like he was a *prima donna*.

Ten.

One of the smaller men grabbed a whiskey bottle off a table and took it over to the bar. He tried to smash off the bottom of the bottle, intending to use it to come after her with the stem and the jagged glass. But when he slammed the bottle on the edge of the bar rail, it just clunked, it didn't break. He tried again. No. Annah went over to him, and quicker than he could comprehend, she yanked the bottle out of his hand, smashed it for him, and handed it back.

She nodded and told him, "You are old school, my pal. Good. That is encouraging."

He stood looking at her for a while, holding the broken bottle in his limp right hand. He placed the shattered bottle on top of the bar, went over to

ANNAH TORCH   Jim DeFilippi

the dark corner where he had been sitting before everything had started. He sat down in a chair and folded his hands in his lap.

Nine.

The others started to close in on Annah. She quickly and effortlessly hopped up onto the bar and stood there above them. She said, "*Take the High Ground*, 1953, Richard Widmark." But the nine men weren't listening.

One of them started to climb up on the bar to get to her, but when he placed his hand on the bar-rail Annah crushed it with her Solomon boot. He screamed, but he must have been one of the more tenacious of the group, because he tried to climb atop the bar a second time, now using his one good hand.

Annah's battle position put her at a perfect level to kick the guy in the face, so she did. With the same boot that already had blood on it from the hand-stomping. The man moaned and twisted like a ballet dancer as he clunked down onto the floor.

Eight.

Annah hopped down off the bar, just to give the final eight a fighting chance. Three or four were closing in on her. One guy yelled to the others, "Look out, she's swift, she's awful swift!"

Annah stared at the man who was yelling and she pointed a stern, commanding forefinger at him. She stared at him. He visibly shriveled. Annah told him, "Go to your place." The man stood frozen, his eyes wide and focused on Annah. Then louder: "Go to your place." The man stayed still for a moment more, looking around at his friends. He walked back to a far table, where he sat and slumped down into his chair. And there he stayed.

Seven.

One of the smaller men lunged at her, arms out, hands clenching, trying to grab her and twist her into a take-down tackle, but she broke his grasp, moved quickly around so that she was behind him, and she gave him a head-butt to the back of his skull. The butt stunned him, he lost his balance and started to fall sideways. Annah grabbed him by the back of his belt and the hair on his head,

ANNAH TORCH — Jim DeFilippi

she lifted him off the floor, and she threw him over the bar and halfway through the kitchen window. He smashed through both the glass and the wooden mullions of the window. He lay there, still, only the bottom half of his body visible to the barroom. After a moment, his ass and legs began twitching. He started making sounds like he was retching onto the kitchen floor.

Six.

Annah grabbed a half-full pitcher of beer off the bar and, keeping it level so as not to spill the contents, heaved it into the chest of a man wearing a camouflage t-shirt. He actually called out the word, "Ooomph," when the pitcher hit him in the solar plexus. He staggered for a moment, turned to the door as if considering a retreat, and then his body folded into itself and onto the ground, where he lay moaning and making incomprehensible sounds that sounded foreign. His mouth was gurgling out red spit over his lips, but he still had a bit of fight left. He pushed himself back up and tried to voice a curse or a threat, but before it came out, Annah drove an upward-aimed fist into his chin, which drove his jawbone up towards his brain, which left him unconscious and concussed.

Five.

The remaining men stood looking at each other and watching Annah move across the floor to the front wall, where she put her gloved fist through the glass of the trophy case, and removed Joe Pepitone's baseball bat. Once she turned back to the room holding the bat halfway down its trunk, like a baton-twirler, the tide of the battle shifted. In truth, the tide had shifted at the first punch thrown.

Two of the five remaining potential assaulters held up their palms and began backing away, like they were twin rats and she was the mother ship. They didn't take their eyes off the label of Pepitone's bat. They were keeping their palms held up.

Annah quoted Roberto Duran for them, but using questions marks. "*No mas? No mas?*"

They just looked at her.

ANNAH TORCH   Jim DeFilippi

Four.

Three.

Two of the remaining men made a desperate, halfhearted charge at her, but she stepped forward just as they reached her, moved between them, shoved them both into the bar from behind, cupped her hands around the sides of their heads, and crushed the two heads together like orchestra cymbals. The clunk sounded like empty coconuts, it was almost musical. One groaned, one yelped, both fell.

One.

The man named Roscoe, the one who had originally bolted the front doors, now ran to the door on the right and started desperately trying to unbolt it. It seemed to be frozen in place. He rattled the door, still locked, he looked over his shoulder at the approaching Annah. He made an absurd squeaking noise, like a mouse.

Annah grabbed him, lifted him high over her head, and slammed him onto the floor, where he lay motionless. She took a bottle of beer off a table, held her thumb partway over the spout and sprinkled it onto Roscoe's face. "*Dominus vobiscum.*" The unconscious man snorted, then twitched and snorted again. His eyes suddenly opened and went from non-comprehension to panic, looking up at the woman standing above him. He held his hands up towards her and started to say something quietly, with a begging, submissive tone.

Annah flipped the man over onto his belly, yanked his right arm behind him, and started twisting it and pushing it up across his back toward the back of his head. He began crying. Ligaments were tearing, something was snapping.

Annah called down to him, "Call me Jesus." The man whimpered. She pushed the arm further up his back, it was almost at the base of his neck. She said louder, "Call me Jesus."

The guy was shrieking and crying. He cried out, "My arm."

Annah bent over and explained to him, "No, this is *my* arm. I might allow you to use it, if you call me Jesus." She gave the arm a sharp twist.

"Oww, okay, all right, you're Jesus. You're a Jesus freak."

"Just Jesus."

"Jesus."

The victor gave another twist, harder, things kept snapping. Roscoe gave out another shriek and begged, "Let go my arm. Give it back to me please."

Annah bent down over him again and whispered in his ear, "Who?"

"What?"

"Who. Who does that shotgun belong to? The one in the picture."

"I don't know." Another sharp twist, more snapping sounds.

"Who? Who?"

The wounded, suffering man, called out through his snot and his tears, "Nico. Nico Madness."

&&&

Chapter Thirteen

Nico Madness was born Nicholas Parva twenty-eight year ago in the Coney Island neighborhood of Brooklyn.

By the age of ten, he could be found at construction sites and bus terminals selling stolen cigarette cartons and nicotine patches.

At fourteen, he had dropped out of school and gained full-time employment as a message runner for a brothel in Flatbush.

Two years later, he was named co-leader of a street gang called the Holy Melengas.

Then, he suffered through his first period of incarceration upon being arrested at a chop shop on the Bay Ridge Parkway.

After serving out his six-month sentence, during which he received his first troubling mental evaluation and psychological report, he relocated to the Albany area where he lived with his maternal grandmother, Rosa Hidalgo. It was believed that the move was made necessary or at least hastened in order to avoid the heat from law enforcement, along with a paternity suit from the lawyers of a young girl's parents.

Within six months of his move to the upstate Capital area, he was charged with selling an unregistered Smith and Wesson .38 caliber Police Special revolver to an undercover policeman. Nico avoided a three-month sentence by agreeing to undergo psychological and drug counseling. He was expelled from the drug treatment program for supplying false information on his entry form.

One year later, on Memorial Day, he broke into the armory of the Black Stone Hunting, Fish and Game Club, in order to steal a cache of rifles and handguns. His prison stay for this offense included another psychological study which listed the following as possible conditions: schizophrenia, delusional and paranoid personality disorder, and manic depression.

ANNAH TORCH   Jim DeFilippi

By the age of twenty-four, his mental condition seemed to be deteriorating. He had numerous arrests for vagrancy and disturbing the peace, with the accompanying police reports speculating on the arrestee's "tenuous grasp of reality."

Recent arrests included being caught with an arsenal of illegal firearms on the campus of Albany State University, and assault with intent to do bodily harm to the medical team at the Urgent Care Center of Albany.

Nico was currently being held on a variety of charges at the Capitol Northeast Correctional Facility in Herkimer, New York. This facility provided detention for arrested individuals as ordered by the courts within Albany County. These courts included Local Justice Courts, Superior Courts, and Federal Courts.

Even though his current incarceration had been for a short time, he had already been disciplined by correctional officers for applying and self-administering body tattoos, often depicting circus performers such as clowns. He had also been disciplined for attempting to send threatening letters to celebrities like the comedian/actor Keegan Michael Key, and the father of the late singer Amy Winehouse. Other letters addressed to the Puerto Rican embassy were permitted to be delivered, but with reservations and deletions.

One letter, which was characterized as "rambling and basically incoherent," was turned into the Albany Police Department and eventually found its way to court officials in White Leunge, New York. The letter contained the sentence, "I was in the room when that college girl got shot. I do nothing, but Ima talk all about it as soon as Ima outta of here." Authorities determined that he had been apprehended two days prior to the Dede Constaghulia murder, and therefore lent little credence to the boast.

Nico had seven months left to serve out his sentence.

&&&

Howard Wyzell was telling Annah, "With your old songs and old movie quotes, I could swear that you came of age in the Sixties, except you weren't even born yet in the Sixties."

She said, "I guess I am just a child of my time, but this does not seem to be my time."

Wyzell had just finished providing all the information he had dug up on Nico Madness, after she explained to him what had happened at Thunder and Stumpy's. When she told him that she had to question this guy, the sooner the better, Wyzell just made a face at her.

"No? Why not? Amanda obviously got the shotgun from this shit-bird."

"I didn't find anything to tell us he was the street dealer that provided Special K to either of the two girls. Or anything else."

"The gun is enough. I have to see him, ask him about Amanda."

"Maybe. I don't know how. Incarcerated. We neither of us are on his visitors' list. And neither he or his lawyer want us there. So this could be a problem."

She asked, "Nico Madness, is that his name real?"

"That's what they booked him under."

"Must be a street name."

"That's what they booked him under. I guess he dropped the Nickolas Parva long before he got to the Capitol area." Wyzell looked off beyond the walls of his living room, pretending to be speculating. "He must be part of the affluent and influential Madness family."

"Sure he is."

"The great granddad, Utter Madness, invented Twizzlers, you know. I heard he made a fortune from it." Wyzell was tugging at his collar, as if wearing a tight necktie.

Annah told him, "Okay now, Shecky, so if the routine is finished, we can try to figure out..."

"Rodney. The old man is still recognized as the Twizzler King."

"I really am going to enjoy my Friday cigar this week. It has been a week of questioning dullards and fighting off thugs. And you."

"So it's a fact, you beat up ten guys, in a bar, all at once, like I've heard tell?"

"Twelve."

"Twelve. Huh."

"Twelve, but they were not that impressive. Neither individually nor as a group. Sagging muscle shirts, drooping tattoos. Half of them did not want to be in the battle to begin with. Since the plan was to rape me one by one, not all at once, that is also how they chose to attack me. Or to not attack me. They stuck with that one-at-a-time protocol you see in Bruce Lee movies. Very polite, but inefficient."

"So they each took a number, like at a bakery?"

"Unofficially, yeah. It helped."

"So you managed to clear out an entire bar, the worst one in the Combat Zone."

"It would have been harder to do before the Fever. More crowded."

"Denser population."

"Oh, this population was pretty damn dense all right. More MAGA caps than face masks."

"I just thank God you didn't kill anyone."

"I did not."

When Annah was faced with having to use physical ferocity, Wyzell knew that his employee could turn into a stone cold killer. At times, her actions had reached levels that Wyzell found extremely uncomfortable. He had never been physically present for any of these instances, but he had been told about them, had intimated the details, and they left him with chapped lips, a dried-up soul, and a worried mind. "Annah, let's try to get through this without killing anybody, okay?"

"I am no killer."

"You're not? What about Crayton?"

"Who?"

"Never mind. Annah, I don't like any of this at all. You can't be doing things like this. Twelve men. Good God, girl."

Annah shrugged and told him, "Well, Counselor, it could have been worse."

"How?"

She started singing, "If I Had a Hammer." The Trini Lopez version.

&&&

ANNAH TORCH   Jim DeFilippi

Chapter Fourteen

Annah sat on her Boulder, looking out over the waters of Robert's Pond.

Her Cordura backpack was lying beside her. She reached into its side pouch and gently slid out the *Hacienda Vintage Reserva*. She unwrapped the cigar's plastic, unspooled its band, and slid both into the side packet of the pack. She used her pocket knife to slice off a quarter inch from the foot of the cigar. She licked down all four box-pressed sides, moistened the bottom two inches with her lips, lit a wooden match, held the flame a quarter inch from the head of the cigar and sucked in until the tip began to glow.

For the next twenty minutes, she sucked in slowly, deliberately, allowing the smoke to cloud its way into her mouth, no further, although she knew a fraction of the tar and nicotine would find their way down her throat to her blood stream and lungs and eventually to her brain. The *Hacienda* was providing a light, smooth taste, something that the cigar pamphlets would call "luxurious," but she would go no further than "very decent."

There was no more than a barely noticeable, occasional breeze blowing in from across the water below. This made it a smoke-ring day, which pleased her. She managed to puff out sixteen distinct rings from her first mouthful of smoke, each ring hovering in the air for a moment, the circle forming into a heart-shape before it rose and disappeared. Annah's personal record for a single mouthful of smoke was fifty-eight, set on a hot, humid, windless afternoon last August. Fifty-eight. The same number of home runs that Jimmie Foxx—the Old Double X—had hit in 1932, almost equalling the Babe that year.

Fifty-eight.

Annah had been proud of the number she had put up, until she checked the *Guinness World of* and found the record to be in the hundreds. This of course, disallowing the cheek-tap, a disingenuous and unethical film-flam of a move.

ANNAH TORCH   Jim DeFilippi

Twenty minutes had stretched into an hour, smoking, watching blue rings evaporating out above the muddy water, thinking about what she would be asking Nico Madness when Wyzell got her in to see him.

A rustle from the brush forty yards behind her, off to her left, caused her to look back, stare, and then silently scurry behind a clump of red elderberry bushes. She crouched there and studied the woods. The noises continued, got louder, closer.

It had to be human—no other animal could be this clumsy and awkward in the Woods. And a male. The most clumsy and awkward of the species. Could it be a normal doubled-eyed version of a man, or could it be a recently created Cyclops? Closer. Louder.

Annah picked up a rock. "Good afternoon, Counselor, how did you find me? Did you follow my smoke rings, like the Indians used to do?"

"Annah, it's late Friday afternoon, where else would you be?"

"My method for keeping track of the weeks."

They both sat down on the Boulder, both looking out over the water, staying silent for a time.

Wyzell asked her about the cigar.

"Searching for a compliment, Counselor? Well, it is just great, wonderful. The draw, the flavor, it has yet to flame out even once, even though I have been babying it."

"Prolonging the moment."

"Why not?" She held the cigar out in front of her and studied it. "I suppose the magazines would describe its 'dense, aromatic bouquet, with hints of toast, coffee, nuts, and gentle spices.' To me it's just blue smoke, but thanks for it, I enjoy."

"We all have our guilty pleasures."

Annah said, "No guilt at all, just blue smoke."

They spoke of things general and unthreatening for a while, until Annah turned to him with, "Weaz, there was no rock on our stump this morning. I could have killed you just now. You are a nice guy, but you do not know when to stay home." She said it gently, but like she had been holding back.

Wyzell sighed. "Annah, when have I ever come to you without the rock, without an appointment, without you expecting me?"

"Before this?"

He pointed down at the Boulder they were sitting on. "Before right now."

"Never, I guess."

"Never is right. I know how you...how you want things to be. And I respect that, certainly. I don't do that, show up for a drop-in. You know I always call first. If I could convince you to get a cellphone. I knew coming in like this would upset you a little bit. I apologize for the inconvenience."

"And I accept. So why this time, Counselor? What?"

"I thought you had to know—would want to know—right away."

Annah asked her question of him with a look.

Wyzell told her, "Amanda's awake. She just woke up, came out of it, whatever it was she was in. A coma."

"Really?"

"Yes. And one more thing, I'm sorry to tell you this."

Another questioning stare.

"Annah, I'm really sorry. She's admitting to everything. She's admitting she did it, confessing. She killed Dede."

&&&

Grace Silver asked her husband, "With everything else going on, did I forget to ask you, how was the Pope? Was he cute? Did he have his hat on?"

"Delightful. He's a Munchkin. Grace, I told you, I don't actually meet with him over there. I meet with the real seats of power. They are representatives of what they call the College of Cardinals, for my business."

"It's a college?"

"No, Grace, Jesus, it's not an actual college. They don't have a football team. They don't hold mixer with schnapps and kegs. Are you still on your morning champagne—what time is it—or you're hitting Mare's Legs already?"

"Johnnie, you couldn't come get me, take me with you? She's my daughter too, you know. I wanted to be there. I wish I was there when she first woke up."

"You got to see her, didn't you? I had Murray take you down there first thing, didn't I? Did you get in?"

"I wanted to be there, see her, when her eyes opened."

"Grace, the both of us missed that. It doesn't matter. We see her now. Grace, for Christ sake, I was halfway back across the Atlantic in the Lear when I got word. I was heading into the City, to work on some of the Vatican stuff, before I came up here. I immediately had them divert to Albany. I rushed in to see her. I sent for you right after that. You got there right after I did."

"The cop at the door said thirty minutes, a half-hour you were in there with her."

"It wasn't that long. I had to talk to her. We had things to discuss."

"What things? She hasn't really talked to me. Just answered my questions, sort of. One word. Nothing about except how she was feeling."

"Grace. Grace. Listen. She's going to plead guilty."

"Why?"

"Why? Why for Christ sake? Because she is, that's why. Grace, Amanda gunned down her roommate, all right?"

"That pretty woman, the lawyer's one, she was here. She talked to me, she wanted to talk to you. Johnnie, she told me Grace didn't do it."

"Oh, for Christ sake, I know, I know the Torch woman was here. Look, I know she's working for us, but I don't want you talking to any of them any more —the Weasel guy, to her, to our own lawyers—don't be talking to any of them without me, you understand?"

"Annah. Her name was Annah. She said that she knew our Amanda was innocent."

"Oh, God damn, Grace, that's what lawyers say. That's what we pay them to say. Grace, our little girl was in a locked room, clutching onto a shotgun, and for some crazy, crazy reason, she shot her roommate. So now she pleads guilty. It's the best thing. It's the only thing."

"I can't...in jail..."

"Grace, sit down, listen to me, get me a Pepsi, I'll get it, then I'll tell you."

"Tell me what?"

"Tell you why our little girl won't be going to jail. Let me get something to drink first."

"Tell me now."

Johnnie took hold of both of Grace's shoulders and wobbled her over to the couch. He sat her there, then sat down beside her. He said, "Grace, don't worry about anything. Things will be fine. I am not without influence in Goofy's office. That's the District Attorney."

"I know who that is."

"I've called in some markers, kicked in some chits, looks like we've bought ourselves a deal. There's a type person called a partial body amnesiac. From drugs or trauma. Both. I read a book, *Victims of Memory*, says traumatic memories don't get repressed, just the opposite, but it goes both ways. Amanda remembers being in the room, she remembers the gun, she remembers pulling the trigger. After that, and before that, it's all unclear to her. There's also a thing called temporary insanity."

"Johnnie, my daughter is not..."

"No, wait, don't be concerned with the term, it's just a word, it will not harm us. It will actually help us out, in this case. It looks like we can get six months..."

"In jail. I can't...our daughter can't live for six months in a jail, Johnnie, she's fragile, she's..."

"No jail time. Six months, maybe less, in an institution. A hospital."

"A prison."

"No, Grace, nothing like that. Nothing at all like that. A good place, nice place. Better than Chelsea, even. And she'll probably learn more there than she did back in the school. And she'll be getting help. It will be comforting to her, to us, to have her there. Calming her down. They'll show her how to deal with what she's done."

"Johnnie."

"It's decided. If you'd rather have her do twenty years in Attica, for Christ sake? This, Grace, is a good way to go."

"Amanda wants this?"

"Yes. I talked to her. This is what she wants."

"Let's go see her, we can..."

"Not now. I've already discussed this whole rigamarole with her, her and me. She's not saying much. She just can't remember much. She has no idea what happened between her and Dede. Or about the gun."

"We'll just go see her."

"Not now. I'm taking the Lear out to Vegas tonight."

"Tonight? I thought the tournament was over."

"It is. I just have to get away, play some one-on-one in the high stakes room, with the dealer, with the house. I need it for my own decompression. A few days only."

"When will things be decided? For Amanda."

"Soon. All of this will be put to rest. Eight months tops, she'll get. In a nice, nice place."

"I'll go see her without you."

"Okay, all right, if you want. But don't ask her about the killing, don't get into any of that. And don't stay too long. She needs to rest. She needs to forget. She needs to forget about things."

"We all need to forget about things."

"Yes, we do. I've got my poker table..." he pointed at the large wooden liquor cabinet, "...and you've got that. And Amanda has us."

Grace was staring out across the room. "We all have things we need to forget about."

&&&

Two days later, Wyzell told Annah, "We've got to stop meeting like this. Is there poison ivy? I think I'm getting itchy."

Annah said, "Was your call. You placed the rock. So we are still on the packet, are we? We have not been cut loose?"

"Sure we are. Why cut us loose now? Baby Johnnie knows there's no one better than me for softening up a fall. She did it. She didn't mean to do it. She didn't know the gun was loaded—that's a reference."

"Spike Jones."

"And his City Slickers. Before your time."

"So Johnnie is not interested in us finding out the truth?"

"He knows the truth, Annah. The important part of it. The kid is saying she remembers pulling the trigger. Daddy thinks he's got it all set for under a year it some brain-easing country club. Upscale, very *phroo-phroo*. Maybe they bring Doctor Phil in for pep talks."

"I would opt for the electric chair."

"Baby Johnnie just wants us to put something together, provide a character witness package for the court, only this and nothing more."

Annah shook her head. "No. Uh-uh. Not so fast. When can I get in to see Nico Madness?"

"Annah, you can't. That loony street-dog wants no part of this case, or of us. He's got his own troubles."

"He has seen sunshine, he has seen rain."

"Rain, mostly. I always wondered why James Taylor would brag about that. Who hasn't seen sunshine? Who hasn't seen rain, for God's sake? You have to write a song to tell us? Anyway, Mr. Madness doesn't want to talk to us, to see us, his lawyer doesn't want us talking to him. That's all dead, Annah. We no longer care about how she got the gun, or why she got the gun. As a matter of fact, it helps us more if there's no sane and sensible answer to these questions. She was insane at the time. Maybe she had a *Special K* blackout or something, doesn't matter."

"How do I get in to see Nico?"

"Annah, you don't. You don't. Amanda Silver is saying two things—she remembers killing her friend, and she doesn't want to talk about anything beyond that."

"That is not the truth, Weaz, it is not."

"It's all the truth we have to know. 'You can't handle the truth.' Nicholson's great. Look, I can handle it from here. Go back to live in your treehouse. Be happy up there. I thank you, I do, for your time and your effort. Enjoy your cigars, my cigars. If there's anything else I can do for you, just let me know."

"There is one thing."

"Anything you want. What's that?"

"Get me in to see Nico Madness."

&&&

ANNAH TORCH   Jim DeFilippi

Chapter Fifteen

Annah was alone in Howard Wyzell's downtown office. It was five o'clock in the morning, the lighting had been dimmed, the doors were locked. She checked a large round clock hanging above a glass bookcase of law books, and figured that it would be another three hours before the staff would begin arriving.

She had found an Exacto knife in one of the secretary's pullout desk drawers. She took her expired New York State drivers license from her backpack, turned on the secretary's desk lamp, funneled it down to the green desktop blotter, and began her exacting work.

The license was too old to have been enhanced. It had a header that read, "New York State" in large blue lettering, with a black "Driver License" written smaller below. A "USA" and the Commissioner of Education signature hovered over by the right edge.

The black and white photograph of Annah Torch's face, right above her small signature, took up most of the left side of the card, the rest being crowded with her name, address, sex, height, eye color, date of birth—along with a nine digit identification number, a Class D categorization, and the card's expiration date. Some of the information was current, some of it was correct. The expiration date had long passed, but she figured a well-placed thumb could cover that. Splattered around various corners of the lamination were smaller pictures of her face, outlines of dolphins, maple leaves, bear paws, a small U.S. flag, and a black heart next to the words, "Organ Donor."

Annah leaned over the desk and studied her card. She picked up the Exacto and slowly cut a box around the black all-caps lettering of her name. With great care and a jeweler's touch, she made sure the blade was only cutting the upper level of the plastic as she outlined her name. A few times the blade went all the way through the card. Annah would mumble a quiet curse to herself and continue with the surgery.

ANNAH TORCH   Jim DeFilippi

Wyzell had been holding on to this license for her for years, along with other legal papers that she had no place nor need for—wills, deeds, her birth certificate, her expired passport. He kept them all in a heavy medal box labeled "Torch" at his home office. Earlier, in the dark of night, around four a.m., Annah had gone to Wyzell's house to pick up the license.

Wyzell told her that he didn't want to be involved in any of this. He kept dropping the term "aiding and abetting" to her in a quiet and concerned whisper, but they both knew that he was powerless to resist this arbor-loving force of nature. She had also asked him if he had an Exacto knife. He said he didn't think so, but that she could probably find one in one of the secretary's desks. Annah brought a small, pointed knife of her own, just in case.

With her printed name peeled off from the license, Annah took out a piece of paper that had a list of names written on it. Wyzell had provided this list for her. Prison system authorities had vetted the list, searching for past felons and those currently on parole. The list was four names long, three were the names of public defenders, along with the name, "Rosa Hidalgo."

Annah looked around the office for a printer, then decided to use the one she had scouted out in Wyzell's inner office. She went in there and slowly raised the dimmer switch by the wall. The place sprang to life like a scene from Hollywood. She had never seen this office before—back when he was her boss, the firm had a smaller place across the Hudson in Rensselaer.

The four walls, ceiling, and floor of the twenty-five by twenty-five foot room all combined into an ornate homage to cherry and bloodwood. At its hub was Wyzell's huge, cherrywood desk, with its nine drawers, pewter knobs, and its six-foot-by-four-foot shiny top, perfectly clear except for a small pewter framed black and white photograph of a weasel eating something, maybe a chipmunk.

Two matching leaden sconces, each one crowned by a six-sided linen shade, hung from both sides of the marble framed fireplace. A gas-fed replica of a pile of logs lay silent and dark.

ANNAH TORCH Jim DeFilippi

Six louvered windows, thin but stretching nearly from the floor to the ten-foot high ceiling, were all darkened by green shaded and heavily insulated glass.

Wyzell's desk chair, a huge recliner, and a wing-backed sofa, were all upholstered with black leather and golden studs.

A brown and green, ornate Persian carpet covered nearly the entire floor, except for the shiny strip of cherrywood that peeked out and ran along the bottom of each wall.

Wyzell would have to swing his chair around to access his computer and printer, sitting in an alcove that was holding scones identical to those by the fireplace.

Hanging on the wall above the desktop computer appeared to be two black matted white documents that were actually television screens used for Zoom and FaceTime meetings.

A wastepaper basket by the edge of the desk proclaimed Northeastern University, but it had a green and white *New York Jets* sticker running diagonally across its surface.

An audio system with an attached viewing screen was queued up to play *Bob Dylan's Greatest Hits,* along with the Geezinslaw Brothers. No speakers were visible anywhere in the room.

Tucked in a corner was a rusted, black, ten-gallon milk pail, probably rescued from some defunct Vermont family farming operation. A diagonal bumper sticker across the front of the pail proclaimed, "Death to the Bulk Tank." The pail's top had been removed so that it could act as a flower pot. Huge red geraniums drooped heavily down over the lid.

The wall that held the door to the office was covered with photos in cheap eight-by-ten frames, maybe forty of them, pictures of past clients—some had been exonerated, some found guilty. There were no pictures of friends or family members anywhere in the room.

The only disorganized area in the room was a pile of cardboard boxes and plastic milk cartons, stacked by the side of the computer alcove. Manilla

ANNAH TORCH Jim DeFilippi

folders, loose papers, documents—some labeled by the case name, some not. Next to the pile were three books—*Summa Theologica* by St. Thomas Aquinas, a biography of Dwight Eisenhower, and the novel, *The Friends of Eddie Coyle*, by George V. Higgins. This inner office contained no volumes of the law.

The place smelled of musk and Helmut Lang cologne.

Now, in the headquarters of Howard Wyzell and Associates of Law, Annah loaded ten sheets of Hewlett-Packard photo paper into the Epson printer, and she typed the name "Rosa Hidalgo" onto the computer screen. It took her six frustrating attempts to print the correct size, font, and color for the name, but she finally mumbled, "Aw, fuck it, Dude, let's go bowling," to herself and used the Exacto knife to carefully cut a nearly perfect name from the photo paper, using the dimensions she had jotted down on the secretary's note pad.

Any use of paste or glue would screw up the look. She gently pressed the photo-paper printed name into the rectangle she had cut from the card. She had to shave off one corner a bit, twice, but eventually she could run her thumb across the face of the card without feeling too much of an imperfection. Anyone who closely studied the card would see the rectangular outline around Rosa's name, but Annah kept assuring herself that no one would be all that interested.

The bearer of this card, Rosa Hidalgo, was now an authorized visitor of inmate Nico Madness at the Capitol Northeast Correctional Center.

At six forty-five that morning, Annah locked up the office and drove Wyzell's Subaru over to Billy's Red Barn, a local Costco-like warehouse, where she had to wait three hours for the doors to open. The purpose of her visit there was threefold: 1. to test the potential validity of her doctored and quite obviously ersatz drivers license; 2. to secure a secondary form of identification, albeit an extremely non-official and suspect one; and 3. she hadn't been to Billy's Barn in over five years, she wondered whether that since the Fever, did they still give out free food at the top of each aisle?

She left the store a few minutes after ten o'clock, with a picture ID card identifying her as "Rosa Hidalgo," a proud member of the Billy's Red Barn family.

ANNAH TORCH   Jim DeFilippi

On a lark, she also left the store with a large box of Billy's Organic Trail Mix packets. She knew she would have to store them in a shady corner once back at the hut. M&M's tend to melt.

She drove back to Wyzell's house and parked the car in his garage.

She entered the lawyer's house without knocking. Once she was inside, Wyzell again tried to talk Annah out of what he called this, "half-ass, hair-brained identity theft." He said, "You have to remember, pal, you're done for, you're off the case, we don't need you anymore. All we're doing is a character witness package. You're a nice gal, you don't know when to go home. Thank you for your service."

"Weaz, would you like a Trail Mix? They taste good."

"Annah, let's reconsider please. I don't want to have to come bail you out and represent you in night court. Have to use your swamp turtles and raccoons and whatever the hell else you live with out there for your character witnesses. Also, I myself would prefer not to get myself disbarred."

"Weaz, Weaz, you are not involved. And Amanda Silver is not guilty. Maybe she is a bit off the mark from being completely innocent, but the girl did not murder."

"And you think a few words with a troglodyte like Nico Madness is going to change all that? Even his name..."

"It has to be my next step."

"This case is a simple, Annah, never been opened, always been shut, clichéd but true— locked room, shotgun blast, boom, boom, boom. We hitch up our trousers, fold up out tents and we move on."

"This case is a Black Swan."

"Annah, doesn't matter what color the bird is. You walk into Northeast Central with your grammar school art project there. I mean, with the facial recognition they have today, along with enhanced coding and what else they got, you won't get as far as the metal detector."

ANNAH TORCH   Jim DeFilippi

"Weazy, you have been to Northeast Correctional a thousand times, you more than me. When was the last time a guard or trustee ever did more than take a quick glance at your I.D. and the authorized visitors list? They are asleep. They do not care. And it is a lousy picture of me to begin with."

"Okay, Annah, here's my last try, my last reason for you to drop this charade. You don't keep a mirror out there at the treehouse, but if you did, you would know this—I'll have to tell you myself—you are beautiful. You are what we guys used to call a knock-out, before MeToo ruined everything for us. You are the most beautiful woman I've ever met. Maybe the most beautiful the world ever had, since Hedy LaMar got old and died. I guarantee, the minute you step into the visitors queue at Northeast, every screw, male or female, old or young, will be studying you up and down. And that mostly includes your lovely face, which by extension includes the phony driver's license you'll be flashing."

"Hedy LaMar worked out the key to frequency-hopping, which led to Wifi, Blue Tooth, GPS, which reminds me, I have to use your bathroom."

Up in Wyzell's second floor bathroom, Annah pulled her hair back and tied it behind her head. She used a Sharpie to paint dark bags beneath both eyes, and a hint of mustache above her lip. An old plastic bottle of calamine lotion applied ugly blotches in various places around the face, and gave her complexion an ugly, crusted-over appearance. She pressed a small Bandaid horizontally across one eyebrow. She used a hint of rubbing alcohol to give both of her eyes a red, puffy appearance.

When she finished with her cosmetics, she went to the top of the stairs and called down, "Counselor, can I borrow a sweatshirt, maybe some sweat pants?"

"In my bedroom closet and dresser, Hedy. Jock straps are in the sock drawer."

Annah found a Northeastern sweatshirt and a baggy pair of brown pants. She even took an old trench-coat that must have been left over from Wyzell's Colombo days. She stood before a full-length mirror and practiced a stooped over posture and a slouching walk. She used a hand mirror to practice her sour, depressed, loose-hanging, morbid facial expression.

ANNAH TORCH   Jim DeFilippi

    A plaid woolen scarf was hanging from a bathroom hook. She wrapped it around her head for a combination do-rag and face-mask. She checked the mirror and thought she was maybe ready to try out for Bruce Springsteen's band. In a bottom dresser drawer, she found an old, decomposing leather wallet that gave off a bad smell. She slipped her altered drivers license into its plastic window.

    Finally she came down to the bottom step of the staircase and asked Wyzell, "So, Counselor, am I less outstanding now? Do I blend?"

    Wyzell studied her for a while, then gave a grim, sardonic smile, and proposed marriage to this homely woman named "Rosa Hidalgo."

                                        &&&

ANNAH TORCH   Jim DeFilippi

Chapter Sixteen

Nico Madness looked as young as a boy-band singer and as crazy as a loon.

He was sitting across a plastic picnic bench from Annah in the Visitors Chamber at the Capitol Northeast Correctional Center in Herkimer, New York. The room was gymnasium-big and echoing, clogged with noise, food, the smells of cheap perfume, and regret.

Nico was studying Annah even before he sat down, when he asked her, "Who the hell you?"

"I am your grandmother, Luke."

"You no my gramama. I no Luke. You a new lawyer for me?"

"I am your *abuelita*, so you may call me that."

"You no my gramma, Ima tell you that already."

"No, but I would like to be. If you would allow me."

Annah had gotten to the prison a half hour before the posted visiting hours. The guards were as bored and sleepy as she had hoped. When the entry guard pointed at the visitation log, she leaned in and wrote, "Rosa Hidalgo" under "Name" and "Grandmother" under "Relationship to Internee." She held up Wyzell's old wallet, with the yellowing plastic window showing her forged drivers license. The guard looked at the wallet itself harder than at the license before he told Annah to put it away and tipped his head sideways in a "move along" gesture.

She passed through some airport-like screening, and got the back of her right hand stamped with a red indelible mark. A large metal door creaked slowly open, buzzing loudly for three seconds. Then she and the other visitors walked down the corridor directed by an arrow to a sign with the word, "Visitors." There they were squeezed into a thirty-foot by fifteen-foot steel room, where the

ANNAH TORCH Jim DeFilippi

guard had inserted a key into a slot in the wall, causing the steel door behind them to buzz loudly, hiss itself closed, and click itself locked.

The group waited there for five minutes. Annah used the time to observe the forty people in her group, a mix of kids, girlfriends, wives, and parents, maybe twenty-five percent white, sixty percent hispanic, fifteen percent black. Television cameras in each corner were aimed down at them.

They had all been instructed about strict rules prohibiting provocative dress. A few of the younger woman had attempted to look as hot as they could within the allowed boundaries, but they had failed. Wyzell had told Annah that guys in prison get visits from their girlfriends, females in prison get visits from their mothers.

The group waited and stayed quiet, morose, deflated, going through the motions required of those pretending to harbor sympathy for a convict.

Annah couldn't identify any lawyers in the group, she wondered if they took a different route, maybe to a more private meeting.

Finally, a second guard in front of them used his key to unlocked the front door of the room, and it hissed mechanically open, with the now familiar loud, long, warning buzz.

This door led them to an outdoor tarmac with a chainlink fence and spartina-razor wire curled along the top. Forty feet across the tarmac, on the other side of the yard, was another mechanical door which was opened more quickly, but with a buzzing that was just as loud and annoying as the previous two. They finally entered the visitors' building. They turned to the right and entered a long room filled with cheap plastic chairs, round banquet pedestals, and wobbling picnic tables. This was the visitors' chamber. The room had a dropped ceiling of yellow-stained acoustic tile hanging above decomposing linoleum flooring. The windows seemed to be of heavy wood and thick glass, with no bars across them.

At the far end of the chamber, a steel door buzzed and hissed, and a group of maybe thirty prisoners were allowed in. Each prisoner wore a short-sleeve dark green shirt, matching pants, and heavy black boots. Most shirts showed the top of a white undershirt at the neckline. A guard escorted Nico

ANNAH TORCH   Jim DeFilippi

Madness to Table Six, where Annah was seated. The guard went back with a few others to stand by the prisoner door.

After Annah admitted to Nico that she was indeed not his grandmother, she told him that she was a lawyer for Amanda Silver, and she just wanted to ask him a few questions.

At first Nico sat looking confused by the statement, but pretty quickly he was confident and off to the races, sounding like a man who no one had listened to in a decade. He told Annah that yes, indeed, he knew Amanda Silver, but that she would never be President of the United States.

Annah agreed.

"See, why, you can be learnt a lot by Mr. President of the United States of America, you can get you religious commandments there, but the best lesson we all forgot, we learn once by watching the eternal light, right, don't we? Working as a team, up and down and all shined, till that shine, all its energy, create a rainbow, you understand? Ima not remember what happened after that though, you can teach me, if you want, Ima be listen, but, but, but, what happen when all that eternal light shine them feelings with all that mighty energy on something, all at the same time, huh?"

Annah shook her head, said she didn't know. She added, "I wish I did."

"Ima tell you what, what happen there. Ima tell you, no, wait, I show you..."

Nico jumped up from the table, had his green shirt unbuttoned and off, and was yanking away at the back of his undershirt to display a large blue tattoo of a clown which was covering his left shoulder, before a guard got to him, instructed him to get back in uniform, sat him down, and told Nico one more event and he was out of there, back to the block.

Nico apologized to both the guard and to Annah. As the guard was walking back to his post at the door, Nico was calling to him that this lady here was his *abuelita*, his grandmama.

ANNAH TORCH   Jim DeFilippi

Annah tried to moor this dirigible to some sort of a docking tower, but the winds of delusion were mighty. "Nico? Nico? Can we talk about Amanda Silver?"

"Why not."

"You knew her. I think you met her at Thunder and Stumpy's, didn't you?"

"I ain't no street pharmacist, man, you understand?"

"Of course, of course you're not."

"So just before you go jumping ina my box, lady, know Nico can pop up, pull up, break in, stake out, car chase, kidnap, and shoot out. Nico do all that."

"I bet you can."

"And more."

"And more."

Her years in the Woods had taught Annah the value of patience. Before she had lived within that paradise—still out in the Fever world—she tended to be impulsive and impatient. But living in the woods of northern New York State, waiting for each spring to arrive, for every tree and bush to bloom, it teaches one to be patient.

When Nico went silent for a moment, she asked him, "Can we talk about Amanda some more now, please, Nico? About how you…"

"If you my bitch, no niglaw be able to get conversation outta me, outta you."

"Well, maybe just a word or two."

"Ima good, like a dream on mushrooms, micro dousing, a running too fast, off track, on track, weebled, they wobble but they don't fall down, but don't never fall down to the best resistance, be getting to the top, be the best you can, best, best, never rest, get you the bestest safety line you can get, and then you control it, you gotta control it, like the drip, drip, drip, of some skag, or some skag with two O's behind it, you understand, grandma?"

Very patient. "Yes, I do, a little bit of it, not all of it though. I forget how you and Amanda Silver got together."

"We never been together."

"No, no, I mean, how you guys, you two, would meet. Down at Thunder and Stumpy's, wasn't it?"

"Bitch bar."

"I have been there."

"I ain't no street pharmacist, all right?"

"No, I'm sure you're not."

Nico leaned back off the table, looked around the echoing room of babies crying, mothers weeping, inmates hunched over and looking sad, trying to look tough. He took in a large lungful of air, let it out slowly. He looked across the table at Annah like he was wondering how she got there. He leaned back onto the table with both elbows. He said, " 'ciety girl."

"Yes, she was."

"High."

"Right."

"I ain't no street pharmacist."

"No, you are not."

"I deal in bang."

"Bang?"

Nico made a pistol-shooting sign with his hand. "Bang."

"I understand."

"Sobriety girls. Both of them."

"Amanda and…Dede, you knew Dede too, the both of them?"

ANNAH TORCH   Jim DeFilippi

"Both of them, 'ciety girls."

"Yes, they were."

"They come in down there, they homies, they act like one elbow gots the other one's shoulder."

"I do not…"

Nico crossed his index and middle finger, held the hand up to Annah.

Annah asked, "They were friends, then? Best friends?"

Nico kept the crossed fingers in front of her, and shook them, like he was making a point.

"What happened, you think, Nico? They wound up…uh…not getting along?"

"We in there one night. They like this here." Nico held up his crossed fingers again. "They both getting high. They on Special K. They be talking. They tripping. They getting along." Here Nico seemed to lose focus and stared up at the ceiling, his eyes glazed over.

Annah tapped on the table top, gently. She called out, "Nico? Nico? What happened then? To the two girls. Did they have a fight?"

"Ima tell bitch shuck she don't like."

"You told her stuff she didn't like? What? What stuff? Which? Which bitch was it?"

Nico raised his face to the ceiling and started barking like a dog, then howling. The guard started coming over, but Annah raised her hand, indicating she would get Nico quiet again. The guard seemed to prefer that.

"It's okay, Nico, all right, that's fine."

"Her bootie offa her, you understand?"

"Yes…no…sort of."

"Everybody know bout food stamps and Ramen Noodles, but they don't never know bout walking to the laundry mat with big bags of boiling water and

ANNAH TORCH   Jim DeFilippi

lighting up candles in the house cause the electricity it don't work, second hand, sleeping on the couch, on the floor, don't know about getting your food from the Pantry and the luck line, tune on the stove if it work, cause the heat don't work, washing clothes at the sink at somebody else's house."

Annah had run out of ways to respond.

"Yo, grandmama, this what made me what I am today. I ain't no street pharmacist. I hustle bang. Bang." He made the pistol motion with his hand again.

"You sell guns. Do you, Nico, you sell guns?"

Annah saw Nico smile for the first time. He kept repeating his own name. "Nico, Nico, Nico...she got a shot-gun, little one..."

"A Filipino-Blitzer .12 gauge."

"Right, right-o."

"Nico, did you sell Amanda that gun?"

"Saw-off."

"Sawed off, yes that's the one. A sawed-off .12 gauge. Did you sell it to her, Nico?"

"Ima cut that piece off myself." He held his two palms up to show them to Annah. "These two hands. I cut and cut and saw. Like a clown, working all morning. I show you my clown tat?"

"Yes, Niko, I saw that. But tell me, Nico, you have to tell me, all right?"

"All right, shoot." Nico grinned to himself, like his "shoot" was an unintentional and inappropriate joke. "I sell her that bang. Five hundred. Five." Nico held up five fingers. "Maybe Nico gets a bit more in the deal too. Some cooz. Could of got me more of the money, I suppose, being if I wanted to. But bitch was a high-sobriety girl. Five though. Ain't cheap. Not bad for a night's work. You looking to buy, grandmama? Was a good working gun. Very tasty for the hand. Ima got a lot more, but, don't blame me."

"So you sold it to her then?"

Nico smiled.

Annah moved in closer to the table top, closer to Nico. She asked him, "Nico, did she tell you what she was going to do with that gun? Did Amanda Silver tell you what she was going to do with that gun?"

"I tell you everything you got to know, take thirty second, tops. If you not listening too good, thirty-two second. If the screw's coming over, ten second, quick."

"Sure, please, go ahead."

"Dudda white bitch..."

"Which? Amanda? Dede? The other one? Which one? Amanda?"

"She ax me for a gun. I tell her, Nico do that. But make sure you dump it on the flip side, you understand?"

"Nico, what did Amanda intend to do with the gun, she tell you that?"

"Yeah, I do." Nico was smiling again. "She say to Nico, 'Ima kill that bitch.'"

Annah leaned back and sighed. She was working for the defense, but she seemed to be strengthening the case against Amanda.

Nico said again, "Say to Nico, 'Ima kill that bitch.'"

&&&

ANNAH TORCH   Jim DeFilippi

Chapter Seventeen

Neither man would ever admit it in peer company—and if accused would immediately plead the Fifth—but Homicide Detective Sergeant Simon L. Gumm and Special Investigator for the Office of the D. A. Leo Protski both loved to gossip as they drank beer, gossip like a pair of old hens at a mahjong tournament.

Drinking beer to the tune of gossip floating in the air—ecstasy.

Gumm belonged to the Black Stone Hunting, Fish and Game Club, a group that would convene each month with a meeting consisting of a guest lecturer, followed by firing off some rounds in their underground rifle-range. The featured speaker could be a local gun-shop owner and enthusiast, describing and then live-firing a new weapon of choice.

To be followed by some beer. And some gossip.

Sometimes a lawyer would lecture the group about their rights as gun owners under the U. S. Constitution, afterwards dissecting any new court decisions that would impact their right to bear arms. They liked to call themselves the 2A movement, referring to the Second Amendment.

One time, a younger group member with longish hair and a snootful of Miller High Life suggested to the group that they occasionally bring in someone with a different stance—an opposing point of view. Maybe someone with a speech titled, "Ain't Nobody Coming for Your Stupid-Ass Guns, " or something in that vein. Or maybe that madman in the newspapers who was going around pushing his "GUNZ R4 Pussies" movement. The young man's suggestion was roundly hooted and criticized as being confrontational for the sake of confrontation. It got voted down. Voice vote.

As its last guest speaker, the club had been fortunate enough to have an Olympian biathlete. He described the most effective method of firing accurately when the shooter has shortened breath. It was simply a matter of breath control and mind control. It was a very instructive lecture, some members were even

ANNAH TORCH   Jim DeFilippi

jotting down notes. The question and answer session lasted for over half an hour. But in truth, everyone was there for another purpose...

To drink beer and gossip.

Protski was in a bowling league, where the talk ran from strikes and spares to tourney seedings and shoe powder. Or maybe the best way to convert a seven-ten split. Every member rolled at least three frames each week, and many stayed afterwards to polish up his skill with a few extra frames. But in truth the bowlers were all there for only one combined purpose.

To drink beer and gossip.

That was what the two men—Gumm and Protski—had in mind as they sat in a booth at a bar called Rudolph the Red's, in the town of Rensselaer, just across the Hudson from Albany, close to each man's workplace. There was a second Rudolph's down the pike in East Greenwick, but that one played its music too loud for comfortable gossiping while drinking beer.

Both Rudolph's featured a large neon sign of the famous reindeer out front, with its red, powerfully blinking, five-hundred Watt nose. The year-round theme of both bars was Christmas, which both Gumm and Protski tolerated. In their preferred Rudolph's, the soundtrack—Christmas standards ranging from Brenda Lee's "Rocking Around the Christmas Tree" to Bob Dylan's "Must Be Santa"—was kept at a lower level than the one out in Greenwick. So both men were able to drink their beer and gossip. Other than the wintertime sports tie-in, no one could explain why the only photograph hanging in the place was an autographed picture of Tonya Harding landing her triple axle.

In a tip of the elf cap to Hugh Hefner and his Playboy Clubs, the waitresses were dressed in sexy Christmas elf outfits, which made customers think back to how much testosterone their blood streams had flowing during those years many decades ago. Rudolph's made Hooters look progressive and tasteful.

A feature both men claimed annoyed them—but which secretly pleased them both—was that the bar retained its "Fever Red" protocol. Each booth was surrounded by three-inch wide strips of plastic, dangling down from a metal

ANNAH TORCH — Jim DeFilippi

frame. Each booth was "smoked and sanitized" immediately after a party had left. The pretty elf, with her breasts peeking out of her red and rhinestoned vest, would leave the drink order outside the plastic, on a little table, then she would smile and leave. The customer would reach through the plastic and grab his bottle or glass.

This set-up was supposedly healthier, more sensible, less dangerous, but the two men also liked it because it lessened the danger of someone overhearing the gossip that they were sharing in-between sips.

Protski was especially concerned about being overheard. He knew that if his boss—District Attorney Sarah "Goofy" Guffleberg—were ever to catch wind of him talking without sanction about any current cases, he would be immediately fired. With his desk cleaned out, he would be scrubbed from the data-bank, his computer would be wiped clean, and a uniformed officer would escort him to the exit with his cardboard box of personal belongings. No recommendations would be forthcoming from this previous employer.

But what the hell, Protski figured, a few beers and a bit of gossip never hurt anybody. Too much. Anyway, both he and Gumm were on the same side of the law, they were both in the business of putting scumbags behind bars. And scum-baguettes too, girls—girls like little, rich Amanda Silver. Both men were fascinated by the Silver case—not so much because of the players involved, or because of the wealth of the players involved—but more by the fact that the case remained so utterly simple and so utterly complex at the same time. Neither man could remember any case like this one. The locked room—the shotgun toting, sweet looking killer—the smiling, gutshot corpse.

Both men agreed that little Amanda would wind up behind bars—it was just a question of where she would be housed and for how long—but some sort of heavy sentencing was being carved into stone. Bad little girls who did what this one did deserve to be punished, and this one would be.

"But I'll bet on this," Protski was telling Gumm, "some little girls I'd rather punish them by putting them over my knee and giving them a good spanking. This is, if my boner didn't get in the way. Oh, and have you seen that girl that the Weasel has working for him?"

"Mmm."

"She's a stone fox all right. She came by to ask me some questions. Didn't get anything she didn't already know, but I sure enjoyed the corroborating. I'd submit to corroborating with that one anytime. I wish I could have thought up some more stuff to tell her, just to keep her around."

Gumm took a sip of his beer. "Never spoke to her much before this. I'd heard about her. Lives out in the Adirondacks in a cave or somewhere."

"Nature girl."

Gumm said, "That's her, that's what they say all right. But now I got her involved in a completely different caseload, something completely not related, lucky me. Maybe I get to see her again."

Protski leaned in to hear the kill. He took another sip of beer. The only thing better than lightly-buzzed gossip was lightly-buzzed gossip about a pretty woman. "Tell me about her, about it. What's going on?"

"I'll tell you that tale later. First, you dish about Silver and her Daddy. What kind of new shit on that one?"

Protski sipped. "Well, as you know, Goofy loves to bargain a plea. She lets all her minions know, 'Stoop first, ask questions later.' If some loser kills his wife, mother-in-law, and you get him to cop a plea to reckless endanger, that's fine with Goofy, go ahead and do it. That's not what people think about Goofy, the image they have of her, tough on crime and everything, but that's the office practice, the code of operation, the S.O.P."

"Why's that?"

"Because taking a plea is a conviction. Goes in the books that way. Goofy keeps her success percentage high, clear, and clean. She's shooting for one-thousand percent, and damn near got it. It's not about preventing crime, or punishing the individual, or vengeance for the victim, or justice for the victim's family, it all has to do with political expediency. So Goofy can look like a hard-ass crimefighter, so she takes her next rung up the political ladder, on her way to the stars, see?"

ANNAH TORCH   Jim DeFilippi

"Yeah."

"So, with this case, the Silver girl, it's what we all expected. Daddy's money, his firm's lawyers, he even brought the Weasel in, with that beautiful honker, the woods girl—you're going to tell me about that later, don't forget—so we are all expecting a nice plea bargain. You know, manslaughter, reckless endanger, something sanitized like that, something as sanitized as this booth will be after we get up to leave."

"And that didn't happen?"

"Sort of, not yet. But not exactly. The father, the baby Johnnie guy, has all the riches in the world, so he figures he's got a bigger set of balls, a mightier swinging dick, than Goofy does. So he decides, they'll go to trial, screw the plea bargain, they'll get in court there and bring up temporary insanity, temporary amnesia, the kid gets off without a conviction, no jail, no police record, just some fancy-assed mental institution, where they knit mittens and watch Judge Judy all afternoon. Baby John even somehow arranges McDonaldson to sit on the bench, to run the trial. You know him?"

"I don't think so."

Protski put his fingertips into the chest pocket of his Hawaiian shirt, like he was searching for a loose cigarette. "He sells to the highest bidder. Johnnie can buy him with pocket money, loose change, pennies. So it's all set up. This is just what I hear, you understand. There's none of it going to hold up in court. It's just, we're two guys talking, having a few, chatting, am I right?"

"Of course we are."

"So it's all set up, at least in Baby Johnnie's mind it is. Not guilty. No plea bargain. We take our case to court. Once there, it's 'The girl's insane, Your Honor. There's no jury. It's all up to you, what do you say?'"

"And the judge says...?"

"Judge McDonaldson pounds the mighty hammer, and declares, 'This little girl was insane, but just for a little while. I sentence her to two weeks knitting mittens in some pleasant surroundings.' McDonaldson sends her off to the Oneida Therapeutic Institute, some country club such as that. Watch some

ANNAH TORCH   Jim DeFilippi

TV. She's not inside long enough even to watch a decent Netflix series, *Tiger King*, all the episodes. 'Sorry, missy, you'll have to watch those last few epi's on the outside. You're free to go now. No criminal record, no big thing. Behave yourself. Bye-bye."

Gumm said, "Well, that would be the damnedest thing. Money can buy almost anything, certainly freedom from justice. For the right amount. I thought the best she could get is they'd bargain it down to Second."

Protski said, "And that's what they had all planned."

Gumm was impressed. "So that's what's happening there. Thanks for the input."

Protski shook his head. "No. Nope. No, it is not. That's not what's happening at all."

"It's not?"

"You remember how Baby John called her 'Goofy' a couple times on TV? Said it was a slip, Freudian or whatever, but apologized, all is forgiven, you remember that?"

"Yeah, I think so."

"Well, Goofy, she's an elephant, she's the Count of Monte Cristo, she's Johnny Cash looking for the man who named him Sue. Goofy does not forget, much less forgive. She plans—you never heard this from me—she plans to pull the old switch-eroo on Johnnie as the gavel bangs. She's got shit on Judge McDonaldson even the devil doesn't know about, only his confessor and his hairdresser knows for sure. He plans to put the metal screws to young Miss Silver. 'Yes, little girl, you might have been nuts at the time of the gutshot, but that doesn't make you innocent, I sentence you to...to...to who knows what.' Somewhere where the head-shrinkers are all ex-Nazis, their shoes hurt, they got dyspepsia, their wife's run off on them—like mine did—so they're in a foul mood. Take it out on the accused. Torture chamber. A type place where your time of release is measured in decades, not years, not months. So we shall see what happens to the young prep school damsel with the sawed-off. We shall see. But it won't be pretty."

ANNAH TORCH   Jim DeFilippi

Protski finished off his beer, wiped his lips and sat back. Proud of his performance.

Sgt. Gumm was impressed. "Wow," he was saying. "Wow."

Protski leaned forward again. "So, you were saying there's something going on with the Weasel's girl, that thing of beauty? Tell me about that. What's going on there?"

"Fair enough." Gumm took a sip of beer. He was up. His turn on stage, dim the houselights, except for the one on his bald patch. "Well, I've got a meeting scheduled tomorrow morning. Meetings. Three of them. Not one, not two, but three different times. Ten. Ten-thirty. One after lunch. I take an early lunch. It's about the Weasel's gal. The babe's name, the looker, it's Annah, Annah Torch. Just like the one you been carrying for your ex all these years."

&&&

ANNAH TORCH   Jim DeFilippi

Chapter Eighteen

Ruck had decided for himself, and for Horn and Box, that the only thing better than one criminal complaint against the jungle slut would be two complaints, and the only thing better than that would be three.

The three men were in the empty backroom at the Lodge—the White Leunge Fishing and Hunting Casino—and they were observing their "first-round of silence" mandate. They sat, silently drinking their Yuengling Black and Tans, each from the bottle, each mentally preparing his presentation.

Ruck's right arm had dropped the sling, but it still hurt around the elbow if he slept on it wrong or if the weather was changing. The black patch was covering the spot where his left eye had been. He had grown used to the inconvenience, enjoying the studying of his new face in the bathroom mirror mornings, and in public restrooms during the day. He thought it gave him a mysterious aura, although he was still not used to the lack of depth perception, still walking into screen doors, still having to slam on the brakes of his six-pack Dodge at the last minute.

Around the house, Blanche had mostly just shut up about mentioning either of the wounds—she wouldn't ask a question, except some generally vague and traditional one about how things were going. She never asked about what had happened out there in the Woods that day. Instead, she seemed to be playing the part of the concerned wife of a one-eyed partial-invalid. When she wasn't busy nursing some grudge or another, her words spoke of caring about her husband and his troubles, but Ruck couldn't shake the idea that she kept circling to her right as they spoke, like she was trying to stay out of his sight, a prizefighter trying to lesson the impact of an opponent's mighty right hand.

Ruck had only hit her once—well, twice, if you count—but just taps compared to what a professional prizefighter's right hand would do to her, like

ANNAH TORCH Jim DeFilippi

that head-buster Mike Tyson had delivered to his wife, the sexy black girl who divorced him for it. That one had been a thing of beauty.

Ruck and his two buddies had coordinated by phone and were meeting at the Lodge with the intention of "lending some coordination" to their respective stories—get to twerking and tweaking, suggesting, fine-tuning, criticizing, improving them. As the conversation commenced and progressed, and the beers kept being delivered and disappearing, each of the three men began taking more and more stubborn possession of his own story—fighting to protect it against the onslaught of his buddies' suggestions for improvement. Each storyteller was taking his tale more and more to heart, and listening to the suggestions for improvement more and more resentfully. Little Box always ended up editing his, falling in line with the demands of the others. Ruck of course had the last say over all three final drafts. Each of the men had an appointment the next day with the WLPD, planning to register his criminal charge against the jungle slut.

"Okay," Ruck sipped and said, "Let's tiptoe over each of them again, just one more time, just to make sure all the stories got that straight and narrow bent to them."

Horn and Box were getting bored with the repetition, but Ruck was Ruck, he was the boss, so they both shrugged and agreed.

&&&

As in the preceding rounds, Ruck was the first to tell his story. He knew that his tale was by far the best, and all three agreed that his came the closest to what had actually happened out there in the Woods. But in truth, they all knew that Ruck's story was still a gun's throw over a tree and into a lake away from the actual truth.

In Ruck's complaint—to be registered officially tomorrow morning at ten—he had gone hiking in the Woods, alone, quiet, peacefully, trying to commune with nature, although he kept misspeaking the phrase as "commute with neighbors." Horn and Box had tried correcting him the first few time through, but they had given up by now.

ANNAH TORCH   Jim DeFilippi

"So, officer, I'm out there commuting with neighbors. I got my brand-fucking-new .480 Ruger Super Redhawk strapped on my side, just for protection, you understand, not for anything else. I brung in the sales receipt for it. No cheap weapon. The bear population is intense out there, especially this time of the year, in this pre-hybernation-al time of year, when they're looking to fatten themselves up for a long winter's nap."

Box grimaced and felt he had to point out to his leader that the term 'pre-hybernation-al' might not be a suitable word for the occasion, might not be a word at all. Ruck responded that it was a term of nature, referring to that period of the year right before bears went hibernating for the winter.

Horn pointed out that even though it might be a word of nature, maybe even an English word, it wasn't a legal one, which is what they were striving for.

Ruck agreed to take the word choice under advisement.

"Anyway, I tell this cop that all of a sudden, without warning or enticement, this giant of a woman jumps out of the bushes at me. She's certainly gone crazy, and she's got this stick—she's going to tell you it was just a stick, but in truth if it was, that stick was a hockey stick, more likely a club like a sword or a lance or even a spear even—and she sticks the damn thing right into this missing eye of mine, right here—this is when I point to my eye, where it used to be—even offer to flip up the patch to show him the damage."

Horn interrupted, "Chief, make sure you tell him how much the gun cost, was worth."

"I ain't even up to that part yet, but I will. I sure will. Twelve hundred fucking bucks, that's how much. But anyway, she blinds me, I'm totally, totally blinded."

"One eye."

"Totally, totally blinded. She takes the opportunity and advantage of me to reach into my holster there and grab the Redhawk, steals it from me cause I'm a blind man by now. Totally." He gave a sharp look at Horn, making sure he stayed shut up.

Horn took the cue, and instead of offending, he offered support. "But you fight on."

"Of course I do. Of course I fight on. I am blinded but I am not finished. I fight on like Demetrius the Gladiator in that old movie on Turner TV. The Classics."

Horn said he saw that one, with the old good-looking guy, Vincent somebody, but he wasn't sure if Demetrius had been blinded, or if he just got a haircut from Salome.

Box had never seen the old movie, never even heard of it, so it was assigned to him to watch.

Ruck continued. "So, anyways, I manage to fight on, I'm swinging out around thin air, hoping to hit something, hoping I don't bunk into that spear she was carrying, but by now she's gone, she's disappeared, taking my twelve-hundred dollar Redhawk with her. Never to be seen again."

Ruck smacked his lips and looked around, silently denoting, "End of story."

Both audience members nodded their approval.

&&&

Horn's story had not one iota of truth to support it. He was out in the woods just walking his dog, Stella, who always carried a tennis ball in her mouth. Never went anywhere, even around the house, without the thing. Ruck's wife Blanche called Stella "Roger Federer," because she never saw Stella without a tennis ball. Anyway, they both—both him and Stella—get themselves accosted by this jumbo of a woman. She probably ran close to two-fifty—no joke—although from what Horn could observe, all of it was well-placed and evenly distributed.

This banshie-woman was carrying a knife, flashed it about, and demanded that Hook hand over all of the money in his wallet, which was considerable, almost four-hundred dollars. He had cash because he had won big at the OTB. The giant woman also demanded he hand over his binoculars, a fairly new pair of Nikon Monarch HG's. Ten-by-thirty mag. Close to a thousand bucks. Gone now, maybe forever.

ANNAH TORCH   Jim DeFilippi

"Can you beat that?" Horn was asking his friends—and by extension the cop next morning—rhetorically. "How can you ever beat something like that?"

Horn said he lunged at his mugger a few times, but she always managed to parry his thrusts with her knife. It was a big knife, a Bowie type, a lot bigger.

After the robbery, when she was done stuffing his money and his binoculars into her backpack, she told him to strip down.

Horn asked the table, "Should I say, 'What do you want my binoculars for, honey? From what I can see, you got yourself a pretty good pair there yourself,' or would that cheapen the scene?"

Ruck and Box both shook their heads. No, keep that part to yourself. Then Box's face came alive—he got it— but still the answer would have to be a hard No.

So anyway, the woman stuck out the knife at Horn and told him to take his pants off. Right now. Then and there. Horn refused. He told her no way he was going to do that. He told her that she could take all his money, his cash, and she could even take his field-glasses, but she would never take his virginity.

Box snorted and asked him, "Aint't that already been took?"

Horn realized his mistake. "Shut up, fuck-stump. No, no, oh yeah, I didn't mean that. I meant something else. My morality. I meant she couldn't take my morality. That is what I was meaning to say."

&&&

Box had done his homework as far as researching the lie that he was prepared to tell the cops.

He was watching from the underbrush as Mrs. Bigfoot there built herself a huge bonfire. A cooking fire, he supposed it was. She had a stone fire-pit, huge, maybe ten feet across. Maybe more so. And she went and started the damn fire by using a can of kerosene. Really. She poured on kerosene from this red can she had there. Could have started the whole Woods ablaze, easy. Pouring straight kerosene on the pile of logs and weeds there. Crazy. Just plain crazy. Illegal. Against all mandates and park rules.

And then, chopping down lots of trees to feed that fire too. Most of them from an endangered species, Box suspected. Same thing with animals. She was jacking deer out of season, probably eating them too.

He was sure she was. Must have been.

&&&

With all of their stories sharpened to a thin and perfect point, the three each laid a hand on the tabletop before them and vowed to get this thing done. One for all, all for one.

All they had to do was stick to their stories. Go into that interview confident and sure, tell the cop they wanted this bitch put away. And their property returned to them.

Horn told the others that he was making a mental note to hide his Nikon binocs at home, just in case the cops came searching, trying to corroborate, which they wouldn't do.

All they had to do was stick to their stories—the cops would probably make each of them tell it any number of times—and don't make changes in the retelling. Remember the details and repeat them the same way, every time through.

And don't admit knowing each other. Well, everybody in White Leunge knew that they hung out, so that was all right, but they were never in the Woods together. This was the way it happened, three different crimes, with them as victim or witness of each, with no overlap.

Of course, some overlap could have been used as corroboration, but it was too late to start unspooling that thread now. So it would be three separate crimes, three separate instances, the only common factor being the jungle slut herself. Who would soon be turned into a jailbird slut, hopefully like those ones on television.

The three men each checked the time of their appointments.

What about clothing?

ANNAH TORCH   Jim DeFilippi

It should be natural, innocent looking, regular, nothing fancy or flashy. Nobody had to go out clothes shopping, that was for sure.

Jeans would be fine, camo would be good. Maybe a splash of hunter orange here and there.

And dead serious faces. All the time. Three faces of men who had been wronged. Three victims, victims not of circumstance, but of perpetration.

If all went well, and it certainly would, the bitch would be held without bail by the end of the week, the end of the month at the latest.

The three men finished their beers and went home to get a good night's sleep.

They had to be fresh and clear thinking, come the morning.

&&&

ANNAH TORCH   Jim DeFilippi

Chapter Nineteen

Detective Sergeant Simon L. Gumm had been borderline ecstatic four and a half years ago when he had been named head of a brand new department of the White Leunge Police—the Major Crimes Unit. The weighty title carried with it neither a promotion in rank nor an increase in salary, but there had been unspoken hints of increasing the size and prestige of the office.

None of it happened. Gumm was still a detective sergeant, no closer to being a lieutenant, and he was still in charge of a one-man department—himself. Now cruising into his late to upper forties, Gumm was still where he was four years ago, and except for a few aberrations where he was given the lead on a high profile crime like the Amanda Silver killing, he was mostly just stuck with shit jobs and boring cases, taking statements from people with vacuous lives and minds. Like the three he had scheduled for today.

In all fairness to the brass of the WLPD, one had to ask just how many major crimes were committed each year in White Leung, New York, to begin with. Despite the town's reputation of being a cauldron of festering crime and immorality—"White Leunge on the bottom rung"—recent murders and rapes were nearly nonexistent. Almost all crimes were of the petty street level variety—drugs and domestic abuse, or else financial and clerical—the type that for the most part remained undetected and not prosecuted.

If given the opportunity on some television game show to choose what was behind one of the three doors on stage—better pay, more prestige, or a job promotion—Gumm would have to take the cash and run. Money was tight and getting tighter. The wolf wasn't quite at the door yet, but Gumm could see it out there in the front yard, hungry and approaching. Both his alimony and child support were in arrears. Various unsanctioned factions were pressing him for payments on past wagers. If someone offered him three-to-one odds that he had a debilitating gambling addiction, he would have to take the action.

ANNAH TORCH   Jim DeFilippi

Any success he had once enjoyed at the betting window—at Saratoga, OTB, or any of his five bookies—had run out with the arrival of the Fever. Before the Fever had heated up and exploded, he could pick a winner—especially in the NFL—a lot more often than not. For an inveterate gambler like himself, fifty-one percent was the magical winning margin, and he had continually scored well above that—week after Sunday week, month after seasonal sport month, year after point-spread year.

It was as if he had within himself *something*, something almost magical, some sort of undefined skill that had been mingled within the very marrow of his bones, something that would heat up his fingers and the back of his neck as he slapped his money down and picked up his ticket, and later on, his winnings.

It wasn't just a case of a team's roster, or who they had starting at key positions, or of that week's opponent or venue, or how they were managing to compensate for the names on their injury list, or how Bill James would chalk up the statistics with his Sabermetrics—it was something beyond all that. It was a certain instinct he had for picking winners, something related to how they took the field before a game, or how the star cornerback was standing behind the microphone at the postgame press conference.

But all of that had been frozen by the Fever. Lately he had been on a downhill slide, unmatched since Job's cold streak got reported in the Old Testament. Things had twisted, and Gumm had yet to figure them out, had yet to regain the confidence required to point at a team or a horse and call it a winner for the day.

And so he simply had to beat his way on, a boat against the constantly flipping odds board, borne back ceaselessly to the fifty-dollar window—just get the odds right this time, stretch the paycheck until right before it snapped—and keep hoping for his luck to change, or at least to perk up a bit.

The three interviews he had set up today—two in the morning, one after lunch—were just three more squat-downs in a long line of crap jobs. He had barely ever met any of these characters—at least as best he could remember—but everyone around town knew them as lower level woodchucks, good old boys who were never all that good and no longer boys, just three buckets of tree sap, old

ANNAH TORCH   Jim DeFilippi

and getting older. And dumber by the day, and more steadfastly committed to their ignorance.

Gumm didn't think he had ever come face to face with the ten o'clock—Ruck Ruckhouser—but Gumm knew his wife all right, the former Blanche Leunge. She was very smart, she was clever, and accommodating. The two had begun dating a year after graduating from WLHS, and things got pretty serious for a while, right up to the time that she had married this Ruckhouser crud for some God-only-knows reason. For months after the nuptials, at least nine, Gumm kept waiting for a birth announcement—but nothing.

Why did smart women so often fall for morons? It must be something evolutionary. Had Darwin ever written about this phenomenon? It must be related somehow to Survival of the Shitiest. If not for a woman tapping them on the shoulder in warning, most of these guys would be using a welding torch to get the cap off a propane tank.

Gumm and Blanche would sneak off together every few months or so, meet at one coffee shop or another for a round of shared tea and mutual sympathy, with both of them thinking it might go further, but so far had not. He would lay out his troubles of holding a shitty job in a shittier town. She would tell him that her Dad had last-stage Alzheimers, but could still carry on a more coherent conversation than could her husband.

So this cop besieged with gambling debts was commiserating with a lady married to a dimwitted game-poacher, and in all likelihood things were destined to remain that way. Blanche would use her Dad's condition to get away for a harmless rendezvous, but usually she really was over there at her Dad's house, listening to his incoherent and constantly repeated stories while ladling soup into his mouth.

Gumm checked his watch. Nine forty-five. Time to make the donuts. Time to meet the numb nuts.

&&&

Less than four minutes into the interview with Blanche's husband, Gumm realized that this guy's story about being attacked in the woods by an Amazon woman was at least ninety percent clam-wax. Gumm pretended to listen, pretended to write down some notes, but he was unable to come up with any questions more meaningful than, "Then what?"

The guy was trying to present himself as someone who could handle a situation with fists or a gun, and wouldn't mind doing either.

Finally, Gumm couldn't take any more of the bloated pablum and the boredom, so he invented and then introduced into the conversation the term, "Perjury Protocol."

Ruckhouser stopped talking in mid-sentence to ask, "What's that?"

Gumm leaned back in his chair and took a sip of tea. "Well, it's a very simple process we have. When any suspicious activity occurs, such as this, I, as a member of the court, am required to investigate and study it. At this stage, an arrest might be instituted or at least forthcoming."

Ruck's eye had enlarged. Gumm guessed that there was similar activity going on beneath the patch. "Wait. You talking about me or about her? What are you trying to pull here?"

"The District Attorney in the district court seeks an indictment from the Grand Jury. If enough evidence of perjury is presented, then the case is not dismissed, but rather it proceeds to the prosecution stage. By the way, the defendant or his defense have no opportunity to present exculpatory evidence at this stage. It is a one-sided ball game. Guys like me, police officers, offer the Grand Jury their expertise and their opinion. I might make a statement something like, 'You could tell the stupid clamshell had just made up the whole story and was trying to sell it as truth.' Perjury. False reporting. That is the very definition of perjury."

Ruck's smirk had hardened into a scowl. He said, "That's not this, though. What the hell?"

Gumm went on. "No, I'm just painting you a portrait of how things proceed. You asked, didn't you?"

"Maybe I did."

"So, the state presents its evidence of guilt to the Grand Jury." Gumm stopped talking, turned slowly around, and he pointed up at the video camera in the corner of the interview room. Ruckhouser's eye followed Gumm's finger.

Gumm said, "I like to videotape all depositions. We'll determine with the Grand Jury if there is enough probability to bring charges against you."

"Against me? What the fuck. This is fucked up."

"Sit down. Against the perpetrator. It's theoretical at this point."

"Good. It better be."

Gumm continued. "Sure enough, so let me go on. From there, the defendant may either surrender, or he is arrested by the U. S. Marshals Service. He appears before a magistrate judge to hear the charges that are being brought against him. In this case, he is charged with perjury."

"Perjury. Like shit."

"Perjury. Again, we're talking hypothetically. So far. So if the government attorney seeks to have the defendant detained until trial, a detention hearing is held. The defendant is then..."

"The guy who did the lying. If there was any."

"That's right, that's the guy. The guy who lied must be present at the detention hearing, along with his lawyer, as well as at all future hearings."

"If I can't afford a lawyer, you guys get me one."

"Absolutely. But we're not talking about you, sir. But yes, that would be supplied by the Public Defender Office. It's usually some fuzzy-cheeked kid right out of L-school, still brings a sandwich with him for lunch, has you and fifteen other clients going on at the same time, doesn't even remember your name, what you did, couldn't care less anyway. You are basically fried at this point, done for, if you have to depend on a public defender."

"I got money. My wife has plenty money."

"I know your wife. We went to school together. How's her father doing?"

"No good."

"Too bad. She's a good woman, Blanche is. She is strong and tough and smart, as I remember. Taking care of her dad like she does. She wouldn't need anyone taking care of her, if, God forbid, something happens to you, but I'll be glad to look in on her from time to time."

"Damn it, what? What you saying? I don't know how to take that."

"Take it intelligently, it's the best way."

"I guess. It better be."

"The defendant is either released on bail or kept in custody until his next court appearance."

Ruckhouser looked around the room. "In here?"

"Capitol Northeast Correctional Center, most likely. It's over there in Herkimer. Nasty place. Guys are taking it up the kazoo all the time over there."

"Not me."

"Of course not. When the perjurer is advised of the charges against him by the magistrate judge, he enters a plea of 'Not Guilty,' although everybody on both sides know that he is. This is called the arraignment."

"I know what you're doing here. It's bullshit."

"If the plea is changed to 'Guilty' at a later time, which it usually is, the perjurer meets with a probation officer, who prepares a pre-sentence report. The defendant appears before a district judge to be sentenced."

"I know what you're doing. I'm not guilty of anything."

"Good, that's very good. Stay that way. Then if the plea is 'Not Guilty,' like you're saying it is here, then both attorneys prepare for trial. Well, the state's attorney prepares for trial. Your attorney, the public defender, he just eats his brown bag sandwich while he checks LinkedIn for a new job, a real job, something he can actually work at. And get paid for."

"I uh..."

"The government must disclose all the information and evidence that they have to this guy, like video evidence," Gumm glanced up at the camera, "but as I say, the P. D. just tosses it in the corner and goes back to eating and looking for a real job on the Internet."

"All right, all right, all right."

"The pretrial motions to suppress..."

"All right."

"At that point most cases are just plea-bargained."

"I said, 'All right!' God damn it. Look, officer, I know exactly what you're doing here, but I can see where this is all going to, so you win, for now. I'm just gonna get up and get on out of here. Forget I ever come in. Jesus, talk about the deck being stacked against the common man."

As Ruckhouser was leaving the interview room, Gumm called to him, "Hi to Blanche for me, okay?"

Ruckhouser turned back. "You know, if you people ain't going to do something about it, then I'll have to. Justice will be served. I need that gun back. So I'll be using that or somebody else's." The guy looked like he meant it.

"Mr. Ruckhouser, don't do anything like that."

"I will. I will. You bet I will."

After the subject had left, Gumm shook his head and said to the empty room, "There's nothing worse than a stupid man with a gun."

&&&

Gumm's second interview that morning went roughly the same way as the first.

The interview room they were using was designed and furnished to intimidate. A single, six-foot by four-foot hard plastic table, with one chair on the subject's side and three on the officers' side. The officers' chairs were three inches higher than the subject's. The table had iron U bars that looked like rebar sticking up through the hard plastic. The bars ran right through the tabletop to the frame of the table below, where they were bolted to the floor. A set of handcuffs, with one ring clipped to the rebar, and the other dangling loose and open, was lying on the table on the subject's side. The floor of the room was gray cement, troweled so smooth that it was almost slippery. All four walls and the ceiling were acoustical tile held in place by cheap aluminum framing. One wall had a blackened window that was meant to look like a two-way mirror, but in fact was nothing more than a sheet of darkened plastic. The camera was mounted in one upper corner and aimed at the table.

This second guy was even dumber than Ruckhouser. He gave his legal name, but said everybody called him "Horn." He swore that he had no idea why.

He spent most of the time gazing off into space, somewhere miles beyond the wall of the interview room. At one point he offered to bring in the stolen binoculars to show how really expensive they were. Then he quickly changed his story and said he meant to say that he could bring in a pair of similar binocs, ones that he had bought since the first ones had been robbed.

This time, Gumm didn't have to go into as much legal detail before the guy got up and left, with an apology. Of course, any references to Blanche were edited out, although at one point Gumm asked this guy Horn if he thought his wife would be capable of supporting herself on her own.

The guy kept looking off into space, even when he got up to leave. His leg banged hard into one corner of the table.

&&&

Gumm ascertained that the three nitwits must have shared a lunchtime meeting, because the interview after lunch began with this guy Box saying that he wouldn't mind having a lawyer present.

"Of course, of course you can." Gumm offered to lend him his iPhone. "Call any attorney you want."

"I don't know any." This guy was tiny, just a bit over five feet, he started twitching with nervousness.

Gumm wasn't sure he had even seen that before. "Oh, that's too bad. Not even one? A school chum or someone?"

"Can I go look one up?"

"Now? From here? No, you just have to guess."

"I just want to leave then, okay?"

"Of course."

"Is that okay?"

Gumm pointed at the door of the interview room.

&&&

ANNAH TORCH   Jim DeFilippi

Chapter Twenty

Hard-boiled egg sandwiches at the beach.

For every anniversary, for so many years, this is how Grace and Baby Johnnie Silver celebrated the day. With hard-boiled egg sandwiches at the beach.

The tradition had stated with their first anniversary. Johnnie was still performing back then, and he and Li'l Gloopy were playing some decrepit little village playhouse all the way up on the Upper Peninsula of Michigan. They were broke, hoping that by the end of the tour they would have enough money to pay the rent on their tiny walk-up back in Lower Manhattan. Maybe with even enough left over to take out some insurance for themselves and any family member that the stork might bring along in the future. Both sets of parents had offered to help them out with money, but they wanted to make it on their own.

Broke but happy. Happy but in love. In love but broke. Broke but happy.

Michigan is a land of a thousand lakes. They found one they had driven past in their old touring Buick. The lake didn't have any name that they saw, but the sand was warm for the fall, and the trees and bushes were cut back nicely to offer them a view of the hills beyond the water. Grace had made some hard-boiled egg sandwiches with the motor hotel hotplate—one of the few things she was capable of cooking back then—and they took a wicker basket down to the water, along with two Seven-Ups, a bag of pretzels, and some cartons of Good and Plenty for dessert.

They ate and smiled at each other between bites, and Johnnie offered up a toast. May this paper anniversary melt into cotton and clay and silk and lace and ivory, eventually to silver and gold. Johnnie was such a romantic. Even back then he could name every anniversary, from the first to the seventy-fifth.

The horse flies on the shore were the size of bumblebees. Johnnie started telling wonderful lies, stories about how each of the flies was special, had

ANNAH TORCH   Jim DeFilippi

a distinct personality, and he could talk to them, and they liked him because of his jokes.

Married for a year, and this was the first date that he had not brought Gloopy along on. It was just the two of them.

And the hard-boils on the beach tradition continued through the years.

Their third anniversary—leather—was the one they first got to share with a daughter, who spit out the egg and made a face that made them both laugh.

For their fifth—wood—they were back in Manhattan, and they drove out to Jones Beach with the sandwiches. West End One. Johnnie explained how Robert Moses had built all of this, creating one of the greatest beachfront attractions in the world. They drove to the main boardwalk, where Johnnie pointed out all the subtle details Moses had insisted on—the garbage cans shaped like smoke stacks of an ocean liner, the Needle, the delicate design of the bath houses, even the gentle roll of the sand dunes. Johnnie said that someday he would leave behind an image like Robert Moses.

On their seventh anniversary—wool—they were once again out on Long Island, they brought the sandwiches right out to the tip of the Island, Montauk Point, where they tried to break into the lighthouse so that they could climb the circular stairs to the very top, and look out toward Europe.

By the time their marriage had turned to clay—the ninth—they were rich, although Johnnie insisted they were merely "comfortable," not even "really well off." Nevertheless, this year the beach was called Miami Beach, and they were leasing a house in the same neighborhood—just a few blocks over—from Gianni Versace. The sand was white and warm, and although their passion had cooled, the sandwiches tasted as good as ever. They snickered about the other snobs at the beach who subtly let them know that the smell of boiled eggs and mayonnaise was not appreciated.

For their twelfth anniversary, they went to Hawaii, to the Big Island, the town of Kuala Kona. They were celebrating a month early, because Johnnie was scheduled to spend six weeks *incommunicado* in a Soviet Bloc country. He wouldn't tell her what he would be doing over there. Business.

ANNAH TORCH Jim DeFilippi

They got up early, before the sun, to hear the cannon go off for the start of the Ironman Triathlon World Championship. At the roar of the cannon, Johnnie had pretended to be startled and asked her, "Is that for us?" They took a top-down drive out of town, down the coast to a beach that had black sand, to celebrate their day. By midnight, the athletes were still finishing up the event, and the announcer was calling to every single finisher, "You are an Ironman!" Johnnie would salute each of them with the champagne glass he had been carrying with him all day. He stopped drinking soon after that. Grace did not.

They were in China, Johnnie on business, Grace tagging along, bored and tipsy on *Baijiu*, for their fourteenth anniversary—ivory. Johnnie had their egg sandwiches flown in, and they ate them by a lake whose name was unpronounceable back then and long forgotten now.

Johnnie told her that their twenty-third anniversary would have to be special, because it was the silver-plated one, and they were the Silvers. She told him all the years were all special. They drove from Florence all the way across Italy to the Amalfi Coast, and ate their sandwiches as they looked out at the Adriatic Sea.

And today, they were at Buckingham Lake Park, a few miles west of their chateau in Watervliet, trying not to think about their daughter in jail. They had brought some cheap champagne and caviar along with the sandwiches. Johnnie had caught Grace trying to also pack the fixings for her Mare's Legs, but he had frowned and she had placed them back on the counter. She gave him her sheepish, little girl, tilt-headed smile. "No?"

"Grace, you can do without for a couple hours. It's our anniversary."

She agreed. And Johnnie agreed to sip the champagne.

The park did not have an actual beach, but it did have a lovely little lake, much longer that it was wide. They sat down by the water and tried to enjoy the day. A few people would pass by, mostly in two's, behind them on a sidewalk that ran alongside the water. A few yards up from them, a couple had pulled their bicycles off into the shade of a copse of trees, and they were leaning over, examining the man's back tire. He would hold the frame of the bike up off the ground, spin the back wheel, and then clamp on the brakes.

ANNAH TORCH Jim DeFilippi

Right next to these amateur bike mechanics was a lovely iron footbridge, a gentle arch of beams that was reflected in the water, so there were two bridges, right side up and upside down, and together they formed the smile of a clown.

Green and yellow patches of leaves and weeds were spread out along the shore. The sky was blue but mostly cloud-covered above the trees surrounding the far side of the lake.

Grace drew in a long breath of air and told John that the smells were wonderful. Johnnie agreed. They sat and ate their sandwiches very slowly, savoring the taste, prolonging the celebration and—like every other year on this date—they tried to match memories of places and dates that they had shared. It got a bit harder each year.

Grace mentioned the smell of hard-boiled eggs mixing with those coming from Amanda's full diaper one year—where was that?—but at the sound of their daughter's name, the celebration ended.

"Does it still look like, you can...you can...do something?"

"Of course I can do something, Grace. I can do anything. It's just that these gnats, these houseflies, these local fucking politicians, they try to make it as hard as they possibly can for us, for our girl. This D. A. has a hair up her crotch for me, so now she's trying to renege on the deal we had mapped out. They are leeches, all of them."

Grace smiled and said, "You called them horseflies."

"I said house flies." Johnnie smiled. "But you remember, don't you, the horseflies up on the U.P., our first year?"

Grace was smiling, but her eyes were tearing. "You said you could train them. Talk to them. I knew then that you could do anything."

"Remember how pleased you were that I left Gloopy at home?"

"Yes. For just one day, we were childless."

"Where is that little rascal anyway, I can't remember."

"Oh, you remember, you remember just fine. Storage. New Jersey."

"That's right. I forget."

"So we do have two of our children locked up, don't we."

"Not for long we don't. I only wish dealing with this fucking District Attorney was as cut and dried as dealing with the storage facility."

"My Baby Johnnie can do anything."

"Yes, he can."

"Johnnie, I think that big beautiful woman in the suit can help us. The one who works for your Weasel."

"Wyzell. Yes, she's a strange bird, I've heard, but very capable."

"She came to see me, when you were in Rome."

"I know. I know she did."

"She told me that she believes Amanda didn't do it. That she'll prove that."

"I told you, Grace, don't believe that shit. They have to say things like that, everybody knows it's just a chant. An incantation. Like chanting *Oooomm*. It doesn't mean anything. It's just a sound. I told you, don't talk to anyone anymore."

"She sounded sincere."

"Grace, you were drunk."

"How do you know that?"

"Because, darling, you're always drunk. The sun was shining, wasn't it? Or the moon was out? You were drunk."

"You're cruel to me."

"I'm sorry, it's our anniversary, what's wrong with me. I could have used another sandwich. Grace, I've told you before, it was okay that you talked to the Weasel, Wyzell, and it's all right that you spoke to his assistant that once. But that's it. They're on our side, but that's it. Nobody knows who's working what angle anymore. So just don't talk to anyone. Check with me first. Okay? All right?"

"Why would Amanda hurt Dede, her roommate? They got along. She liked her."

"We don't know why, Grace. We probably will never know. Amanda's not talking and we shouldn't be asking her to. There is no explanation for any of this. So forget it. Try not to think about the why's and how-come's."

"I even spoke to that man from the D. A. Protski. Was that his name?"

"Was that his name? I don't know, but whatever it was, for God's sake, cut that out. Grace, they are the enemy, don't you see? They want to harm Amanda, harm us, as much as they possibly can. That's their job. Don't talk to anyone, but most of all, don't talk to cops and lawyers, especially prosecution lawyers. For God's sake."

"I don't think Protski was a lawyer."

"He's an investigator. For the D. A. That's even worse. An investigator just means he was too dumb to make it through law school, so that's his job now. At half the pay."

"He didn't seem dumb. He seemed nice. He was very good for me, to me. He seemed like a good man. I think he's just after the truth."

"Oh, right. Sure thing, he's just after the truth, and Dumbo is a big elephant who can fly, and I can talk to horseflies and tell them jokes. Grace, what's the matter with you? Haven't we been married long enough that you can tell a little bit of what the world is like? What people are after? Grace, know this —everyone you meet is either after my money or my scalp. That's it. He's just after the truth? Come on. Grace, take that dream and burn it. These people are out to burn us, so just don't allow them in the house any more. Don't go talking to them on the phone. Drunk or sober, it won't help. Only hurt. Block their texts, block their tweets, block out whatever the hell they're sending out."

"Johnnie, I just want to hear someone saying our little girl is pure and simple."

"She's pure, all right, and you're simple. I'm losing that anniversary cheer, aren't I? I'm sorry."

"I just want to hear people telling me that Amanda did nothing wrong. Is that so right? I mean, is that so wrong, wrong of me?"

Grace had packed some Siberian Sturgeon caviar along with the sandwiches. Johnnie was scraping a smear of it off his paper plate with a plastic spoon. He put the plate down on the grass. He tossed the spoon into the lake. He slid himself over to Grace, pressed his hip against hers, took hold of both her shoulders, and said, "Grace. Gracie, my little darling. Happy anniversary, my love, but listen to me. Our little girl locked herself in that room, with Dede, her roommate, and with a hand shotgun. She fired it, the gun kicked back, smacked her in her forehead, and she went unconscious for days. And Dede was dead."

Grace was looking at him, staring, like she was trying to find something hopeful. "Dede. They say she died smiling."

"Yes, she did. She died happy. We don't know why, but she did. But the main thing is, Grace, is that she died."

&&&

Chapter Twenty-one

Blanche was gone for the weekend, headed over to Rotterdam to take care of her father—he had started blowing out the gas flame on his stovetop. The day-nurse couldn't decide if he was trying to kill himself or just getting confused, but the flickering blue and red flame seemed to alternately scare him and enthrall him. Both Blanche and the day-nurse agreed that things were getting worse by the day. The old man was still fighting institutionalization, but soon that might be the only viable solution to his mental disintegration.

For over a year now, Blanche had been going over almost every weekend, then driving back home Monday mornings. Now the old man might have to be watched not only all day, but for all seven nights of the week. Until Blanche could make sure that Medicare and Medicaid would pay for everything, she would be spending more and more time over there, and less time at home.

Which suited Ruck just fine, Blanche wasn't complaining about it and neither was he.

This current situation gave him his weekends at least—time to enjoy himself without restraint or that subtle, stink-eye criticism of hers. This Saturday night, he was down in his finished basement—he called it "The Dungeon"—with Horn and Box.

The three were drinking beer, eating pepperoni slices, and watching the huge Samsung seventy-five inch TV.

Rape videos.

Ruck had hooked up his iPad to an adapter he got from Apple, and from there to the plug on the side of the TV, which was a mirror-thin screen of a device sitting on a thick wooden shelf hanging from the brick wall. The conversion made the victims' bodies on the screen life-size, almost like they were there in the room with you. Ruck pointed out to his guests that some of the asses being pumped were as big as a breadbox.

ANNAH TORCH Jim DeFilippi

Ruck had wanted to mount the giant Samsung right onto the brick wall, and then tear out the shelf altogether, but his Amazon request for mounting brackets especially designed for brick and mortar was on back order. He kept getting emails with the expected date and time of delivery, but the dates and times would come and go with the wind.

So maybe he should just cancel his order and wait. A new, bigger Samsung, called simply "The Wall," might be worth waiting for. That one would cover the entire wall, make all the brick and mortar and everything else expendable.

For now, the smaller but still big Samsung was glowing above a large arch-topped fireplace that was set into the brick. The fireplace was filled with last night's logs and ashes. Two smaller, useless fireplaces were set into the wall, one on each side. Ruck had never burned in either of them.

Covering the rest of the brick wall, crowded together, horn to horn, shoulder to shoulder, were thirty-one mounted deer heads, with a few walleye salmon mixed among them. Everything would all have to be moved if Ruck decided on the new Samsung. Most of the whitetails had racks, ranging from spike-horn all the way up to fifteen point. The two bucks right above the television screen had their heads tilted toward each other and their horns interlocked. There were so many mounted heads that a few had to be hung out beyond the center brick portion of the wall, spilling out onto the sheetrock on either side. A string of track-lighting hanging from the ceiling lit up the display as if the deer were movie stars, but Ruck had dimmed the lights so that they could watch the TV screen without any glare.

The rest of the room was dominated by other stuffed animals of other species, either standing or hanging out over an ornate and intricately patterned ten-by-twelve rug from Costco, which in turn was laid on top of another rug, this underlying one bigger and plain brown in color. The room smelled heavily of stale, spilled beer, mixed with the musk of recent and poorly performed taxidermy procedures.

Ruck's seventy-pound black bullmastiff-boxer mix—the dog's name was Slave—lay asleep in a corner, half off the rugs.

ANNAH TORCH   Jim DeFilippi

Ruck pointed at the television screen and said, "She's a good one, I'd take that." The black woman was being raped by a man wearing a ball cap and Halloween hood.

Ruck turned to both the boys and told them, "So show me what you brung."

Both Horn and Box had come into the house with large Army surplus duffle bags slung over their shoulder. Both duffles were heavy canvas, clipped shut and fully loaded. The two men stood up—Horn from a wooden upholstered love seat, Box from the couch—and they poured the contents of their duffles out onto the carpet.

Grotesque items were spilled out across the floor. Each item was picked up in turn by Ruck, who passed it on to Horn, who passed it to Box. Each item was carefully studied by each man—the weight, the feel of it in the hand, the heft—and it was either rejected or accepted by voice vote. Most of the rounds of the voice voting ended in unanimous acceptance. The process was only interrupted by trips up to the kitchen fridge, and by Ruck's announcements that he still missed his Redhawk, and by casual quick side-glances up at the TV screen, where a man in a hood was now grabbing hold of a woman's chainlink vest.

The items varied in shape and size and design, but all held a common theme.

Thick leather wrist and ankle restraints with heavy brass buckles, still in their shipping packaging.

Handcuffs, a black hood with a red tie-string around the neck area, a set of ankle irons—these were all voted on and accepted. Horn mimed the hood being dragged over his head, then him trying to suck in some air.

A series of handguns, mostly automatics along with a few revolvers, were held in the palm, shaken, aimed at a wall, dry-fired, and then put back down onto the carpet with nods of approval. Ruck was again mentioning his missing Redhawk. He had replaced the stolen revolver with a new Super Redhawk Alaskan snub-nose. Full house. "But I still want my old one back too, the one what got stolen."

ANNAH TORCH   Jim DeFilippi

More ankle irons, lengths of heavy chain, rolls of duct tape, blindfolds, spools of wire.

Box stood up at one point and slipped himself into an institutional strength straitjacket, but he refused to allow his friends to hook him up into it. He explained that he was no Houdini and he didn't want to be. They called him a pussy.

Two small cotton bags—one filled with sand, the other with ballbearings—were labeled as "saps" by Ruck. "In case you faggots didn't know what that word was."

Black leather gags with a red ball designed to be inserted into the victim's mouth reminded the men of the ones they had seen in *Pulp Fiction*. Horn placed one red ball into his mouth and pantomimed choking.

The benefits of a stun-gun as opposed to a simple taser were talked about and voted on. Box jolted his body like a seizure, showing them what it was like to be hit.

A glass bottle of chloroform leaned against a plastic Army canteen that Horn said also was filled with chloroform. Another identical canteen was filled with gasoline.

Leg shackles and wire cutters.

A compass and binoculars.

A pair of heavy, sound deadening ear protectors, like the ones they would wear at shooting galleries.

Trip wire.

There were two types of lug wrench, the L–with the socket on one end and the pryer on the other– and the X, with its spider choice of four different sizes of lug nut.

Rags, pairs of pliers, three type screwdrivers, various sizes and shapes of hammers and knives all littered the carpet.

ANNAH TORCH   Jim DeFilippi

Ruck told his two men, "I tried to buy a shrunken head one time from the Peabody Museum, over there in Salem, but they wouldn't even admit they even had any. I know they did though."

Ruck had put out a bowl of pepperoni slices that he had peeled off the top of a large frozen pizza that Blanche had left for him. He told Horn and Box, "They make me fart." He sailed one slice through the air toward Slave. It landed on the dog's ear. Slave didn't wake up. Ruck said, "They make Slave fart too. Worse than mine."

All the drinking and tool selection was tiring out the three men. They still hadn't talked about their mission.

Ruck went upstairs for more Yuenglings and a jar of Vaseline Total Moisture Conditioning Cream that he had swiped from the medicine chest in the downstairs bathroom.

The three men sank back onto their seats and started studying the video again. They made various comments of approval or concern at the different clips and activities. Some of the scenes were shot dark and grainy, with the actors almost indistinguishable from the background. Some were shot with clear and bright lighting, of near professional quality.

Ruck passed the jar of lotion around.

As the three men sat and watched the scenes flashing across the huge screen, the room grew silent, almost reverential.

The video was about forty minutes long. When it ended, Ruck rewound it and played it from the beginning. This time through the men started remembering some of the players and the scenes. They would lean forward in their chairs when they would sense that some particularly captivating activity was about to unfold.

Ruck reached down and picked up the sap filled with sand. He kept pressing it with his fingertips, making indents that would slowly re-inflate by themselves.

Horn held a SIG Sauer P365 semiautomatic pistol as he watched the show. He kept sliding the bolt back and forth, in rhythm with the onscreen

ANNAH TORCH Jim DeFilippi

action. The weapon was resting on his lap, his hand around the grip, finger through the finger-guard. He had oiled the weapon and was moving the slide back and forth, back and forth—rhythmically, mechanically, erotically.

Box held a pair of heavy wire cutters in his right hand and would slap it hard into his left palm.

Whenever the rapist on the screen was a black man, boos, barks, and simian yells would accompany calls of "Lock him up." Whenever a particularly attractive female was being attacked, the cheers would drown out the rock music sound track.

Eventually, each man put down whatever object he had been holding.

Ruck went over to the light switch and dimmed it down to the off position. He also grabbed a box of White Owl cigars from the gun cabinet in the far corner. Each made a pretense of unwrapping the cigar, wetting its tip, and lighting it. Ruck put an antique Buick ashtray on the table in the center of the room, and went up and got a serving bowl from the kitchen to act as a second ashtray. Despite all the preparation and pretense, none of the three men took more than three or four puffs before stubbing the cigar out and tossing it into an ashtray.

Horn asked Ruck if he knew how many buck-heads were mounted on the wall. Ruck said he didn't know. Horn asked if he remembered when he had taken each one. Ruck said he didn't. Horn asked if there was one or two that were extra special to him, either because of the size or its beauty, or the massive effort he had to put in of tracking and bringing down the mighty buck.

Box giggled and asked how many had he taken legally, how many of them had tags.

Ruck told them both to shut up and watch the movie.

A series of blond women in fishnet stockings were being grabbed from behind on a wet, dark street, dragged into an alley, where their dresses were stripped off. Each woman was slightly different, but they were all blond, all wearing fishnet, all being accosted in the dark alley. The camera tended to show their faces in a mix of agony and ecstasy, then pan down the naked bodies, pausing at their hips, before continuing down to their legs and feet and the cold, dark, wet pavement.

The blue flickering light of the giant Samsung—showing scene after similar scene—was providing the only light in the room.

Each man kept his eyes straight ahead, on the screen. They were done speaking, as if everything important had been said. They had to wave a hand blindly in the air to locate their beer bottle, then grab hold of it, take a gulp, and put the bottle back down.

They still hadn't talked about their mission.

Box's beer bottle spilled over on the carpet. He looked away from the screen and quickly righted the bottle, but a puddle of beer had spread into the nap. He took a handkerchief from his back pocket and made a few weak attempts at sopping up the wet, but Ruck called him a stable-mutt and told him not to worry about it.

Since last year, when a fight had broken out among all three of them, and little Box had lost a tooth, the rule had been: No touching anybody else. Everybody just plays on his home field.

After a long, silent period of time, Horn gave out a short, loud snort of pleasure and then went silent. Box was asleep, his snoring sounding like moans, his mouth hanging open.

Ruck was wide awake, smiling to himself, staring at a spot on the brick wall to the right of the television screen.

The video ran out. Box snorted himself awake and looked around like he couldn't figure out where he was. He spotted Ruck and asked, "You been sleeping, boss, you asleep, Chief?"

Ruck told him, "No. I been thinking about the future."

&&&

Chapter Twenty-two

After Baby Johnnie Silver had consulted with his mole in the D.A.'s office, he told Howard Wyzell to meet with him, ten o'clock, Johnnie would come in to the offices of Howard Wyzell and Associates at Law. He told Wyzell to have that girl investigator there too. "Grace told me about her. I want to meet her. Have her there."

Wyzell told Annah to wear her big girl clothes.

Johnnie's BMW delivered him at nine-forty, and he seemed annoyed having to wait until nearly ten. Being on time meant being early.

"Sorry to rush you, dude, but I'm off to Las Vegas this afternoon. Pleasure trip. Well needed. With what's going on."

Wyzell said that he understood and introduced Annah.

"My wife told me how impressed she was with you. You left her an imprint. So you work for the...Counselor Wyzell here."

"Not too much."

Wyzell said, "She used to, full-time. Best I've ever had. She's sort of– retired–these days. I keep trying to talk her out of it, to coming back on board."

Johnnie was looking Annah over. "They tell me, I've heard, you've decided to go off the grid. Because of the Fever?"

"No. Before that. Things were making me...sleepy, feverish, so I left."

"Fascinating. How do you live? The Counselor here is still paying your bills?"

"I don't need much. My wants are few. Howard keeps a bank account for me."

"You talk like you don't need much money. Only rich people talk like that. I say the same thing sometimes, but only to impress people."

ANNAH TORCH Jim DeFilippi

Annah shook her head, no.

Johnnie said, "But you are rich, aren't you, I bet. Family money. Inheritances. I can tell. I started out..."

"Both my parents were mushroom miners, from western Pennsylvania."

Johnnie's eyebrows went up. "Mushroom miners."

Wyzell told him, "Annah likes to fool around, when she's meeting human people instead of animals." He looked over at her. "Sometimes she doesn't know when to hop off the clown car."

Annah smiled at him.

Johnnie asked, "You're a lawyer? You were? For Mr. Wyzell? Before?"

"I was an expeditor for the retail association."

Wyzell turned to Annah. "Annah, please, come on."

Johnnie asked, "What's that?"

Annah told him, "I don't know. It's just something I tell people."

Johnnie and Wyzell looked at her. She said, "I'm sorry. I apologize. I'm wasting everybody's time here, and I shouldn't do that. We should be talking about Amanda's case."

Johnnie winked. "Yes, yes, by all means, I dislike business meetings that veer off into the personal. I don't permit it. But, in this case, I was a bit intrigued by your life's story, so just tell me please, quickly if you must, what convinced you to go so aboriginal on us? Was it a busted romance type thing? I bet it was. Who was he? I imagine he was some doozy of a lover."

"Ben Franklin."

"Huh?"

"'Tho treated with all imaginable tenderness to prevail with them to stay, yet in a short time they become disgusted with our manner of life and take the first good opportunity of escaping again into the woods.'"

ANNAH TORCH — Jim DeFilippi

Johnnie didn't say anything.

Finally, Wyzell said, "I treat her with all imaginable tenderness all the time. She doesn't stick around." Wyzell seemed to relax, his shoulders dipped, he pulled at his necktie. Johnnie smiled and Wyzell went into his lawyer spiel. "Yes, let's start, if we could, Mr. Silver. Your daughter..."

Johnnie said, "My little girl is in a very fragile state. I don't want anyone bothering her. Your only job now, Counselor, is to get D. A. Goofy to back off. Your task is the alleviation of Amanda's punishment, not Amanda herself."

As Wyzell started to speak, Johnnie held up his hand. "My daughter shot someone. We all can agree on that."

Annah said, "Damn, it's me again, sorry. Mr. Silver, she didn't do it."

Johnnie tilted his head, like he hadn't quite heard. "She didn't do it? What? Did I hear that?"

"Yes. She..."

Wyzell cut in. "Annah has a theory. I won't ask her to explain it to you. I don't think she can explain it to me, or to herself even. I think this is a path not to be taken, that we shouldn't be on. Let's just talk about what happens from here, like you said. You said on the phone that's what you wanted this meeting for."

Johnnie looked from one to the other. "That's right. That's right. I think you've been kept up with what's been happening. I was led to believe that we had a deal worked out with D. A. Guffleberg. Amanda would plead not guilty..." He looked over at Annah. "Not guilty is a legal term just, of course. We would go to trial, the case would. My lawyers—not you, the real ones—you're real, I mean, I mean my staff lawyers, would introduce legal insanity. Temporary legal insanity. Amanda would pay for her crime, pay dearly, but fairly. She would be institutionalized for a time, until the proper medical authorities would certify her being cured. Then..."

Wyzell said, "The plea could be Not Guilty, Not Guilty by Reason of Insanity."

ANNAH TORCH   Jim DeFilippi

Johnnie said, "Yes, either one. You can tell I'm a business man, not a lawyer. But the important thing was, is, for Amanda, that we are guaranteed a soft deal. Not 'soft'—fair, a fair deal. Now I'm being told that D. A. Guffleberg is reneging, is intending to go strong arm on her. So I'm here today telling you both to make sure that does not happen. I won't have that. We can't have that. It could kill Amanda, it could kill my wife."

Wyzell said, "We are here to see that Amanda gets a fair treatment for her crime." He looked at Annah. "If indeed she did commit a crime." Back at Johnnie. "Mr. Silver, you vetted me before you hired me, I'm sure you did. You know how I operate. I don't throw up smokescreens, I don't prevaricate, I don't elude or collude or misuse the law. We will do our best, my entire firm and Ms. Torch here, to get the best possible treatment for your daughter. If you've been promised something by the District Attorney's office, we will make sure they'll make good on that promise."

Johnnie held up his hands. "That's all I want. That's all we're here for. That's the only assurance I've come for."

"Good. We are good. Annah, we are good, are we not?"

Annah said, "We are good, Howard."

Johnnie said, "I'll only be out in Vegas for a few days. Decompression. When I get back, I hope you'll be able to tell me everything is all set."

Wyzell said, "Your wife told me you play in poker tournaments out there?"

"I do. Not this time. All this mess with Amanda, plus me over to Rome, I missed the World Championships. I'll just play some personal high-stake penny-ante, if that's not a contradiction."

"Enjoy yourself."

Johnnie started to get up, but sat back down. "It's the only brand of poker I'm any good at. It's called *Pai Gow*. Oriental, originally. Have you ever heard of it?"

Wyzell shook his head.

ANNAH TORCH   Jim DeFilippi

Johnnie turned to Annah. "You, Miss Torch?"

"I have heard the name."

"It's really fascinating. It's like anything else, it's like practicing the law, I presume. The rules are well laid out and childishly simple, but if you train yourself to play with precision and dedication, then you win more often than you lose."

Wyzell said, "I see."

Johnnie went on. "It's poker, but both you and the dealer, or you and your opponent, each get seven cards. Forget about the pocket bets, the side bets, they're pipeline dreams, waste of money."

Annah told him, "Go on."

"So, seven cards. Poker hands are five, of course. Each of you break your hand into a five card–that's your long hand, and the two left over–your short. Your long must always be better than your short."

"I see."

Johnnie seems amused. "That's it, that's all there is to it. If both your hands win, beats your opponent's, then you win, if both of your opponent's hands win, you lose. Everything else is a push, okay?"

Wyzell asked, "You can have a flush, or a straight, with the two-card hand? That'd be awful easy."

"No. High card or pairs only. There's no flush or straight without five cards. In your long hand, a pair of nines or better are going to win most of the time. In the short, it's an Ace or any pair, that's the Continental Divide. Every player knows these odds."

"Sounds simple enough."

Johnnie said, "And it is. Simple as Amish pie. Any dope can play, can win. It's like blackjack."

Wyzell said, "Everybody plays blackjack."

Johnnie said, "Yup, it's a thousand times more popular. I don't know why."

Annah asked, "Tournaments?"

Johnnie smiled. "That gets a little bit more interesting. You have one-point-five seconds to make your play, to break up your hand. It kills some players. Doesn't seem like much time—a second and a half, they have a timer that dings—but it is. I've been lobbying the casinos to get the time cut down to an even second."

Wyzell asked, "And if you don't make your move in time?"

"Then *ding*, you lose. You got no dog in the fight. You no longer got skin in the game."

Annah asked, "So with things being so simple, so easy, why doesn't everybody have an equal chance. How come you win all the time?"

"How do you know I win all the time?"

"You win all the time."

Johnnie was smiling more broadly. "You're right, I do. I do win all the time. At everything."

"How?"

"Well, see, there's a very obvious, very simple thing that players don't realize, don't utilize. Amateurs. The pro's know it, but psychology gets in the way. That bell's about to go off, so they go with instinct, which is wrong most of the time."

Annah asked, "What's that one simple thing?"

Johnnie looked like he was about to burst open with joy, with cleverness. "Here it is—your short hand is just as important as your long hand. Okay, so you got a flush, but that leaves your short with just an eight and a two. You're not gonna win, you got a push there. But you pull that Ace, destroy the flush, put it over in the short hand, match the eight with one's already there, you got a shot, then. Get it?"

Wyzell said, "I'm lost. I'm still back at the bunkhouse looking for my boots."

Johnnie looked at Annah. "You?"

She said, "I think I get it. So you step back, in that one and a half seconds that you have, and you look at everything, you look at both. One thing is as important, plays into the solution, as much as the other thing does."

Johnnie nodded. "You got it."

Annah nodded.

Johnnie told her, "You're a smart girl, I could tell. I knew you would."

Wyzell told them, "I used to watch Texas Hold 'em on TV. Hey, I can do this, this isn't so hard. But I got to the table at Foxwoods, there's no announcer telling me what's going on. There's no little TV camera showing me everybody's hole card. Makes it more difficult."

Johnnie was still smiling. "Did you lose?"

Wyzell said, "I won a bit, but I had to go back up to my room with a headache, I couldn't take it. The pressure. The confusion."

Johnnie pointed out, "But you do it in the courtroom, everyday, right? You do that. You're brilliant, I've heard tell. You take all that pressure, and all that confusion, and you turn it against your opponent, you use it, don't you?"

Wyzell said, "That's the courtroom, not the poker room. Both high stakes, but it's different."

Johnnie turned to Annah, "How about you, Annah, can you do it? Can you take all that confusion and make something or it?" He seemed to be challenging her.

Annah said, "Mr. Silver, may I ask you a few things about Amanda, about her and the case?"

"Of course, go ahead. Anything that will help. Put poker aside, that's what we're here for." Johnnie shifted in his seat and his iPhone beeped. "Oh, excuse me, let me take this." He held the phone up to his ear and said, "Silver."

He began listening and nodding. Then he said into the phone, "Let me hear it. Let me hear the message." He listened and nodded some more. "Tell Rome it's a question of time, not of money. Tell them that." He listened some more while shaking his head. "No...no...not that way...can't work. Tell them the Pope can go shit in the woods if that's the way." Grinning, he looked at Annah. "No, don't tell them that. You can imply it. Okay."

Johnnie clicked off the phone and slipped it into his inside jacket pocket. "I'm sorry. I apologize. My daughter's wanted for murder and I'm arguing with rock-headed Catholics."

Wyzell said, "And heading off to Las Vegas. I'm sorry—that came out wrong."

Johnnie said, "No, it didn't. That's what you've been thinking, so that's what you said. I appreciate that. I'm not wounded by it, but I accept that. What people think has never been the thing with me. Even when I was doing my dummy act, up on stage, years and decades ago. What people think didn't matter. That's probably why I wasn't very good at it. Not like my father was. That's why I got out of show business. Got into the business of business. Where it doesn't matter what people think of you, just how things turn out when the deal gets done. That's all that matters. I'll be back in just a few days. You'll report to me then what's happened, what's been done. You'll report to me then that things have been set straight for my little Amanda."

Saying no more, Johnnie got up and left.

&&&

Chapter Twenty-three

After Baby Johnnie Silver had left the office, heading off to LasVegas, Wyzell and Annah remained sitting there. Neither was talking. Wyzell was used to being patient with Annah, just letting her sort through things in her mind. He studied her face as she processed.

Wyzell's secretary came to the door holding a clipboard, when she started to enter the room, Wyzell held up his hand to her. She nodded, turned around and left.

After five minutes Wyzell said quietly to Annah, "You know, Sherlock Holmes could trace Dr. Watson's thought process just by observing his facial movements. But your face doesn't move. So I can't do that."

"Shut up, Sherlock, I'm thinking."

"Okay, but don't call me Shirley."

Five more minutes of silence. Finally, when Wyzell sensed that Annah was coming out of her trance, he looked at his watch and said to her, "Annah, the lease on this place is running out. C'mon, what did you think of all that? What are your thoughts about Baby Johnnie Silver?"

"I learned."

"You learned what, how to play poker?"

"I learned many things."

"Thank you, Swami. Did you know this guy used to be a ventriloquist? With a dummy and everything? Like Jeff Dunham. Doesn't seem right, does it? But that is supposedly how he started out. From his Dad's act, took it over. This was before he became an ego-crusted Warren Buffett. Was just a second-rate ventriloquist."

"I could see his lips move."

ANNAH TORCH Jim DeFilippi

Wyzell reached into his desk drawer for a pencil, took it out along with an old fashioned ice-cube sized pencil sharpener. He started shaving the point of the pencil in the little plastic-held razor-blade. He would take the shavings and drop them into the North Eastern wastepaper basket by the side of his desk. "It sounded like unless we have everything settled for sweet girl Amanda by the time Papa John gets back, we'll be out on the street again. I don't think I'd mind though. I really haven't been enjoying this packet at all. Everything is too simple, too confusing."

"How long did he say he would be gone?"

"I'm not sure, maybe a couple of days. I wasn't listening at that point. He lost me back at the blackjack table."

Annah said, "A few days might not be enough. But it might be settled by then. I have to check some things."

"Settled? Settled? Annah, this is the law we are dealing with. The wheels grind exceedingly slowly. Settled, you say? You know, I used to wish I could enter your mind for five minutes. I don't wish for that anymore. Not without some spelunking equipment. And a helmet for when I fall off the ledge. Or walk into a wall. Or into a mirror. Annah, things are a long way off from being settled."

"Weaz, have you read a book called *The Black Swan*?"

"What's it about, how to play poker?"

"It covers how to think."

"Oh. Then I'm not interested."

"It investigates events that happen so infrequently, that are so rare, that they almost don't exist. But they do."

"You mean like a young girl smiling as she's about to take a shotgun blast to her stomach?"

"Like that."

"Like a college girl, a prep-school girl, executing someone like she's an old fashioned assassin?"

ANNAH TORCH Jim DeFilippi

"Like that."

"And like a supposedly brilliant crime investigator who keeps telling me the girl with the sawed-off is innocent?"

"I keep seeing that smile, damn it. The death smile. I cannot rid my mind of that photograph. Maybe I stared at it too long."

"Me too. Pretty girl. Died smiling." Wyzell was shaking his head in sadness.

"The guy who wrote the book said that the human mind, by our nature, the instinct is to try to find simplistic answers to these Black Swans, to these aberrational events. It makes them easier to think about, puts them in order."

"Probably true."

"But Black Swans aren't that for everyone. Getting killed is a Black Swan for the turkey, at Thanksgiving, but the farmer knew about it all along. All that grain he was feeding the bird had a purpose to it."

Wyzell said, "Yes, the murderer knows what's coming. Pre-med. Amanda knew what was coming when she squeezed that trigger. Maybe she didn't know the gun would kick back and knock her out for a week, but she knew where the buckshot would end up. And what kind of birds are we talking about here, swans or turkeys? They don't mate, do they? Can they? A swurkey?"

"I am just sputtering out my thoughts, I am going in circles on this packet. I am."

"I've never seen a swan standing up, have you? They're always floating along in the water when you see them. You've got them out at Robert's Pond, don't you? I know you watch them have their babies in the spring. But do they have feet? Do they even have legs, do swans?"

"So you think Taleb should have called his book, *The Standing Up Swan*?"

"Maybe."

Annah said, "Every spring, I watch the male, a cob, patrol the waters bringing food to his mate, who is sitting on the eggs. For a month. He's protecting her, feeding her, chasing off the Canadian geese and snapping turtles. He is the bully of the block. Mothers get all the ink, but a father's instinct is just as strong. Johnny Silver loves his daughter, he's trying to protect her, I can tell."

"I'll give him that. Rich guys can be human too, I suppose."

Annah told him, "You're rich, are you human? I guess so. And yet, I've watched you eat spaghetti, so I have my doubts."

"I always wear a red shirt."

"Weaz, I am getting closer. Dede Constaghulia was gutshot. Amanda Silver was holding the gun that killed her. Amanda's parents feel she's guilty, but will do anything to protect her. If Johnnie thought he could have rigged a jury, or bought a judge outright, and gotten his daughter off free, not guilty, he would have done that. We know he's working every angle he can to relax the punishment, the sentence. We know that Nico Madness supplied Amanda with the gun."

Wyzell said, "But you told me Nico..."

"Nico was not lying, and he was not telling the truth. The poor slob has no idea what either of those two things are. My instinct of him indicates innocence, other than dealing the gun to her."

"But he also told you what Amanda was going to do with that gun. She was strolling off to kill her friend."

"He also—he was almost impossible to follow—he also said something about telling her something that she didn't like hearing."

"What was that?"

"I don't know. It was like talking to a Scrabble board. But something happened between those two girls in the bar. Something that turned two fairly close friends, two happily coexisting roommates, something that turned one into a shotgun wielding amnesiac, and the other one into a corpse."

"A smiling corpse."

"Yes. Yes. I am getting there, Weaz. All the chocks will fall into place. Eventually."

ANNAH TORCH   Jim DeFilippi

"They always do for you, Annah. You've never come up empty on anything I've ever sent you out on. And I've sent you out on some really unlikely quests. You always come back with the Holy Grail. Go get them, Archie."

"Thank you, Nero." Annah was smiling at the gag, but seemed unsure about everything else, uncommon for her. She was clamping her eyes tight shut, moving her head from side to side. "Weaz, I just cannot yet see how this thing works out."

"Annah, can't we both just decide to do what baby Johnnie is paying us to do? Let's just make sure Goofy doesn't screw her. That she gets a fair shake—whether it's a shorter prison term or a stay in a state hospital—she gets what is deserving. Can't we just shoot for that?"

"Counselor, this girl..."

"I know, she's innocent. Okay. You told me."

"Weaz, I am moving forward, I am getting closer, I really am. Let me..." Annah stopped talking in mid-sentence. She sat and stared out the window for thirty seconds. Wyzell sat silent again, watching her. Then she looked back in at him and said, "That was interesting, what Johnnie was telling us about that poker he plays. *Pai Gow.*"

"I'd never heard of it."

"There is always a long hand, and a short hand. And they are both equally important. One might be a Black Swan, or they both might be. But they are equally important. We have to look at both."

Wyzell snapped his fingers twice, waved his hand in front of Annah's emotionless face. "Annah, there's something else. Something I have to talk to you about."

"Go ahead."

"Si Gumm came in here yesterday. The Major Crimes cop. You know him, I think, he's a good guy. He's trying to put the scumbags away, I'm hired to save their ass, but we get along. He came in here as a favor to me."

"What for?"

ANNAH TORCH   Jim DeFilippi

"He came in here to warn me. Well, to warn *you* actually."

"About what?"

"Annah, he had these three shit-birds in his office the other day. Trying to file reports, about you."

"About me. Who?"

"Those three guys. Gumm talked them out of it pretty easily. They were bogus to the core. But here's the thing—Gumm seems to think these three lunatics have it in for you. He believes there's a real chance they'll be coming after you. Out there to Topher's Woods. He's concerned."

Annah was smiling.

"Annah, these guys are not to be played with. Everybody in White Leunge knows these three. Shit-birds to the core. Poachers, bullies, wife-beaters probably. And with plenty of guns. Plenty, plenty, lots of guns. Here's the thing, Gumm thinks they might...you know these guys? You know them. Seems they hate you. They have a reason to come after you specifically?"

"They think they do."

"Gumm said something about them wanting their gun back. You know anything about that?"

Annah didn't answer him.

"So you know them. What happened between you and them? It was out in Topher's? Must have been out there. What? What was it?"

Annah got up to leave the office. She said, "Nothing of consequence. Thank you, Counselor, for the fair warning, but please don't worry about it. Thank Sergeant Gumm for me. Tell him not to worry about it too. It is nothing."

"Here's the thing, Annah. Gumm thinks these guys are more than just mouth warriors. He thinks...they've been involved before in serious matters, deadly matters, they've never been directly implicated...but Gumm thinks they're more than capable of killing."

ANNAH TORCH   Jim DeFilippi

"Killing."

"Yes, killing more than a whitetail buck, killing more than an out-of-season doe. Killing people." Wyzell pointed at her. "Killing you. Annah, I don't know what these guys have going with you—Gumm doesn't know either—but he thinks you have to be careful. Please, why don't you come sleep in the bus for a while, couple of nights, maybe a week. Just till we see what's going on. Until we know you can be safe."

"Weaz, don't be concerned. They will not harm me."

"Gumm thinks they might. He's thinking that's exactly what they're getting ready to do. To harm you. Annah, these guys are hunters by nature."

"Not good ones they're not. Not skilled, not moral, not intelligent, not even sane. Nothing to worry about."

"But still, they are hunters. That's how they see themselves. They might be so psychotic that they see heading into the Woods with their camouflage suits and their carbines to hurt you is the same kind of weekend as heading in to hurt squirrels, wild turkeys. Maybe they're screwed up, but they think it's the same thing. Gumm said to me that there's nothing worse in this world than a stupid man with a gun. Except maybe three stupid men with three guns. And three stupid men with guns coming after you. Annah, be careful. Come stay in the bus. I'll heat up some Swiss Miss for you in the morning."

Annah was at the office doorway, holding the door open. She turned back. "Weaz, listen, Bob Dylan would call this whole topic 'breadcrumb sins.' It's nothing. Whatever these mutts intend to do, I can take care of it."

"But I don't know if you can. You have a nice comfy vest you wear out there in the Woods. Keeps you warm. A nice thick parka. But those thing aren't made of Kevlar, they won't stop bullets. You have to keep yourself safe."

Annah was still smiling. "Maybe I should wear a mask. So I don't infect them. So I don't infect them before I attack them, before I do away with them."

"Annah, that's not what I'm saying. I don't want you getting out your Daddy's Hammer on this. No need to go that far at all. I want you as an investigator, not as a client."

"Weaz…"

"And please don't put anyone in the hospital if you can avoid it."

"Weaz, Weaz, Weaz."

"What?"

"I will take care of it."

&&&

Chapter Twenty-four

Blanche was gone—gone back to live at her father's again, maybe for good this time.

Last summer, she had been over there for a good month, with his fall, and Ruck hadn't missed her at all. "Thank God they're saying it's not his hip. Nothing's been broken," she had told Ruck over the phone. "With the hip, of course, they always tell you, it's the beginning of the end. That's a cliché but it's true. Statistics show."

Blanche's father had fallen in the kitchen, reaching up for a towel. They were at the emergency room with him, she and the day-nurse. It was one of those walk-in places in Rotterdam where all the doctors were teenagers and grumpy. "We had to wait for almost an hour to get in. And he's an old man. It was all these construction guys first, pretending they had a fever to get off work. He was in pain the whole time. I had to keep reminding him where we were. He kept wanting to just go home. I told him, 'X-rays first, Dad.'"

Blanche had told Ruck that she would be over in Rotterdam for who knows how long. She wouldn't say. Said she couldn't tell. "At least until Dad gets back on his feet again. Could be a while." Turned out to be month.

Blanche had made Ruck take the old fossil hunting with him once. Talked the whole time. This was back when he was still mostly together. Just talk, talk, talk, telling the same stories over and over, and with him knowing that he's told them all before, he just didn't care. Just wanted to hear those stories again, coming out of his own mouth, along with the spit and the drool and the giggling. Ruck dropped him off at the McDonald's, told him he could walk from there, and back home Ruck had told Blanche, "Never again," and he meant it. He had stuck to it.

Ruck had told Horn many times that he wished Blanche's old man would just stagger off somewhere and die, like a buffalo or an eskimo or something. Everybody would be a lot happier.

ANNAH TORCH   Jim DeFilippi

Ruck had told Horn that at least with the old man dead, he could maybe get a decent meal once in a while. Tonight's supper had been some warmed-up frozen gnocchi, a hotdog that had been fried a second time on a stick on top of the stove, and some kind of orange paste Blanche had left for him in a plastic Ziploc.

Sometimes he would admit to Horn that he wished Blanche was dead along with her father. She contradicted Ruck all the time, disagreed with everything he ever said. Ninety percent of the time. And the worst part, later on, he would think about it and have to admit to himself that she was right. He would never tell her that, but it still annoyed him.

He didn't think that he had ever voiced to anyone any plans to actually kill her. Not like the three of them—him and Horn and Box— had done with the jungle slut. Who still had his Redhawk.

But this time, Blanche was probably gone for good. She had always been on the mouthy side, telling him all the things that she knew and he didn't. So it had finally gotten to be too much. He had thrown her against the brick fireplace wall. When she bounced back off, she told him he had broken the bone in her cheek. How would she even know something like that? But she was probably right. She always was.

When she had finished up with her crying, she came at him, so he had to put her down. A couple punches. To the side of the face, one to the stomach, then up to the face again. All right hands. His arm wasn't hurting anymore. The TV commentators would have called it a combination, maybe even "a killer combination."

So for now, Ruck would be cooking for himself. Once the gnocchi was gone.

After the lousy supper, Ruck brought a six-pack of Youngling and a half bottle of Wild Turkey down to the Dungeon to watch some porn for the night. He enjoyed the cool chasers more than the hot whiskey, but the hard stuff was what got it done.

ANNAH TORCH   Jim DeFilippi

This porn was a pretty good one. Some investigative reporter was doing a story on a health spa. Ruck didn't know why, but she was. The reporter had jet black hair down to her shoulders, and a mole above her lip, and these big eyes black around the edges. Her breasts kept peeking out from the front lapel of her reporter suit. The spa was full of beautiful women and guys with stubble and no shirts. Soon, the reporter was being screwed by one of the boys, but when Ruck blinked his eyes awake, she was being screwed by some other guy, with a shaved head and tattoos, in a hot tub, so Ruck must have fallen asleep. There were two other people in the hot tub with them, but they were just floating there not even watching. This second screwing seemed to go on for a long time. Ruck wondered how they filmed these things. Other guys were screwing other girls at the spa, off and on.

Finally, he clicked off the television, flopped himself from the couch down onto the rug, and he managed to pull himself up two flights of stairs, up to the bedroom. Whenever he was in a condition like this, he had to pull himself up the stairs, using the railing like a towline. Grab, pull, yank, up one stair, grab again, pull, yank, all the way to the top.

Taking his pants off, he heard a whimper from down in the living room and remembered he hadn't fed Slave. The damn dog would keep him awake all night with complaining, so Ruck went down to the kitchen, opened up a can of Alpo, spooned it out, and tossed the empty can in the sink. Slave always had to shit right after he ate, so Ruck opened the kitchen door and moved him out into the back yard, using his foot to hurry him along. Ruck shut the door. Slave could stay out there all night. It wasn't so cold and he wouldn't complain.

Back on the second floor, Ruck used the bathroom, stripped down to his boxer shorts, and flopped into bed.

He tried to say some prayers. He got up and flipped on the ceiling fan. It helped him sleep better. He picked out one blade on the fan and tried to follow it movements round and round with his left eye. He had to keep that one good eye in shape.

He began feeling a bit sick and dizzy, so he got up out of bed and went over to his bureau, top drawer, to get his new Redhawk Alaskan. It was a nice gun, double action snub nose, but it could never replace the giant Redhawk that the jungle slut had stolen from him. He spun the barrel of the Alaskan a few times, aimed it at different pictures and flowers around the bedroom. Another reason he didn't mind Blanche being gone, she would complain about him doing that.

He slid the Alaskan into the nightstand drawer and closed his eye to get some sleep.

He had been ashamed at how he had handled himself back at the cop's interrogation. The cop had been working him, playing him with all that perjury bullshit, and the memory left a battery acid taste in Ruck's mouth.

Some nights when he couldn't get to sleep, he would call up Horn, and they would talk about what a little shit Box was. With his baby shoes and baby clothes, and always agreeing with whatever the big guys said to him. Always agreeing to do whatever the big guys told him to. He would be coming with them into the Woods, of course, to hunt the bitch, but he'd be looking over his shoulder the whole time. They had de-pantsed Box once at a Fourth of July party, with his wife and his kids watching, trying to laugh at him.

A noise from downstairs—maybe from the kitchen. It sounded like someone had clanged the bottom of the old spaghetti pot with a wooden spoon. Ruck went down to investigate. Nothing there. He went to the kitchen door and flicked on the backyard light. Quiet and still out there. Slave was asleep in the corner patch of pachysandra.

Ruck went back upstairs. The minute he was back in bed, the clanging noise came again. Just one time. This time he brought the Alaskan down the stairs with him. He started looking around, first down in the Dungeon, saw nothing, found nothing. One flight up on the first floor, he checked every room, every closet. When he was about to leave the kitchen, he saw the wooden spoon lying on the counter beside the sink. He didn't remember leaving it there. He must have.

Ruck climbed back into bed and forced himself to think of all the things they were going to do to the jungle slut. He wished he could get in a good punch at her, like he had with Blanche. But this one would be big and naked and they would be passing her around. She would be crying, her hair all messed up, her make-up dripping, and she would be begging Ruck to let her go, so she could get his Redhawk for him and bring it back. He would keep saying, "Yeah, in a little while, bitch, soon as I'm finished here."

He kept his good eye closed.

When he opened it back up again, she was there in the room with him, but she was dressed now, in a parka and wool hat, and she had the sharp edge of a trenching shovel pressed up against the bottom of his jaw.

Ruck tried to say something, but the blade of the shovel pressing hard up against his throat made it tough to talk.

She was asking him, "You want your gun back, partner?"

He tried to nod out a Yes, but the blade of the shovel made it hard to do.

She said, "Here it is." Suddenly she was holding the Redhawk. It looked clean, shiny in the dark, he almost reached out for it. But the barrel had a horrible twist to it.

She kept waving the Redhawk in front of his face. Ruck couldn't move. She said to him, "Sorry, I propped it up between a couple of rocks and gave it a good yank. It's a well-made weapon. Took me some trouble, some real pull. Once I start to do something, I finish though, so here it is. Maybe you can use it to shoot around corners."

Ruck kept staring at the deformed barrel.

She was looking at it too, turning it around in the glow of the tiny shaft of moonlight coming through the bedroom window. She said, "Now, neither of us would want your dick to end up like that, would we?"

Ruck shook his head. His good eye was hurting, but he couldn't get it to close.

"Well, okay with me, but not you."

He kept blinking at this shadow of her.

"Sorry I do not have your eye to return. I looked everywhere for it."

ANNAH TORCH   Jim DeFilippi

Then, she dropped the Redhawk on the bed and she was gone. He looked around the room. Ruck started crying. He sucked in big breaths of air and he allowed his eye to tear and his mouth to sob. He got up out of bed, went into the bathroom, and threw up his supper into the small sink. Then more of it into the toilet bowl. He looked down in, he didn't recognize the gnocchi, but chunks of hotdog meat were mixed with the orange paste and his bile.

Back in bed, he lay there uncovered, trying to figure things out. Drunk-dreams. Because Slave hadn't barked, had he? There hadn't been any warning, so it had not happened. Maybe she had taken Slave's head off with her sharpened shovel. He would check the back yard in the morning.

He pulled the sheets back up over his body, but the material touching his hips felt wet and warm. He got up and ripped the sheets off the bed and held them up to his nose. He stuffed them into the hamper in the closet. He lay back down on the naked mattress.

He had been dreaming.

He went into the bathroom and looked in the mirror. His neck and the top of his chest were red with sticky blood. He took a white washcloth and wiped himself off. As he was climbing back into bed, he saw something silver sticking out from under the knitted spread over on Blanche's side. He reached down for it. It was the huge, heavy Redhawk, with its barrel bent, horridly deformed.

He didn't make it all the way to the bathroom this time, so he grabbed a wastepaper basket and pulled it up to his face. He dry-heaved into it, nothing left to come up. He was lurching so violently that he pulled a muscle, something in his chest, right below the ribcage. It hurt each time he took in a breath.

Ruck walked around the bedroom looking for his cell phone. He found it in his sock drawer. It was still three o'clock in the morning, but he called up Horn. It took a minute to get Horn awake and listening. Then he gave him the message. "We gotta hold up a minute on this thing, buddy. We gotta think some more about doing this."

Horn imitated Larry the Cable Guy. "Let's git er done, for Christ sake."

"No."

ANNAH TORCH   Jim DeFilippi

After the phone call, Ruck spent the rest of the night outside, in the rocker on the back deck, the yard light on, his good eye focusing and refocusing into the darkness beyond the light. He was leaning off to the left, so that he could keep his left hand nestled in the hair on top of Slave's head. In his right hand he was holding onto the Alaskan snub-nose.

&&&

Chapter Twenty-five

❝ You know, my husband says I shouldn't even be talking to you."

Johnnie Silver's wife was sitting close to Leo Protski on her oversized sofa. She kept flicking at her hair. He could smell her perfume, but didn't know what kind it was.

She had called him up and said she had to talk to him about Amanda, and the case. He asked her if it was something she could tell him over the phone. She said she'd rather not. But since he had gotten to her chalet—Johnnie was in Vegas—she hadn't told him anything that he didn't already know from their first interview. Twice she had suggested he join her with a drink—some strange mix of bourbon and maple syrup and Tabasco or something that would have made him stomach-sick after a few sips.

"Mrs. Silver, you wanted to tell me something about Amanda."

"I do. I do. I did."

But she didn't say anything else. She just sat there, half-smiling at him. Protski could tell that this woman was getting old, but not beyond caring about herself, about how she looked. She had powdered her skin, and touched on some blush—he thought that was what it was called. Her eyes were a deep Hollywood blue, so blue that they must be colored contacts. Long, sparkling earrings reminded Protski of wind chimes. The top of her white ruffled blouse was held loosely by a single string tied behind her neck. It showed a bit of the centers of her tanned breasts, not just the tops. They'd been worked on, Protski was sure. Between those breasts hung a pendant that was blue azure and white, shaped like a woman's sandal or flip-flop. Black pants, tight on the ass he had noticed on the way in, no shoes or socks.

Did she look like this everyday? Protski tried to think back to what she had been wearing for their first interview. He couldn't remember, so it couldn't have been anything like this.

What was this all about? Him?

She was taking a sip of her drink, then gazing down into the tumbler.

The woman looked like someone in the movies, but he couldn't remember who.

"Mrs. Silver, if you have something for me, don't be concerned, I'll only use it to help Amanda, or at least not hurt her."

"I need to talk to someone," she was saying. "I remember when you asked me questions that first time, you were someone I felt I could talk to. Even though we're on the opposite sides, I guess—Johnnie says you guys only want to lock up Amanda and swallow the key. Do you swallow keys or just throw them away?"

"We, uh... we don't use keys that much, I guess. Anymore."

Drunk. The woman was drunk and what Protski's Mom would have said, with a disgusted look on her face, "All gussied up."

"Look, Mrs. Silver..."

"Grace. Like in church. I'm your saving grace. You need grace to get into heaven, right? That's a little joke."

"Grace."

"Or you could call me Gracie even."

Protski wondered how many of those bourbon sweet'n'hots had she gulped down before he got there. "You have something to tell me. About Amanda. Her case."

"Well, I do, I surely do." The woman hesitated, maybe unsure of revealing a secret, more likely just trying to think up something to tell him. "She had seizures. One. When she was eleven or twelve, I think."

"One?"

"Yes, that one time, but she got cloudy-headed and out—gone—just like she was when she was in the hospital, after she shot the girl. But shorter, for a shorter time."

"Did you have her examined? Take her to see a doctor?"

"It was just that once, so I can't remember. Does that help?"
"It might. Everything."

"And I wish I had more I could tell you about the poor girl who got herself shot. We didn't know her all that well. She didn't deserve what happened to her, but of course neither did Amanda. The girl must have been attacking or something. It's such a shame she got shot. She had such a sweet smile."

"Probably still does," Protski mumbled to himself.

Protski decided that this woman must be ditzy from the first thing in the morning on, even before her first drink. How could her husband put up with something like this?

When she went back into the kitchen to refill her glass tumbler—after talking to herself, "Grace, be an angel. Sure"—Protski looked around the room and the furnishings. The place seemed as confused as Grace Silver. The huge white bearskin rug hanging from the partial wall, Christian crosses, two of them, old fashioned rocking chairs, the oversized couch that could have sat five people, but where she had them crowded together on one end.

When Grace got back in, carrying a full tumbler and sitting down next to him, Protski looked around the huge room and asked, "How long have you been here, you and Mr. Silver?"

The question seemed to disturb her. She said, "I can't remember. It's been not too long. How long have you been where you are?"

"I, uh...I just moved...but your daughter..."

"My brother was a cop. A cop in uniform. Just like you, Leo. Leo's your fist name. I looked it up."

"Yes, it is."

"I looked it up. I asked around. My brother had a different name. It wasn't Leo, but he was a cop just like you, in uniform."

ANNAH TORCH — Jim DeFilippi

"Well, I used to be a cop. I'm an investigator now. I can't arrest people. I just go out and get information for the D. A.'s office."

"Johnnie says she's a high-caliber bitch, that woman. He calls her Goofy, but says she's not. She's goofy like a fox, is what he says. My brother wore his uniform every day to the job."

"Yeah, yeah, I used to do that too. For a lot of years." Protski was telling himself that he had ethics. He was a man with a moral code, but he was thinking these things while staring at a drunk woman's chest.

She said, "I'm trying to picture you in a uniform, Officer."

"Not really an officer any more."

"Blue. It was of the blue color persuasion. Wasn't that a movie, *Blue Persuasion*?"

"I don't know."

"I wasn't in it. I was never in the movies, but I was an actor once. They called us actresses, but that's bad form now, I guess."

The girl on "Friends." That was it. The dark-haired one on that old show. This old gal was nowhere near as young or as pretty, but that's who she reminded Protski of. The smooth black hair down to the bare shoulders, hair that flipped out at the end. The smile. The tilt of the head. The clean and clear good-girl look. This woman was an older version of the girl on "Friends." She might have even been shooting for that look when she got dressed and made herself up for Protski's visit this morning.

She was telling him, "I'm trying to picture you in your uniform. Leo. You look good. You have the shoulders for it. And the gait. I mean, I like your shirt too, it's somewhat Hawaiian, but a uniform, that's different. Policemen always have that certain flair, like they could stand on a curb or something. They could call it a 'uni.' Let me go get you a drink. I'll need one too, soon."

"All right. Please, but just straight." What the hell. She looked good. And why remain loyal to a woman who left you for a stableboy?

ANNAH TORCH   Jim DeFilippi

When Grace was back in the kitchen again, mixing their drinks, Protski leaned forward on the couch so that he could see her ass. When she came back in, he pretended to be looking around the room. "What a place. With that flying bear up there. It's all very impressive."

"It's all Johnnie. That thing is up there because Johnnie has a story about it, so when people come in and see it and ask. Everything here is him. We have this butcher-block island out in the kitchen. Can you see it? Slide over closer to me, see the corner of it? I hate it. I think I'm in a Chicago slaughterhouse when I'm filleting a steak. You get blood stains on it, they don't come out. You have to scrub and scrub with one of those Magic Erasure things. Johnnie had it put in. We had all Silestone when we moved in. All ripped out. This wood monster thing instead, and it stains. With blood. That's the nice thing about sheets."

"Sheets?"

"They wash right out, whatever you stain them with. I don't mean blood. Cum mostly, right?" She was grinning, looking at him, lifting her shoulders, putting her finger to her lips, trying to look like an embarrassed school girl.

Protski knew what was happening, but he wanted to make sure. "He won't let you change things? Do things for yourself?"

"If he picks something out, it stays. He picked me out, and I stayed. I have. It's the furniture, the art work, me, it's all his contribution to the culture of the place. Does this place have any? Culture? No. It's the same, every place we have. He keeps paintings on the wall, that hideous bear up there, all because he knows the story behind each one. The artist. His life and all. Or who killed the bear. He does that in all of our homes. So when somebody asks about it, he can step forward and explain, tell the story. In all of our places, it's the same thing. Mostly here, the art is just junk."

"That's too bad."

Grace said, "I like my men to be tall and mellow. I like looking up at the bottom of their chin when they talk to me. Johnnie's five-seven, but he tells everyone ten, and they believe him, because he's sitting on his wallet."

ANNAH TORCH   Jim DeFilippi

Protski said, "Adding a couple inches to the profile. Like the NBA scouting reports. The NFL combine."

Grace asked, "Combine what? With what? Who?"

Protski just shook his head. "I don't know. You said you had this place long?"

"I don't know. It's not much more than a screw-shop for the wealthy, pardon my freshman English. I'm tipsy. I mean, sure, it's close to Amanda's school, when we come visit. Will they let her back in? She's ready for college anyway. We don't really live here. We just come for short notice visits. We come up here from wherever we are, the mountains are nice, with the snow. Last year we hardly got any at all. You know that. You've been here."

"We get some barren winters upstate."

"Of course you do. Barren as hell sometimes. We had a snowy place in Vail though. Beautiful. I hated it. I hired some high school kids to break in and spread the trash around. Where was that? Alberta, I think. Lake Louise. Vacation. Skiing."

She leaned in and put her drink on the coffee table. She stared at it a while and then said, "Tell me about when you were a cop. You were a good one. Handsome too."

Protski leaned forward, took his glass and sipped at it, put it back on the coffee table. "When I was a cop. Long time ago."

She said, "We don't worry about coasters, they just get in the way. So you were a policeman? Around here?"

"Over in Schenectady."

"Were you married?"

"I was then. Not anymore."

"A single cop. I bet you had so many..."

"I was married back then. I worked undercover for a while. Drugs. That was the only interesting time on the job."

"You were like Serpico."

"Not too much."

"Al Pacino. 'Attica! Attica!' You were like Robert Blake, the cop he played on TV. I can't remember what his name was."

"Yeah, that was an old show, I guess, but real undercover isn't at all like that, it's mostly just boring..."

"He killed his wife."

"Who? Robert Blake?"

"He got off, but he did it. You could tell. Why are you not married anymore? You didn't kill her, did you? I'm gagging you around, just shitting."

"No, we got divorced."

"Why? She didn't like you wolfing around on her, behind her back?"

"Well, it was sort of just the opposite. She got involved with my partner, another guy on the force, he also ran some security up at Saratoga, after I came in from the cold."

"Did you end up killing them both? I'm shitting you now."

"No."

"Did you want to?"

"Just for a little while. I got over it. But it turned out fine. They bought a racehorse together, and it died."

Monica. Monica was the girl's name on "Friends." She was married to some actor for a while, he might have killed himself.

Grace was pointing at his glass. "Drink up, drink up, my little corgi. Did you fool around on her too?"

"A little bit, but she didn't know about it, so she had no right to do what she did."

"Who lied to who first?"

ANNAH TORCH Jim DeFilippi

An hour later, with Protski on his third round, she running up an untold amount, he couldn't remember how long he had been there. They hadn't touched. He was telling her about the last girlfriend he had. "She was a real estate photographer. She takes your picture for you if you want to sell your house. She can really make anyplace look good. Uses a fisheye lens, the place looks huge. She took me zip-lining for the first time ever."

Grace said, "I bet that's not all she did to make you feel younger."

Protski put his drink back down on the table. This was not going quite like he thought it would, but he was closing in for the finale now. "We broke up. She was good. She could make a hobo jungle look like a cabana. Everybody wanted her. We broke up. She was traveling too much. All the damn time. We broke up."

"But you still sleep with her sometimes. I can tell."

"Sometimes. Only when's she's around. She travels."

He sat and watched this woman, older than Nancy but much better looking, sipping at her drink now and looking over the top of the glass at him.

"Grace, you asked me over here to tell me about the case, right, about the shooting? Do you want to tell me anything?"

"Leo, you can ask me anything you want. About Amanda. About Johnnie. About anything at all." Her voice had gotten very soft, almost too quiet to hear. Her fingers were playing with that blue diamond pendant hanging at her chest. Monica. Definitely Monica. From "Friends."

"Did you marry him to get your hands on his money?"

"We were broke. He had a puppet to work with. We didn't have a dime in our shoe."

"Do you love him still?"

"Sometimes, when I'm not hating him."

"Do you ever think about taking on another man? That's purely hypothetical, you understand."

ANNAH TORCH   Jim DeFilippi

"Isn't everything?"

"How would that work?"

"A woman would invite a man over. Pretense. Husband gone."

"To Las Vegas?"

"Anywhere. Vegas would be fine."

"Are you thinking about it right now?"

"I thought you'd never ask."

                                &&&

ANNAH TORCH Jim DeFilippi

Chapter Twenty-six

After Leo Protski had left, Grace went into the bathroom and used a jar of Million Dollar Cold Cream to remove her makeup, some of which had gotten smeared during the sexual squirming. Then she sat in the tub for twenty minutes, let her body soak, especially the muscles in her thighs and hips. She was no longer young.

She dried off, got dressed, laundered the sheet, and started to clean the house.

No matter where in the world they were living for that week, no matter which house on whatever continent, if it were Thursday, Grace would be cleaning the place. In Florence, and in most of their Caribbean places, the locals would get so insulted being passed over that Johnnie would pay them just to come in once a week for a sloppy, halfhearted job. She would always pull the curtains and do the entire place over again—the right way—after they had left.

One time somewhere in Asia, she couldn't remember where, a work crew had snuck into their place and cleaned it while they were out. Johnnie had told her, "Don't worry about it, that's just the way they do things over here. It's the Orient."

She said, "You can't call it that for a long time now, it's just Asia, you have to say it like that."

He said, "What, say what, you mean the Orient? I know, I know. Oh, for God's sake, it's not like I'm calling them all Chinamen or something."

Out on the Point at their Montauk place, along with the beach sand being trampled in, pollen and dust would settle on everything, and that would lead to both of them sneezing and blowing, so she had hired a cleaning service. Afterwards they had tried to live in an A.C. world. So the place was spotless and vacuum-sealed, but she still cleaned it every Thursday.

ANNAH TORCH   Jim DeFilippi

And so throughout her life, if it was Thursday, whether she had just finished off a new lover or a bottle of old bourbon, it was still just her and her dust clothes and some Swifters and the vacuum cleaner.

Here in the chalet, with the pollen and mud—soon to be snow—she had the chore all to herself, with no interference from anyone. She preferred things that way.

This afternoon, it was even cooler than the seasonal norm, she was dressed in her old but sturdy and comfortable Jackie Blue Archer jeans, the ones with the embroidered denim and neutral threads, the ones that she could still squeeze her slightly sore-from-sex ass into. On top she wore a V-Neck of cotton and silk fine gauge. Johnnie called this her "Hilda the Maid Outfit," and he would ask her every time, even after all these years, why she didn't mind doing the chores all by herself. She would always tell him that the cleaning helped clear her head.

With Amanda conscious but insisting she was a killer, and saying little beyond that, to anyone—not to the police or the doctors or to Johnnie or to her own mother—Grace was especially thankful for the normalcy of a mop and broom. The place had central vac, but she rarely used it. The suction was weak and it was difficult to find new bags when the sack got filled. The vac was all right for the garage, but not here in the house.

Grace told herself that things had changed forever the moment the police had told her about Amanda, but still, the cleaning would go on, no different than before.

Sometimes as she worked she would listen to Carly Simon, or one of the newer ones whose names she always got wrong, on the old iPod that Johnnie had gotten for her, back when they first came out.

She would mix up a fresh Mare's Leg—the three fingers of Wild Turkey 101, the splash of soda, ice, a tumble of maple syrup. At first she couldn't locate the Frank's Hot Sauce in the fridge, and she thought she might have to go with the Tabasco in the pantry, but she found the Frank's at the last minute, just as she was about to slam shut the refrigerator door. It was hiding in the back, behind some almond milk.

ANNAH TORCH   Jim DeFilippi

She would transport the tumbler of booze with her from room to room, occasionally refueling after finishing off a round or one of the rooms. She had placed a number of coasters strategically around the chalet, at least one in each room. Half the coasters were in the shape of a maple leaf, the rest were circles that read "Hopsters." She only bothered with the coasters sometimes, if they were within reach.

Grace always began with the dusting, moving nearly everything except on the shelves that were so choked with Johnnie's nicknacks that it would have taken her forever. Then, putting off the kitchen and baths because those were her least favorite, she went instead down to the laundry room closet and pulled out the Shark Stand-up vacuum cleaner. She carried it to the top floor, where she would start and work her way down. This led to a crazy meandering route in a house designed like a maze.

In Johnnie's bedroom, she took a sip of the Mare's Leg, placed the tumbler on Johnnie's night stand, next to his Alexis, and she began vacuuming the floor, switching the toggle back and forth from "Enhanced Bare Floor" to "Deep Shag."

She could never get the vacuum head all the way under Johnnie's kingsized bed, but she thrust it as deeply in as she could, from both sides and the foot. For a second she thought about being with the cop—had it been fun or not? —but she put that thought out of her head. She snapped the vacuum flat and drove its vacuum-head deeply in from the footboard. She heard and felt the hose click against something small underneath the bed, so she turned off the machine and knelt down underneath to check. She eyed something black and small and plastic, just out of reach. She went downstairs to get the telescoping Swifter Sweeper. She used it to hook and retrieve the thing.

It was a USB thumb-drive—black, two and a half inches long, three-quarters of an inch wide, with a red slide button and the red word "SanDisk" on its top. She held it in her hand for a while, flipping it over in her palm, studying it. Finally, she took the device into Johnnie's office, next to the bedroom, and she slipped the thumb-drive into his desktop computer. She rarely used this computer, but now she clicked and switched and wiggled the mouse around until things started humming.

ANNAH TORCH   Jim DeFilippi

Finally, a loud musical note sounded, it startled her, and the screen popped to life, but it stayed darkish, with an unrecognizable image for a while. Grace thought it might be asking her for a password. If it did, she would go back to her vacuuming. She checked and made sure that the thumb-drive was pushed all the way into its slot, then she tapped "Play" a few times. There were more humming noises, the screen stayed darkish, and just as she was about to give up and return to her cleaning, the screen came alive with an image.

The side of her daughter's face was pressed up against some material that Grace couldn't recognize, either a bedspread or maybe some carpeting. Amanda's eyes were half closed, her mouth was open. Grace made sure the mute was off–she wanted to hear what was going on–but it seemed that no sound had been recorded. Studying the frame, Grace could only see most of Amanda's face and her right shoulder, which was bare. She seemed to be kneeling and pitched forward. She was being jarred from behind by something, someone, causing her cheek to slide across the dark material, again and again, each time she was jolted. She seemed to be in neither pain nor ecstasy. The movement went on and on. Grace checked the time of the video, twelve minutes all together. She watched for what she felt was a long time, minute after minute.

From time to time she could catch a quick glance of Johnnie's hairy right hip on the side of the frame.

The screen went dark, but the video was still playing. Grace sat and watched the screen. Her expression didn't change.

After a few seconds, the screen sprang to life again, a longer shot. The scene showed Amanda, flopped over, face down, on the thin top edge of a plastic table, the one down in the rumpus room. She was facing the camera. White plastic chairs were on each side of her legs. The sleeves of her white blouse were pushed up, the blouse's top button undone so that Grace could see the tops of her daughter's breasts. Amanda had on white socks that were pulled up almost to her knees. Her blond hair was fixed into two ponytails, tied on each side of her head with white scrunchies, like a school girl, and the ponytails were bouncing with the rhythm. Johnnie was standing behind her, his hands were on her hips. His dark blue trousers were still on, so he must have had his fly open.

ANNAH TORCH   Jim DeFilippi

He was wearing no socks, but had on his Puma running shoes. And his white shirt.

This section of the clip went on for forty-five seconds. Grace watched it all. Her expression never changed.

Every so often Amanda's lips would compress, like they would when she was a child and she had been given an ice cream cone. She was glancing at the camera, then turning around to look back at Johnnie, then she looked back toward the camera and spread her lips in what might be mistaken for enjoyment. Sometimes she seemed to be mouthing a word. There was still no sound that Grace could find, but the word that her daughter kept mouthing seemed to be, "Drill...drill..."

Both Amanda's legs and Johnnie's rocked together in a syncopated rhythm.

A few times, after a particularly hard thrust, Amanda's legs would shutter and her mouth seemed to be moaning or singing. The mouth would open wide, as would her eyes, then both the eyes would slam shut and the lips would be pressed together. Then the mouth and her eyes would remain closed, almost as if she were asleep.

In the last few seconds of this segment, Amanda pulled the collar of her shirt back to reveal her black bra. Grace recognized the tiny birthmark above her daughter's left breast. How old was Amanda here? Did she still have that shirt? That bra? Grace couldn't remember. She tried to judge the age of her daughter's face, but things were too distorted.

A third sequence was shot from across a room. The iPad or iPhone must have been propped up on a table to do the filming. Johnnie was flopped back in an easy chair that Grace couldn't place. What chair was that? One of theirs somewhere? What room was this? They had so many chairs, so many places, in so many states and countries and...sometimes she just couldn't remember if something belonged to them or not. Johnnie had slid down, almost flat, in the chair. His shirtsleeves were pushed up to his elbows and his arms were hanging over the sides of the chair. His face was looking up towards the ceiling. His mouth hung open, his eyes were closed, but when they opened slightly, they

ANNAH TORCH   Jim DeFilippi

seemed hazy or glazed over. Johnnie seemed to be begging something of the ceiling, of the heavens. He was Jesus on the cross. His pants were pulled down to his ankles. Amanda was on her knees, her face buried between his legs. Her head was moving and her pigtails were bobbing in rhythm.

This one sequence Grace did not watch all the way through. Instead, she pushed the Pause button, then the Exit, and she sat staring at the blank screen. Her face still held no expression, nothing in her eyes had changed.

She clicked the video back on, fast-forwarded it a bit, but eventually the screen went black. Grace waited, but that seemed to be the full contents of the thumb-drive.

Grace sat and stared at the blank screen for a while. Her expression did not change.

Finally, she rose from the computer desk and took the thumb-drive back into Johnnie's bedroom. She placed it on his bureau. She went over to his nightstand, opened the single drawer, and riffled through the messy contents until she found a pad of yellow Post-its and a Sharpie pen. She wrote on the top Post-it, tore it off the pad, and stuck it on the thumb-drive.

The note read, "Darling, who leaves things like these around like this? Imagine if the wrong people found them—giggles—Your Grace."

She drew a small Smiley Face under the words.

&&&

Chapter Twenty-seven

The real estate records were written on paper rather than with pixels, so the work was long and tiresome, but the Woods had taught Annah to be absurdly patient—more than just an attendant to detail, but an actual slave. The under-markings of a mushroom cap could tell you the difference between breakfast and botulism, if you took your time and knew what you were looking for.

Annah had an idea of what she was looking for, but her focus kept changing with the flipping of the old, dusty, fragile pages—sheet after sheet filled with dollar amounts and numbers and locations and foreclosures and transfers and inheritances and sales—mostly sales.

A young efficient clerk with blue-rimmed eyeglasses and stringy black hair had led her down to these stacks a little after nine in the morning. The Albany County Record of Real Estate Transactions was open to the public. The clerk brought a stack of thick, heavy books over to the table and spread them out in front of her. He told her, "We don't get many people wanting to look down here. You can file all the deeds and things right upstairs, on the screens."

Annah looked up at him and nodded, she didn't say anything.

He stood there awhile and then told her, "I'll leave you alone. I'll be upstairs."

She nodded at him again and waved.

After he left, she pulled the top ledger towards her and flipped it open. She had taken a notepad and pen out of her backpack, and she laid them on the table next to the ledger.

A little before seven that morning, she had been at Wyzell's house. He had handed over the keys to his Subaru, one of his extra iPhones, an American Express card, his White Leunge Municipal Library card, his Triple A card, and two hundred dollars in tens.

ANNAH TORCH Jim DeFilippi

Back when she was in college, Annah had taken a course titled, "The Experience of Poetry." She needed something for a prelaw elective, and ranking courses by the time and days they met, it came down to a choice between poems and bowling. She was surprised that she enjoyed the poetry course. The instructor was a thin-faced Italian lady who had published chapbooks of her own poetry. On the first day, the instructor told the class that her husband was a banker in Schenectady, which was a good thing, because she was a poet and an adjunct instructor, their daughter was a dancer, and their son was a drummer in a band, so the Homeland Bank of Schenectady was supporting the entire family.

Annah enjoyed the course so much that she started attending meetings of the local poetry society. Some of the members were doggerel dullards, but a few were brilliant. Gradually the experience with the poets and their poems started cleaving Annah away from the method of thinking that she had been applying to her entire life. Poetry taught her how to break away from linear thinking. Sometimes, she could see that the lines running across a page—like the thoughts running across a mind—were not following a logical path. There were jagged little jumps and quick cuts that could prove powerful and useful.

Years later, the Woods had reinforced that concept. Taking a wrong turn on a path could lead to the right place. Hiking a circle in a counterclockwise direction, a path you had been taking clockwise forever, put you in a brand new place. You had been there a thousand times before, but you had to stop and ask yourself where you were.

Annah collected her notepad and pencil and went up the stairs to the main floor, where she asked the clerk if she should have returned the binders to their shelves. He said, "Oh no, we have to do that ourself."

She thanked him, left the building, and drove to the White Leunge Public Library, where she spent the rest of the morning. She had thought that tracing the real estate transactions would be easy—a couple of computer clicks—but all the hardcopy work left her eyes tired and her mind soggy, so she put off the heavy lifting until later and started out with some breadcrumbs here at the library.

ANNAH TORCH   Jim DeFilippi

At a computer carrel tucked into a corner on the first level, she found an Internet site that boasted a winning strategy at *Pai Gow* poker, but it was all drivel, basic stuff that she had already been told or had figured out. Seven cards, long hand, short hand, almost every deal ending up in a push.

But your short hand was as important as your long hand.

At the reference desk, she put in a request for Nassim Taleb's book, *The Black Swan*, and she brought it back to the carrel with her. Aristotle's *Prior Analytics* was probably the first literary reference to the dichromatic phenomenon at the heart of Taleb's book. Basically, everything was one way until something didn't match. Then, the conclusions of neither inductive nor deductive reasoning could be completely trusted. Ersatz premises led to ersatz results, and shit-for-brains premises would lead to shit-for-brains results. Every swan is white until a black one shows up at the party. Every swan floats in the water until it stands up and shakes its feathers on shore. There are gray swans and red swans out there in the Woods. People just haven't found them yet.

Annah brought the book back to the lending desk and returned to her carrel—she had begun thinking about it as *her* carrel—where she reached into her back pack and took out the autopsy report that Wyzell had supplied for her. She studied it for a long time, flipping back to pages that she had gone over many times before. She studied the words that she was unfamiliar with, looked a few of them up online. She sat and stared at the frosted glass wall in front of her. She studied the patterns of the imperfections in the glass. She went back to the pages of the autopsy.

Using the Internet and Wyzell's cellphone, she managed to talk to the managing director of the Future Entrepreneurs of America, whose office was in Omaha, Nebraska. The organization had been in existence since 1955. Annah asked about the group's national conventions and its keynote speakers. The Director sighed and read off the entire list. It took a number of minutes. Annah didn't have to take down any notes. She was listening for just one name.

After that, she called all the banks in the White Leunge area, but she knew even before she got connected that they would tell her nothing.

ANNAH TORCH   Jim DeFilippi

In the reference stacks, she found a few volumes covering recreational drugs—their dosages, short-term effects, toxicity, detection in the blood stream, other dangers, their history of illegality.

She went to the reference desk and asked for any books they had in the stacks about cadavers. Ten minutes later, a librarian with a butterfly tattoo on the side of her neck brought three books back to the carrel. Annah didn't spend more than a few minutes paging through the indexes and pages of each one. She searched the word "cadaver" on line, and again didn't spend much time with the results.

She stopped at both the research desk and lending desk on her way out and thanked everyone who looked like a librarian.

"Find what you were looking for, ma'am, I hope?"

"Almost. Maybe. Not yet. No, I don't think so."

She hit some resistance getting into the library of the Albany Medical College, but a phone call to the law offices of Howard Wyzell convinced the temp worker at the visitors' desk to allow Annah access to the stacks, as long as she didn't check out anything.

The textbook's title was: *Host Response to Biomaterials: The Impact of Host Response on Biomaterial Selection, First Edition.* Annah thought some editor along the way could have truncated the name a bit, it seemed to be verging on the redundant.

Annah perused the whole text and read every word of "Chapter Four: Host Response to Naturally Driven Biomaterials." Then she sat and gazed at the lettering on the pages, not really seeing them. She read the fourth chapter for a second time, things were pressing up against each other, but nothing was clicking together like a seatbelt latch and its buckle. Annah wanted to hear that reassuring click, but it wasn't there.

It was after two in the afternoon. Annah hadn't eaten since early morning and was feeling a bit giddy as she left the medical library. She took out the roll of bills that Wyzell had given her and asked the temp at the desk what people usually tipped her. The temp hesitated a full fifteen seconds before asking, "What?"

After eating a bagel at the school cafeteria, Annah walked across campus and spent twenty minutes trying to gain access to the medical lab. No amount of convincing and cajoling, no calls to Wyzell's office, no references to District Attorney Sarah Guffleberg, could turn the key.

"I'm perfectly sorry, madam, but access to the medical laboratories is reserved for matriculated students and faculty only."

"I guess that makes sense."

"Yes, it does."

"I am not a doctor, but I played one once in a tennis match."

"Huh?"

"Took me three sets."

Annah gave up and drove to the local AAA office. By using Wyzell's membership card, she gained access to their computer, but she quickly realized it would deliver no more information or instruction than any computer—say the one back at the public library. But she was there, and everyone seemed pleased to have her, would answer any question she asked, so she spent twenty minutes in front of the AAA screen.

Monterotondo is a town of 40,000 in central Italy. It is the venue of the European Molecular Biology Laboratory, which focuses its research on Epigenetics and Neurobiology. Annah was not interested in either, but the world renown and reputation of the laboratory had given birth to many smaller, very specialized scientific research companies and facilities in town. Information on these smaller places was sparse, but Annah learned as much as she could about them, in particular one called *Il Centro Per Ricerca e Sviluppo Chimico*.

Someone at the AAA helped Annah get access to the Internet on Wyzell's phone, and she used that to get into a few medical journals that described what *Il Centro* was working on.

ANNAH TORCH   Jim DeFilippi

Annah was reminded how out of touch she was with cutting edge technology, which changed and transmogrified itself daily, almost hourly, so her next stop was the Apple Store at the Cross Gates Mall, where she had to take a number and wait to be called before getting assistance with her problem. When her number came up, she told a young man who had his head shaved except for a footlong topknot that she didn't really have a problem, she just needed some information about current apps for the iPhone. Annah was especially interested in apps that could be triggered with a gentle prodding of the hip or body when the phone was still in the owner's pocket.

Topknot was pleased to take her and her phone online to the Apps Store, where he download an app called "HipCheck" for her, and demonstrate how it worked. He seemed overjoyed to be showing her this. He said when he got off work he was going to download that very app himself. Annah told him that she was surprised he had waited that long.

It was close to five in the afternoon and Annah realized that municipal offices would be closing soon. As quickly as she could, she began punching letters and numbers into the phone. She was constantly frustrated because of the size of her fingers and her unfamiliarity with the technique, it made quick usage of the tiny keyboard next to impossible. She cursed each time she thought she had hit the spacebar at the bottom of the screen but instead had punched in an unrecognizable twenty-letter long word.

Despite it all, she finally managed to reach the Parks and Recreation Department of the town of Swampscott, Massachusetts. Her luck continued when she actually got to talk to the park commissioner. It was after five o'clock by then, but he told her that ever since the Fever he had been working long hours on the days he was still coming into the office.

Her questions were quick and clipped. Anytime she mentioned specific names, he told her he wasn't at liberty to discuss, but he was very helpful in describing general guidelines for the various properties that his office controlled. He started telling her how the town had been designed by Frederick Law Olmsted, the great American landscape architect, the guy who had done Central Park in New York City and the Chicago World's Fair, the same guy who

ANNAH TORCH   Jim DeFilippi

had done the Chelsea Young Women's campus, but Annah interrupted him by thanking him for the information and then clicking him off.

    Annah found Leo Protski's name on Wyzell's phone's Contact List. He was at home, willing to talk. The call lasted nearly an hour.

    The day had been a long one. Annah dropped the car off at Wyzell's house. He had gone out to Syracuse for the day. She left his cards and keys and nearly all of the money, and she hiked back to her hut in the Woods. To think.

    After the success of *In Cold Blood*, Truman Capote allowed people to believe that he could recall the exact words of the long conversations and interviews he had conducted with the players of his murder story. It was later revealed that his childhood pal, Nelle Harper Lee—who was in the midst of publishing her *To Kill a Mockingbird*—was at Capote's interviews, taking notes for him. He never credited her with assistance. Sometime it's hard for a man to give a woman the credit she deserves. Nelle didn't care.

    Back at her hut, Annah went over each line of dialogue in her Amanda Silver interviews—with the silent Amanda, her classmates, Nico, Grace, Johnnie—replaying them in her mind as best she could. Annah wished that Nelle Harper Lee had been with her, taking notes. She would have given old Nelle her due credit.

&&&

    The next morning, on his way in to work, Wyzell parked and hiked into the rotted stump to check their meeting stone. The stone was still tucked into its place within the stump, but a handwritten note pinned to the bark of the tree read, "A sit-down with Baby Johnnie. Soon."

&&&

ANNAH TORCH   Jim DeFilippi

Chapter Twenty-eight

Annah Torch and Johnnie Silver were sitting across from each other at a picnic table in Tricentennial Park, the middle of downtown Albany. It was at the top end of a cold morning and they were both dressed for the weather, Annah in her North Face parka, Johnnie in a DeSage woolen peacoat with the collar flipped up. Both faces were cold, both heads were clear and focused.

Traffic was light out on Broadway and Columbia. A few people were walking the park, some of them with their dogs and masks on, but the place was basically empty.

Annah and Johnnie were having a very private conversation in a public place. Uncharacteristically, she was doing most of the taking. Over Johnnie's shoulder, she could see the statue of Finn McCool, the mayor's dog, and sitting beside him on a bench with his hand on the dog's collar, was the old mayor himself, Tom Whalen III. If she turned a bit to her left, she would be looking at the life-size bronze casting of a Pilgrim and an Indian, holding between them the four-foot shield of the city of Albany.

Annah said to Johnnie, "You know how to use misdirection, from the old days, from back when you were a ventriloquist, back in your days of talking to a dummy."

Johnnie smiled and told her, "I know I'm not talking to a dummy now. If I'd known everybody would be wearing masks, I would have stuck with ventriloquism. Those were sweet times, in a way. Sweeter than now. So much simpler."

"You knew how to get people watching the puppet's mouth go up and down, the jaw, wood clattering. Watch his head swivel around, his eyebrows go up, the eyeballs start moving side to side. Motion, motion. Motion always attracts and captures the human eye."

"Gloopy was a dummy, not a puppet. He still is."

ANNAH TORCH Jim DeFilippi

"Anything to keep them from looking at your lips, where the real action is going on."

"Keep you jaw loose, the teeth a quarter inch apart. The 'B's are the toughest." Johnnie held his lips together, loosely. "Rubber baby bumper buggy. Rubber baby bumper buggy." His lips were moving, but just a bit. "Tricks of the trade. I've used them well over the years."

"And sometimes, sometimes the best misdirection is to point the mark in the right direction, but only partway there."

"Mmm, I guess so. I was good, but not a master. My Dad, now he was a master of the craft. He kept working on it up until the time he died. I was better at making money. I'm the best there is at that."

Johnnie was pretending to be checking the stitching of his left glove, he was barely looking up at Annah.

"In that poker game you are so good at, people get misdirected, right? They forget—you told me this—they forget that the short hand is as critical as the long one. It should be looked at just as hard, with just as much deliberation."

"So, Annah, we're here to talk poker or ventriloquism? The Weasel said you had something for me."

"Amanda was—is—the long hand in all of this. The short hand is Dede."

Johnnie looked up at the sound of the two names.

Annah went on. "Or in another way, Amanda as a killer is the long hand. But the killer as somebody else, that is the short hand."

"You've lost me. I can usually follow mad ravings pretty well, after all, I live with a drunken lunatic, but you've lost me here."

"Everyone has been asking why Amanda would want to kill Dede. We should have been considering why *anyone* would want to kill her. That is the Black Swan."

"What? What in hell?"

"Sometimes there is a black swan. And sometimes that swan can stand up. From that position it can cause even more upheaval."

Johnnie was pointing across the park. "Did there used to be a duck pond here? Is that what you're trying to tell me? I'm not from around here."

Annah was studying the man's face.

He told her, "Look, if we're not going to talk about anything, then I'm leaving."

"You bought the house in Watervliet a couple years before Amanda was at Chelsea. You did not buy it for her, not just so you could go visit your daughter at school."

Now Johnnie was staring at her.

Annah said, "It was in the realty records."

"So what?"

"You bought it to be near someone else."

"Oh, I did?"

"You do civic work, charities and such. Make appearances. Give speeches. Give money. Lend your name to charity causes."

"Yes, I do all that."

"Three years ago, three and a half, you gave the keynote speech at the national convention of the Future Entrepreneurs of America."

Johnnie's eyes were widening. "I did, did I? I don't remember. I guess I did. So suppose I did?"

"There is a little town in Italy..."

"There's a lot of little towns in Italy. You're taking me all over the globe here. Let's settle down somewhere, please."

"It's called Monterotondo."

Johnnie didn't say anything, but his expression said that he'd just been slapped in the face.

Annah went on. "It is mostly known for its molecular biology lab. But that one place has been so successful, a bunch of other scientific research and development companies have sprung up in town. One of them produces a special substance."

"Does it?"

"No brand name yet. The scientific name is called Ermodemethon."

"Ermo what?"

"Ever hear of it?"

"No."

"Sure you have. It is still years away from being on the market, not even close to being approved by the FDA. What is does is, it dissipates, drastically reduces the amount of insulin in a person's system. They are looking at it as potentially a very effective treatment for diabetes."

"I don't care." Johnnie's voice had gotten weaker.

"Mr. Silver, I do not know if you really are palsy with the Pope or not. Either way, that is not the reason you started going to Rome. It was to black-market yourself some Ermo. I am not sure why you went back there this last time. Just had to tie up some loose ends, I suppose. I hope you did not have to kill any *paisan* over there to keep things quiet."

"I never killed anyone."

Annah said, "When they did Dede's autopsy, I don't know if they bisected that poor girl's rectum or not, but either way, they did a half-assed job."

"You're saying I killed someone?"

"Mr. Silver, the last time we met, in Howard Wyzell's office, I was going to ask you about Amanda, when your phone buzzed and you had to run off. Told me you could not talk just then. You can set off that buzzing whenever you want."

ANNAH TORCH — Jim DeFilippi

"Of course I can. I'm thinking of using it right now, so I don't have to keep listening to all this shit. There's a simple app that does it. I use it all the time to get out of meetings."

"It's called HipCheck."

"Yup, I should be using it right now."

"If you do, you will miss my story."

"You have a story for me?"

"Yes, I do."

"Okay. Okay. I hope it makes more sense than this drivel, this bouncing around you've been doing. You got a story for me? Then please tell it to me. Let me give it a listen."

Annah took a water bottle from out of her backpack and sipped. She said, "I will try to stay linear."

&&&

Annah plodded her way through the whole story for Johnnie, as she had reverse engineered it. She would take sips of water, she wasn't used to talking this much. As she spoke, Johnnie would mostly just smirk and shake his head, as if her words were too stupid to be considered. He would punctuate some of her sentences for her, with words like "Absurd" and "Surreal." At one point he said to her, "You've been out there in the woods too long, my love. They have ticks out there. They get under your skin, then they crawl right up into your brain, don't they?"

Annah knew that some of her story was no more than conjecture and educated estimation, but she kept talking as if all was factual...

Three years ago, Johnnie had seduced Dede at a Future Entrepreneurs of America national convention—he was the keynote speaker, she was just a naive high school kid. It was statutory rape at the time, and as Dede matured, the affair continued. After high school, when she went off to the Chelsea Academy, he bought the chalet in Watervliet as a convenient nearby location for their trysts.

ANNAH TORCH   Jim DeFilippi

Later, he sent his other lover, his daughter Amanda, to the same Chelsea Academy. So Johnnie was keeping two lovers—both illicit to different degrees—a dangerous but thrilling situation. He could playact at being Carlos Danger.

For a smart operator, Johnnie could also be a complete fool with his women. He told Dede about the abuse of his own daughter, probably using the confession to increase his sense of danger and sexual stimulation. Johnnie had been raping Dede since she was in high school, and now he was telling her that he had been raping his own daughter since she was in grammar school.

Grace Silver had told Annah, "Johnnie takes his lovers from all over the world, but mostly right here at home," and "Johnnie is not ashamed of anything he's ever done." But when she added, "And neither am I," she was lying.

At first, Dede swore to Johnnie that she would never tell anybody anything, but she was immature, insecure, Johnnie didn't believe her.

As she grew more hardened, embittered and sophisticated, Dede began blackmailing Johnnie. The two airheads at the Chelsea Academy had told Annah about Dede having a sugar daddy who would send her money. It wasn't her own father sending her those checks, it was her roommate's father.

Dede told Johnnie that she was either going to get paid or she was going to tell everything. To everybody. Come clean. As if either one of them could ever feel clean again. Dede was thinking something like: "I don't even know if it's considered rape anymore. I've come of age, haven't I? But I don't have any more control over it now than I did back then. Except for the secrets I can tell."

Whether Johnnie was really working on a deal with the Vatican or not, he began imagining what business dealings with the Pope could mean for his power and prestige. But the Catholic church had enough trouble with altar boys, they didn't need a story about a business partner with his altar girls and his own little daughter.

He had more than enough money to stay blackmailed forever, but his pride and position wouldn't allow it, so he started making plans to kill instead of pay.

ANNAH TORCH   Jim DeFilippi

The night of the murder, Dede and Amanda were a bit high and getting higher at Thunder and Stumpy's Bar, a place they went to when they wanted to feel endangered and not ordinary, dabbling with illegal drugs and illicit characters like Nico Madness. Amanda had taken some Ketamine—Special K— and was complaining to Dede about her father—nothing specific—as Dede fought the temptation to shock her with the truth. Dede told Amanda something to the effect that she knew what a louse her father was, but she left the bar without her knowledge ever getting unacknowledged.

When Dede left, Nico Madness told the confused and questioning Amanda something that Dede, drunk, had slopped over to a couple of the barflies—that she had been having an affair with Amanda's father.

Nico had said to Annah: "Ima tell bitch shuck she don't like." The bitch was Amanda. The shuck was that Dede was screwing her father.

In tears, Amanda called up her Dad. "Is it true? You and her?" And more important, "Does she know about us?"

He probably lied to his daughter, maybe not. He either admitted half the truth—that he and Dede were lovers—or the whole truth—that he had told Dede about the incest. Either way, he now had two cannons running loose. Johnnie decided it was time to act.

He said into the phone, "Don't worry, baby, Daddy takes care of everything, that's what daddies do." Johnnie was used to putting out fires, solving problems the moment they came up. He packed up some supplies and headed over to Dede and Amanda's place.

Once there, he got Dede high with a few more drinks. By now she was swearing that she would never tell anyone about the disgusting truth—Johnnie and his own daughter. *Just keep those checks rolling in, and my mouth stays shut.*

But why take a chance?

Let's you and me party, Daddy boy. She was enjoying herself, when Johnnie offered to inject her with something that would get her ever happier. *What the hell, why not?*

Maybe he offered to inject her "in that secret spot" of her body, with a dose of Special K. Instead he injected her with enough insulin to lower her blood sugar to a level that would cause a stroke, a deadly coma, or a heart attack. Too much insulin causes low blood sugar, the condition called hypoglycemia. Beyond certain levels, insulin—a natural element of the body—is deadly. Johnnie made sure Dede's dosage was enough to do the job.

Then he injected the body with Ermodemethon, which raises the blood sugar and electrolyte levels, thus hiding the effects of the insulin. Johnnie knew that Dede's body would be found dead from natural causes.

The "slightly elevated" insulin in Dede's blood was important, but it was overlooked by the Medical Examiner and everyone else. It was the "short hand" of *Pai Gow* poker. The Special K, Ketamine, was what the autopsy was focused on, but it was a non-factor, a red herring, not even a long hand.

Dede died happy.

She was smiling. She would never tell anyone anything.

Johnnie watched over her until he was sure that she was dead. He knew she had died happy because he had stood there and watched it happen. Dede Constaghulia was dead. The smile on her face would last forever.

Her body would be found—clear and clean, no questions asked, no investigation launched.

Johnnie locked the place up and he left.

But Amanda had decided to save her dad from the clutches of this devil-girl. She knew that all this shitty truth coming out about her and her own father would destroy her, that as a victim of pedophilia she could never face…anybody.

Victims of childhood abuse and incest often harbor an illogical, unreasonable, emotional loyalty—even a type of love—toward their abusers.

Amanda followed Nico Madness to his place, where—filled with anger at Dede, jealousy of Dede, humiliation and fear of being exposed as a victim of incest—she bought a shotgun, using currency and maybe some sex as her medium of exchange.

ANNAH TORCH   Jim DeFilippi

She was froth with anger—an anger borne of twin bouts—jealous anger and shame. At her father, the pervert? No, at Dede, his victim. Again—abused children are often the staunchest defenders of their abusing parent.

She went to the apartment which she and Dede shared.

Johnnie had locked up the room, but Amanda of course had a key, it was her place too. Still crazy with confusion and drugs and infidelity and perfidy, she entered the room and saw Dede apparently passed out, flopped in a chair. Sleeping with a smile on her face.

Amanda locked the door behind her, in case Dede woke up and tried to run. Amanda pointed and fired Nico's weapon at Dede's midsection—the last thing Amanda remembered was the shotgun bolting back up toward her face.

Later, in the hospital, when she woke up, her father was standing there beside her bed. She looked around and whispered to her Daddy that she had killed, had killed for him.

Her father leaned over, maybe kissed her forehead, then her ear, and whispered, "No you didn't, honey. I killed her for us, you didn't. We're together in this. I'm going to protect you, my dearest. Don't say anything to anyone except that you didn't do it. Or that you did do it. Either way, dearest, I will rectify. Your father will rectify everything."

&&&

An older woman with a shawl over the shoulders of her overcoat was walking by with a large black poodle. Johnnie waited until the woman had passed. "And I suppose you've already taken all of this dreck to the proper authorities, you're not just here to blackmail me?"

"To the District Attorney's Office..."

"That woman doesn't like me. She'd just love to indict me, use an iron sledgehammer to do it. She's a big game hunter, and I'm the biggest game in her town."

"I talked to her Special Investigator. He told me that she would laugh me out of the office, so he offered to do it for me."

"To indict me?"

"No, to laugh me out of his office. I asked him—his name is Leo Protski—about getting Dede's body disinterred—that may not be the right term, it is in a mausoleum—and checking the cadaver for Ermodemethon. I broad-brushed everything for Protski, he pointed out that there was little solid evidence, and there might be jurisdictional problems with Massachusetts over getting Dede's body re-autopsied, but he admitted that his boss would be overjoyed with pulling down a trophy like Baby Johnny Silver."

"But it's a dead end for Goofy, isn't it? You hit the wall."

"Maybe."

"But you're not going to let it drop now, are you?"

"No. What I need is an uncovering of the body and then an autopsy, a real one this time. I will see what I can do."

"Even with all that, and that'll never happen, but even if it does, you won't...but you're not going to let it lie, are you?"

"No."

"And I can't buy you off, even if I decided to. I've got all the money in the world, but you don't use money anymore, do you, you only deal in furs and pelts or something, right?"

"Money? No, not too much."

"So there's not too much I can offer you in the way of incentive then, is there."

"Nothing."

"Oh, there's always something to be done, Annah. I suppose I'll just have to stop this thing in its tracks. In its deer tracks, so to speak."

"Right."

"Yes, I guess I'll just have to hunt you down then. I used to bow-hunt a bit, where you have to get within twenty yards of your prey. But I suppose this time there will have to be more artillery brought in."

ANNAH TORCH   Jim DeFilippi

"Well, you know where to find me."

"Yes, I do."

"But of course, you won't know where to find me."

"No? I won't? You think you can subvert the structure of my life? Do you? Well, Miss Annah Torched-Earth, here's my torch song for you. You should know, think about that little patch of woods of yours as the land lying between Sherman and the Sea. I am about to become General William Tecumseh Sherman, scorching your earth—burn, torch, scorch, lay waste to anything that stands in my way, cutting my path to the sea, leaving a trail of death and destruction across your land. And across your heart. Right through your heart and belly and that sweet body of yours. Are you getting my message, Annah dear, are you?"

"My Mom told me something as a kid."

"Yeah, what's that?"

"Short guys can't do metaphors."

&&&

Chapter Twenty-nine

They were in the master bedroom. Grace was still in bed, the spread pulled up to her belly, her breasts bare. She was wearing her night-blinders. Johnnie would ask, "Can you hear me with those things?" Why would she hear less? Without seeing him, she knew that Johnnie was standing in from of the full-length mirror, no pants, white shirt, tying his necktie. She could tell. They'd been married a long time. He was 'coptering down to the City for the day. Alexa was playing George Harrison, "Do You Want to Know a Secret?"

Baby Johnnie told Grace, "You know me, Sweetheart, I am far from being any sort of a violent man. Peace and joy and turning a profit. That's been my life. But some terrible events, fostered by some terrible people, have been threatening to close in on me. I am forced to go out and find some men who deal in violence, it's justified, it's to put an end to violence. I know that sounds like a contradiction, an oxymoron. Maybe I'm the oxymoron, could be, but with all of our riches, here I am about to go visit the gutter. You won't know why I am forced to do this until it's all over, and maybe not even then. I hope you'll never have to hear about it. I'm only telling you this because I don't have to, but you've always accepted me, my actions in the past. I am a fool who always talks too much to the women in his life, but I never learn, do I?"

Grace said, "You admit yourself, you've told me, sometimes you talk too much."

"I do. I do. But Gracie, my Grace, promise me, never speak of this to anyone."

&&&

Grace was parked in the lot of Henny's Liquors, waiting for them to bring out her case of Booker's. She had Harry Nilsson on the speakers, "Everybody's Talkin'." A pear-shaped man Grace had never seen before came out carrying her whiskey. He had no coat and was wearing a paper party hat, the elastic band under his chin. Grace got out, undid her coat, and pretended to help put the booze in the back seat, leaning in a bit, so that he could see.

After the man had gone back in, Grace took her cell phone and tapped in the name of a "Favorite Contact."

"Leo. Leo? It's Grace. It's Gracie Silver. No, I won't. Listen, Leon, I mean Leo, I've been drinking and drinking, thinking and thinking. I have no one else. Since Amanda has come back, has come out of it, she's not the same. We used to talk, she and I did. But now there's no one. I thought of you, Officer. You were the only one—even though you worked for the people who wanted to put my Amanda away—you didn't, I knew you didn't want that. And you know crime, and criminals, things like that. Remember the nice talk we had, you and me, how much I appreciated you were on our side? I'm very, very drunk right now, but I ask you. Johnnie is looking to hurt somebody, he told me. He wants to get people to beat someone up. I don't know who. I don't even know who. But you, you're a police, like the police, please, please just go to him, explain to him that's not the way to do things. I've tried and tried, he won't listen. I don't want you to scare him, just to convince him. Convince him to just stay home with me, till we get Amanda back. With me and Amanda, who he loves. He loves the both of us. Just talk to him quietly, please, convince him to keep his hands clean. Maybe scare him just a little bit. I don't know what he's been thinking."

She stared out the windshield, the call still live.

"And most of all, promise me this, Officer, not a word of any of this is ever spoken aloud."

&&&

Protski and Gumm were at the underground firing range. Gumm had to qualify for the year. Protski ejected some shells and slipped his ear protectors down to around his neck. He indicated to Gumm that he should do the same. Staccato gunfire was echoing in from the other lanes.

Protski told Gumm, "So here's some scuttlebutt you're not going to hear anywhere else. Remember, you heard it here first. The billionaire, that

Baby Johnnie, he's out there looking for muscle. Looking for some guys, guys, to do some wet work for him."

"Oh, yeah?"

"You didn't hear this from me, right? You didn't hear this at all. Finger to lips."

&&&

Gumm had pulled his pickup right into Johnnie Silver's garage. Back in the bed of the truck was a snowblower. Gumm had changed the plug, gapped it, but the thing was still missing, misfiring. He meant to take it in after this. Gumm was playing around with the soundtrack, looking for Fred Eaglesmith, the one about the Cobra Jet 428. Finally, Silver opened the passenger door and slid in.

"What?" The man was in a hurry.

Gumm said to Silver, "Listen, I'm a good cop, been a good cop my whole life. Still am. But every once in a while even a good man has to shave the edges, take just a little bit off. Shave off the corners. You have so much money, sir, much, so much, I bet neither one of us knows really how much. I'm in need. I just need a tiny little bit of that. You won't miss it. Don't even ask me how I know, that information does not enter. I only know that you are looking for people to do a very special job for you. Some wet work. I would have thought you already knew people like that, that you already had them on the payroll. But I guess not. So let's just say I put you together with this type of people. Get you set up with them. I can give you the names, how to reach them. I got it written down here, I'll hand over this paper. They're not good men, they're across town from being any good. But they're the type who will do the type thing that you want them to do. Okay? Okay? I was thinking, I guess we have to get specific now, talk figures. My troubles would be at the other end of the tunnel, if you could just hand over, for this slip of paper, say, the amount of ten thousand dollars. One-time deal. Never again. I'm a good cop."

Johnnie sat staring at the cop.

ANNAH TORCH   Jim DeFilippi

"Just promise me this, Mr. Silver, this stays between us. Nobody hears a thing about this."

&&&

That night, Simon Gumm was lying in bed, alone. The wind outside was blowing what sounded like a Charlie Parker riff, a celestial soundtrack, making the windows rattle like a snare drum. It sounded gloriously threatening.

Gumm was looking up at the ceiling, talking to God. Explaining that he had been a cop for a lot of years, he didn't feel like totaling them up, but a lot. He had once watched a black man being killed by a fellow officer, but he had never been responsible for someone's death like that. He thought maybe tequila might get him off to sleep, but it took that whole pint bottle, plus a couple Lunesta's. He was still awake. He was still lying there, talking to God.

"Dear Lord, just you and me, can I buy back my soul?" He waited for an answer, then said, "Long odds, I bet."

&&&

Chapter Thirty

Three piles of ten crisp, new, thousand dollar bills sat stacked in front of each of the three men.

Johnnie was saying to them, "At any of my other places than this, like down in the city, Manhattan, Brooklyn, give me half an hour and I'd have a crew that I needed. To do anything. Anything. But up here in the sticks, I'm a bit out of touch. Oh, sure, I could have somebody shipped it, but the logistics of something like that can get confusing, especially if you don't do it every day. I don't do this type thing every day. And with me present at the scene? Never. Never before this one. Plus, I need someone who knows the Woods. Like you guys do. Where we'll go hunting. So I need local talent. That's you boys. When I heard about you boys, I knew you were the local talent I was looking for."

The three were so intent on flipping through the bills, counting them, that they were hardly listening.

Ruck looked up at Johnnie. "I'm glad you didn't try any of that half now-half later bullshit you see on the television. You see that all the time. The guy says to the other guy, 'You get half now, you get half later, when the job gets done.'"

Johnny told him, "It gets done. I've got no worries there. You boys have your full pay. We never see each other again, after the job gets done. We pass each other in the street, down in town, we don't even look sideways. 'Hey, isn't that that Johnnie Silver guy, the billionaire?' You don't even look. You don't say a word. You don't care who that guy is. Right, fellas?"

It was three-thirty in the middle of a cold night—they could see their breaths, even though the garage was heated. Johnnie had seated the three men around a heavy metal, four-foot by six-foot table, on fold-up camp chairs that had been left there by the last occupant, a rug importer whose main place was down in Queens.

The garage smelled of gas and antifreeze, it housed Johnnie's BMW-X7 SUV and his LT Coupe Corvette. The table was set up in one of the two remaining empty bays.

The Queens importer had also left his collection of antique metal gasoline signs hanging on three of the walls. The Orange Circle holding the blue 76. One for "Red Cloud Gasoline." Another for "That Good Gulf Gasoline." The sign dominating the back wall was huge, maybe four feet across, six feet high, a picture of a girl in short-shorts and a halter top, a Mobil gas cap. She was holding the nozzle of a gas line that ran between her legs back to the pump behind her. The pump had the flying red horse and "Mobilegas Special" on it. Across the girl's legs was written, "Fill Her Up!"

Ruck was telling their new boss, "We're not going to jail for this, Cap. We don't want that Gumm cop coming after us for this, you know. He already got us in his sights anyway. Shit."

Ruck was having trouble getting used to being the second in command, but the money was making it easier.

Johnnie told the men, "Nobody is going away. None of us will even be there at the time this thing happens. We're all somewhere else."

Their looks told him they didn't understand. "Here's the mash. I'll be over in Rome. You guys will be out in LasVegas."

Still no looks of understanding. Johnnie thought—if these guys were dogs, they'd all be twisting their heads sideways, trying to comprehend. "Your cell phones will be clicking off towers all day long out there. Mine will be clicking away, over in Italy. That's why I had you bring your cells tonight. Why I collected them from you."

Box asked, "Do we get them back?"

Johnnie told him, "Never. They're buried. I'll get you new ones."

Ruck said, "When the job is done."

Johnnie said, "That's right. For the job, I got you all burners."

Box asked, "They burn?"

Ruck told him, "That means we throw them away."

Johnnie said, "We bury them. Along with the rifles."

Box asked, "We don't get to keep the guns?"

Johnnie shook his head. "Buried."

Johnnie had given them the choice of either using their own long-guns and bringing a top-of-the-line deer rifle for him to use, or else going out and getting whatever they wanted, on his tab. They had shown up at the garage with four new rifles. Two Weatherby Vanguard Series 2's, and two Ambush 300 Blackouts. The Blackouts looked more like a military M-16 than a deer rifle. Johnnie took one of them for himself, so did Ruck. Horn and Box took the Weatherbys.

Ruck asked, "You get us new phones when we're done?"

"Sure. Whatever kind you want."

Box's brain was straining to understand. "We're out in LasVegas, you said? You send us out there? Do we win?"

Ruck and Horn showed Johnnie faces that told him how stupid Box was.

Johnnie went on. "Not just cell-tower pings. There'll be multiple witnesses that will swear I'm over there, and that you guys are out there." Johnnie pointed in opposite directions, maybe east and west. "There'll be airline reservations with your names, dates, times. All punched correctly. You all made the flights and took off. The flight plan on my Lear will show the same thing. Hotel bills—I'm staying at the *Ambasciatori*, you guys at Wynn's. I'll have a few note pads from the place, you guys'll have the cards that the whores give out in the street. You'll all have Uber and cab receipts, records, restaurant tabs."

Ruck was nodding, in understanding and appreciation. "Pretty good, not bad."

ANNAH TORCH   Jim DeFilippi

Johnnie told them, "Somebody will be on the plane for you, don't worry."

"What? Who?"

Johnnie said, "Just somebody. And some grainy videos will show us going in and out of our respective hotels."

Ruck was grinning. "Make mine a good looking guy, like me."

Johnnie said, "Okay. What do we bring with us, into the Woods. You guys have to help me here. First, these rifles. Everybody set? You need practice? You need to sight them in or anything?"

Box said, "Mr. Silver, I'd like permission please to keep mine, after it's done. It's a beauty."

Johnnie grabbed hold of Box's Weatherby, around the stock. "It's not yours. It's on a one-day loan. It gets buried. After some time, a month, I'll get you any type weapon you want, you get to keep the new one. Okay?"

Box nodded hard, three times.

Johnnie said. "Ammunition, of course. We've got that. Or we'll pick up more. Side arms? I don't know. Only if we need them. You guys tell me."

Ruck spoke for his men. "Probably won't need them. We'll see. I got a Ruger Alaskan I'm fond of, but it's traceable, I suppose, so I'll leave it home, I guess. I had a Redhawk too, but it got broken. How do we dress?"

Johnnie said, "You tell me. You guys are the experts."

Ruck made it look like he was thinking. "For something like this, camo probably. No orange, that's for sure."

Horn was ginning. "Ammo and camo, my kind of hunt, right, Chief?"

Johnnie asked the table, "What else?"

Ruck answered for them. "Canteens. Everybody has one filled with water. Plastic. I'll bring an extra. Metal one. Some gasoline. In case we see something. Best grade binoculars. The burner phones so we can talk to each other out there. Get us on some kind of a conference calling. Maps? Don't need them." Ruck pointed at Johnnie. "You want us to have night goggles? Those things are scary real."

Johnnie said, "We shouldn't be out there in the dark."

Ruck told him, "We'll get to the edge before light, near, but you're right, everything will be done by the time the sun disappears. Flashlights, just in case. Good ones. But we won't need them. Things'll be over before then."

Johnnie said, "Yes. Yes, it will. Yes, we will."

Box said, "We'll be back home spending all this here cash by then. I got my eye on a boat."

Johnny said, "Okay, I was thinking of this one thing. Maybe it's crazy, maybe not. Maybe it's overkill. Dogs. What'd you think? Could we use a bloodhound, maybe a couple of them? I could get us that, if we need to. We get hold of something of hers, a shirt or something."

Horn was grinning again. "Her panties. I could be in charge of that, huh?"

Ruck told them, "We don't need no damn dogs."

Box said, "I still like the idea of us being out there in Vegas. I'll tell the kids I won. Won big. That's how I got the boat money."

Ruck told him, "Tell them whatever you want. As long as you was out there."

Johnnie said, "You don't say anything. You don't mention money or Vegas or anything, unless somebody asks, and only if that somebody who asks is someone you have to talk to. Not your wife, not your kids, nobody else. They ask, you just don't answer. Just keep walking."

The three men said they understood.

Horn asked, "Should we camo our faces? Should we paint them up?"

They all looked to Ruck, who told them, "We're not out there in the dark. It wouldn't hurt, but I don't feel it's necessary. We can do without it."

ANNAH TORCH   Jim DeFilippi

Box said, "With all the camo, faces too, there's always the problem we'll be shooting each other, shooting at us, instead of at the target. We could be dodging our own bullets."

Ruck told him, "We don't dodge bullets, we catch them in our teeth." He looked at Johnnie for approval.

Johnnie nodded, not impressed. "How about our strategy, our plan once we're out there? Mr. Ruckhouser...no wait, let's never use names...nothing fancy, like in the Tarantino movies, just one, two, three, four." He pointed at himself, then went around the table, "One...two...three...four. But now, Two, what's our plan, once we get out there?"

"Well, One, Mister One, we boys know how to flush out a deer. We been doing that our whole life. No offense, but when you were in diapers, down there on the Wall Street, making all that money, we been up here out in the Woods, gunning for something to eat for that day. Putting food on our table, our family's table. So we know how to do it all right. We'll do that the right way. Once the time comes. We'll have to check the terrain, the weather, the sky, the light. A lot of tracking and killing depends on the particular occasion and the situation."

Ruck was feeling a bit in charge again. He liked that.

Johnnie told him. "I trust you. I can tell I've chosen the right crew. One reason I'm the most successful trader you'll ever see, down there on *the* Wall Street, is because I know that my personnel means everything. A man can only do so much by himself. It's his staff, his executive board, the personnel department. You boys are my underpinnings. You'll get the job done for me. I'm out there with you, we'll get it done."

Ruck was smiling. "Yes, we will, yes we will."

Johnnie asked him, "What else about the tracking? How do you find something you're hunting for in the Woods?"

Ruck went on. "Yeah, yeah. Well, you ask yourself, can we find the spot, can we spot the area where the game's been sleeping, spending the night? How about–do we know the general area that's being frequented? Are there

ANNAH TORCH — Jim DeFilippi

deer paths that are always being used? Tracks? Can you recognize their tracks when you see it, even though it's almost not there to begin with? It'd be great if a little snow was gonna fall, but it's too early for that. There won't be any tracking snow for us, but we'll be tracking okay without it."

Horn asked, "Ruck, I mean Two, Mister Two, you gonna mount this head on your wall, down there in your dungeon, along with all the rest? Could be a real pretty addition, couldn't it?"

Box said, "Hey, that brings up something serious though. What about the dead carcass? What do we do with that? We carve it up? Bring it on home?"

Horn said, "Or have some fun? We have fun with it?"

Johnnie looked at each of the three men, "We don't do anything with it. We leave it where it lies. Right there."

Ruck looked around at all the others and said to them, "Well, fellas, I do believe we got ourselves a cunt hunt."

&&&

Chapter Thirty-one

" Girl, listen please to me, these guys are to be watched, please. You cannot just shrug this thing off. These lunatics mean to do you some harm."

"Weaz, can you get me a bra?"

The request confused Wyzell, a common state when talking to this woman. "So, what, you're going to fight them off using a bra? What, like a slingshot or something?"

"Something like that. No need to come in all the way. Just leave it by the stump. I will pick it up there."

"I didn't even know you wore a bra."

Annah just looked at him.

"Annah, listen, let's be serious for a moment. Gumm told me, he hinted, both Baby Johnnie and the three rustic dullards are coming out here to hunt you. They wouldn't mind teaching you a lesson. I don't know all what's going on, what bad blood there is. I suppose you *do* know, but you're not talking, as always."

Annah said, "Everything is fine. I am fine."

Wyzell told her, "For some reason, I don't know, I thought Sergeant Gumm looked sort of guilty when he was warning me to warn you. I don't know why."

"I knew Johnnie was contemplating violence against me, but I thought the other three had given up the fight."

"I guess not. No. Not from what Gumm says."

Annah held an open palm out toward him, making a point. "Weaz, you should remember, these are very stupid men, the three of them, I mean. No matter where you place them on the spectrum of stupidity. There is a story about

ANNAH TORCH   Jim DeFilippi

a hunter in the snow. When he hiked an inadvertent circle, he came upon a set of human tracks. Not recognizing them as his own, he decided to track them. Suddenly, there were two sets of tracks. After that, the group of men he was tracking kept growing larger and larger. Finally, when there were more than ten men in the group, he died alone."

"An okay story, but it doesn't give me solace."

"Stupid men, sir. Left alone, they would probably end up all shooting each other."

Wyzell was shaking his head. "Baby Johnnie though, he's not stupid."

"No, he is not."

"He won't be out here with them when they come after you. He hires people to do his grunt work for him, his whole career. His dummies get the job done for him. Are they planning to beat you? To kill you even? I don't know."

Annah said, "Johnnie and I have talked. He will be there, hunting me. Do not worry, sir, strong women are out of season, go check the Hunting Guide."

"These guys are poachers, Annah. Women or doe, they don't care what time of year they go after them. Listen, I'm afraid that you yourself are going to get poached by these guys...poached like a soft-boiled egg gets poached."

Annah had started grinning. "But I am hard-boiled. Can you get me that brassiere or not?"

"Annah, please, let's forget about your undergarments for now. This could end up very bad. Badly. Let's get you some official police protection at least. Gumm said to keep him off the record on this, but the WLPD should be notified."

"Then what, to drive a patrol car past my hut every half hour?"

Wyzell was shaking his head again. "You know, love, I'd come out here and stand guard myself, I would, but I have...pickle-ball." His grin was a grim one.

"I understand...except for—what? Pickle?"

ANNAH TORCH   Jim DeFilippi

"I shouldn't be hacking around about this, Annah. These guys could hurt you. One's rich and three of them are wildly aggressive. It's a bad combination, aggression with money behind it. And at least three of them can be physically violent. And the other one does his hunting on Wall Street, the most cut-throat, dangerous place there is. So I'm worried."

"No need, sir. I can take care of myself, I have shown you that."

"I know that. I also know that you yourself are capable of unbridled violence."

"I am not."

"You're not? What about Crayton then?"

"Who?"

"Crayton Callahan."

"Oh, Callahan. Him."

"Annah, you killed him. Remember?"

"I did."

"With a punch."
"I did."

"So?"

"What about him?"

"So you punched him, Annah...out...really out. All the way out."

"There was nothing better I could have done about it."

"And what did you feel about it afterwards, after it was done?"

Annah was tending the fire in the rock pit, pushing the burning logs around with a green stick. "I ate supper that night."

"And you kept it down, I bet."

"I kept it all down." Annah hesitated, threw the stick onto the fir. "Home fries with carrots."

"Callahan had a gun when you killed him, but this time it'll be four men. Four men, not one. And from what Gumm hinted, these will also be carrying guns with them."

"Four men, but only seven eyes, Weaz, and probably none of them real shooter eyes. I will be enjoying my dinner, afterwards."

"See, that's what I mean. Annah, you have to drum up some regard for human life, especially when it's your own."

"Please, I will be fine. Just get me the bra."

He stood looking at her for a while. Then he shrugged and asked, "What kind you want?"

"Doesn't matter."

"What size then?"

"No matter."

"What color?"

"Anything."

"Okay, I'm done asking, but you *do* mean it then, you really need a bra?"

"I do."

"Okay, I'll pick one up for you at Victoria's. She can keep a secret."

"And some bongos too. You know what I mean—like bongo drums I can beat on?"

"Okay, sure. They'll be coming in with their power rifles and their hunting knives, so you'll be out here in your bra, playing bongos for them. Is this going to be a death match, or is it some kind of party you've got planned that I'm not invited to?"

"Thank you."

ANNAH TORCH   Jim DeFilippi

Wyzell stood there a moment, contemplating. Then he said, "Annah, I don't care, I'm coming out here to stay with you. I'll bring a weapon of my own. Where can I sleep?"

Annah's voice changed into something western. "Go on home, Herb, go on home to your wife and kids."

It took Wyzell a minute to catch the reference. Then, he said, "Oh, *High Noon*, right? You're Gary Cooper."

"Yup."

"Well, Marshall, I hope that when they step down from the train, they won't be able to find you."

"They will find D. B. Cooper before they find me."

&&&

After Wyzell had returned to civilization—back to its ersatz semblance of what was called normalcy—Annah hiked along a deer path to her Smoking Boulder. The Boulder was the size of a small car and it sat high above a cliff, a cliff that bottomed out at the waters of Robert's Pond. A thin trail ran along the edge of the water.

Annah had loved this Boulder ever since she had first come to the Woods. A topographical map would put the height of the cliff at just a few grass-blade-widths under one-hundred feet. This was her favorite spot, even dearer to her than the clearing that held her log hut and its stone furniture. Even in the fall of the year, if the sun was out, she could enjoy lying atop the Boulder, getting sandwiched by the heat, direct sun-rays soothing the front of her body and her face, the radiated heat rising back up off the stone from beneath. Most of the rock surface was covered by an intricate diamond-shaped pattern that looked almost manmade.

Fridays she would sit there and smoke her *Hacienda*, or whatever cigar Wyzell had brought her. Looking down at the waters below. Honking, irritable Canadian Geese and regal white swans controlled this waterfront for ten months of the year. Both of the two feathered species were tough, but the swans were definitely the schoolyard billies. They could keep the geese corralled and away

ANNAH TORCH   Jim DeFilippi

from any area that the swans decided to control. The swans would silently float toward the geese and make them back up in subjugation. When they were swimming with their cygnets, it would take something stronger than a Howitzer to back them off. They controlled their environment.

So would she.

Beneath the surface of the water, the snapping turtles ruled.

Incredibly, each June these snappers would make the hundred-foot sheer climb up to the top of the cliff, onto the area surrounding Annah's Boulder, where they would nestle a spot into the soft sand, lay their eggs, and incubate them for days. Annah would walk up to the expectant mothers, smile down at them, speak quietly to them. These prehistoric, sleepy-eyed creatures, with their shells a foot across in circumference, never even bothered to look up at her. They had no intention of leaving their eggs, of running away from this big strange creature.

When she had described their ascent of the cliff to Wyzell, he asked her if it was a non-technical climb or if the turtles were using ropes and pitons.

The turtles were capable of behemoth feats in order to preserve their life style.

So was she.

Annah slid off the Boulder, ran her fingers across its warm surface in a tender caress, and gave it a kiss.

At the edge of the cliff, using her trenching tool—with its sharpened green blade—she began an excavation. She was digging the dirt away from the front of the rock, removing soil from the edge that faced the cliff and the water. She dug very carefully, cautiously, putting her palm on the surface of the rock every few minutes.

When her digging hit some thick roots that had spread out from the surrounding bushes and balsam firs, she stopped to adjust her shovel. The tool, purchased from an Army-Navy store years ago, had a wooden handle with only remnants left of its original black paint. Its head fit into a canvas holster that held two large brass snaps, and an attached sheath that could hold a bayonet.

ANNAH TORCH   Jim DeFilippi

She ran her finger along the edge of the shovel blade. The last time she had used this tool, it was to intimidate a sleeping moron in his bedroom. Now, Annah loosened the locking bolt at the head of the handle, turning it counter-clockwise and spinning it down. When the bolt was loose, she bent the blade to a forty-five degree angle from the handle, and she retightened the bolt. The shovel had become an ax. She used it to chop through the roots, then to scrape away some of the loose dirt. With the stubborn roots severed, she readjusted the tool back into its original form, it was a shovel again, and she continued her dig. She would use the blade to scrap away dirt from the face of the Boulder, then dig some more, until most of the dirt had been removed on the side of the Boulder facing the cliff.

She turned and walked down the trail a bit until she found a gray and white triangle-shaped rock, about the size of a basketball. She pulled it out of the ground and brought it back to the Boulder. She propped it beneath the front surface of the Boulder and the earth, checked its security, and then dug away a bit more of the dirt. She stepped back and stood staring for a minute, then approached the Boulder again and continued her digging—even slower now, even more cautious than before, with more frequent hand-checks after every few shovel-fulls. She used the blunt end of the trenching tool's handle to tap the dug-up rock into the dirt between the Boulder and the ground. The rock had become a chock.

She kept digging until she heard the Boulder groan and shift a millimeter. Then she stopped.

The excavation took Annah more than an hour and a half. By the time she finished, she was losing the light. She stood back and admired her work. She stood by the Boulder, put a hand on its surface, and leaned over to look down at the path running by the waterline, a hundred feet below. Then she patted her Boulder gently, once again gave it a kiss—it was a goodbye kiss—and she headed back to the hut.

There, she built a fire and massaged her shoulder and arm muscles. Before she climbed into her sleeping bag for the night, she lifted the mahogany case that she had taken from the poacher, the potential rapist. The box was made of darkened mahogany wood, with copper hasps and staples. She lay the case on the ground by the fire-pit. She opened the case and took out her Daddy's Hammer. She slid the tool into the side loop of her left pants leg. She slept with it there, using somnolent mind control to keep her from rolling over on it.

    She slept peacefully and steadily through the night, as she always did. When she woke in the morning, she slipped out of her sleeping bag and sat on the ground, holding the Hammer, studying its wooden handle and its metal head.

&&&

Chapter Thirty-two

Johnnie Silver had picked up the three men at the Albany International Airport in a charcoal black Mazda 5 that he had gotten clean from a staff person who could be trusted. Johnnie told Grace that this should be his last trip to Rome for a while.

Ruck, Horn, and Box had piled their Las Vegas suitcases into the hatch back and climbed in—Ruck riding in shotgun, with Horn and Box in the back. Horn and Box had told their wives that they were heading out to Las Vegas for a while to do some gambling and drinking—don't ask when we'll be back. The wives were surprised and confused, this was something new. Ruck hadn't heard from Blanche since the punching. That was okay.

Silver drove them to a spot at a bend on Potters Corners Road that Ruck had described for him. No one was speaking.

Potters Corners was one of those typical country roads that had been repaved by the town so many times without any scraping that the center line, if there had been one, would be a foot higher than the edges of the pavement. Silver had to fight the steering wheel the whole trip to keep the Mazda from running off into the ditch.

Ruck pointed and Silver pulled the vehicle off into the underbrush as far as possible, but not so far in that it couldn't be driven back out in a hurry. It was still dark, the sun wouldn't be coming up for another half hour. No one was saying much as they worked—Horn and Box cutting branches and laying them across the hood and cab of the Mazda, as Silver and Ruck quietly went over the plan.

The four men would fan out into an ice cream cone shape—a half mile across at the top, one mile down from the top to the point at the bottom. Ruck, Horn, and Box would form the semicircle of a scoop at the top of the cone—the north end—with Horn in the middle, Box to his right—the west—Ruck to the left—

the East. A mile south of them, at the bottom point of the ice cream cone, Silver would be waiting.

The configuration would be centered on the spot where the slut had taken out Ruck's eye. The three men would work their way slowly south, flushing their prey toward the bottom of the cone, toward Silver and his Ambush 300 Blackout.

By six-thirty, they were all in position. The sun had come up and the three men slowly began working their way down. Each man was carrying a rifle and a cellphone.

To the south, Silver had found a fallen log, two feet around, maybe twelve feet from the trunk to its twisted top. He was resting the muzzle of his Blackout on the blackened wood. The log had been hollowed out by rot, black lines of bark twisted around it like a barber's pole. There was a strong smell, but Silver couldn't identify it.

Up at the north, Ruck held his phone up to his lips. "We're moving."

Silver: "Ready here. Come."

Ruck: "Fellas?"

Horn: "A big 'Yup' from Three."

Box: "Yup here too. I mean Four."

Despite everyone's effort to remain completely silent, each man could hear through the phone line the others' footsteps crunching across the top of the dry land. It hadn't rained or snowed for a week.

After twenty minutes of staccato, brisk phone conversation, with the three men working their way south, looking for signs of their prey, Ruck radioed: "Wait, wait, wait, let me see here…"

Silver: "What? See what?"

Ruck: "Hold on, partner. Everybody just stay where they are for a minute. I might have come on to something…"

ANNAH TORCH   Jim DeFilippi

Silver: "Hold up, men. He's got something. Stand at the ready, where you are."

Four minutes later, it was Ruck on his phone again: "Well, now, looks like I found something. Heapy, I'm at the spot where she lives at. Everybody get on over here quick. I'll direct you all."

Silver: "Okay, we halt the flush for now, gentlemen. Two's found something. We'll talk to each other, get us over there. Number Two, where are you? Can you direct us?"

Fifteen minutes after that, the four men were standing at the site of a crude, makeshift lean-to. Logs had been chopped and lashed together to make up the two sides, a low back end, and a roof. Large gray stones helped form the skeleton of the place, as well as the fire-pit toward the front. Various tools and pieces of equipment were stashed around the place. Everything looked rough, but fairly new and definitely lived in. They were all poking around, flipping over logs, pressing their boots against the various objects inside, clutching their rifles, as they checked the nearby Woods for any movement.

With a voice dappled with quiet pride, Ruck was telling the others how he found the place. "We were all coming down, doing our flushing out, when my eye caught a path, looked like more than just deer to me, looked real well used, looked to be human all right. So I go out on my own for a minute, it leads me right over here. Boys, we found us the camp. Number One, what do you want we should do with it?"

In accordance with Silver's instructions, step by step, gasoline from the metal canteen was poured over the wood of the walls and the roof. The two large canisters of water were pulled to the side and stood at the ready. Silver took out a DuPont cigarette lighter that had been a birthday present from Amanda a decade ago, and he ignited the gasoline. Flames immediately exploded ten feet into the air, twisting hot against the sky. The roar and popping of a gasoline fire differs from other types. The men stood back and watched the crude place burning, feeling the heat on their faces, smelling the smoke. It took no more than a few minutes for the structure to be reduced to ashes. The rocks were letting off clouds of steam.

Box and Horn were stepping through the smoke, pouring water on the sizzling, smoldering remains, when Silver pointed at a spot in the Woods and called out, "There! Look, I can see her!"

"Where?"

"Over fucking moving there, right there! She was moving. In the bushes, those damn bushes where I'm pointing."

"Where?"

"Never mind."

Silver raised his 300 Blackout and started firing at a spot in the bushes, maybe thirty yards away. The three other men raised their rifles and began firing into the same area. None of them was doing much aiming, just pointing their rifles and firing, firing, until the clips and the chambers had been emptied. Reload, keep firing.

The sound was deafening and seemed to go on forever. Clouds of smoke were drifting skyward from the firing squad, mixing with the smoke still coming from the burn. Spent cartridges were jumping to the ground like seeds. The clump of bushes being targeted was ripped and shredded down into a leafless, smoking brown mat on the soil. Finally, the sound of gunfire morphed into the sound of four men breathing heavily with excitement and pleasure.

Someone asked, "Did we get her, you think?"

Someone answered, "Must of. We must of."

Silver said, "Go see."

They all went over to the decimated bushes and began shifting through the remains, scraping through the dead branches and leaves with their hiking boots, looking for blood.

Ruck said, "She's wounded and she's running. Now we gotta go get her."

Silver asked, "But no blood?"

"None we see at least. Doesn't mean it's not there."

ANNAH TORCH Jim DeFilippi

Silver said, "I saw a quick glimpse of her there, running. I couldn't see much once the shooting started."

Ruck agreed. "I seen her too, just quick, for a minute. Nobody's gonna survive what we pumped into these bushes. She's bleeding and she's running. Boss—Number One—I say we gotta act quick now, we go get her, huh? Before she bleeds out."

Silver pointed back to where they had started the operation. "If we can't track her from here, no blood trail, then we go back, form up the cone again, we keep flushing, looking for blood spores."

Ruck said, "That's just what I was gonna say."

Twelve minutes after, they had reformed into their ice cream cone, the three men were moving slowly south again, carefully checking the ground as they went. Silver was again behind the rotted stump, with a full clip in his Blackout.

Box radioed: "Wait a minute, I hear something. What's that? Horn—I mean Number Three—Number Three, you hear that? Off to the right there. Off to the...what's that?...the west?...off to our west. Can you hear that? Anybody hearing that?"

Ruck and Silver asked together, "Hearing what?"

Box: "Number Three, you hearing that? It's mostly coming from our side of the line."

Horn: "No. No, I don't. Yeah. Yeah, now I do. What's it sound like?"

Box: "Sounds like music to me. Somebody beating a drum or something. Off to the west. It's crazy."

Silver, on his phone: "Number Three, Number Four, you two go see. Go track it. See what it is. Careful though, if it's a trap, avoid it. Watch your ass. Number Two, you stay stationary, stay right where you are. I'm staying right here. Three and four, let us know what you find, soon as you find something."

Box said, "Roger," and had to smile to himself. He had never said "Roger" like that before, and the saying of it felt good.

ANNAH TORCH   Jim DeFilippi

The rhythmic beating sound didn't seem to be far off. It led Box and Horn to their right, west, until they came to the edge of Robert's Pond. The waters were still, the men were standing on the path which encircled the pond. The beating sound had stopped.

Horn asked, "What'd you see? See much?"

Box said, "Not much," as he raised his SkyGenius binoculars up to his face, studied the water, then the path, sweeping the lens back and forth.

Horn asked him, "So what'd you see? Let me take a look."

"Wait up." The binoculars had stopped their sweep, were training in on something. Box was saying, "Wait...wait...what is that?"

Horn tried to study the edge of the pond where the binoculars were pointing. It was a spot at the water's edge, just below the high cliff that ran up to higher ground. He leaned his head a bit forward, squinting. He asked Box, "What it that? Something hanging? What is that white? Can you see it? Let me use the glasses. Give me the field glasses, damn it."

Box, pulling the binoculars away as Horn was reaching for them, started grinning. He raised them and looked through the lens again. "Well, Jesus H. Christ, God-damn, God-damn, hot God-damn. You know what it is? Out here? I'm pretty sure it's a tittie-lifter."

&&&

Box and Horn were standing by the edge of the water, below the cliff, where its rock met the path. They were grinning at each other, passing the bra back and forth between them.

Horn was asking, "You want to take a sniff of that, do you, Number Four? Go ahead, give it a snarl."

Box told him, "I will, but you don't gotta call me that. Nobody's around anyway."

From somewhere far above them—it could have been from somewhere at the top of the cliff—a rhythmic clicking sound was getting louder, sounding like a hammer hitting stone.

Both men were looking up but couldn't see anything. The morning sun was in their eyes.

Horn said, "That's not the drum beat we were hearing before. This is something else altogether. I didn't hear it for a time. Now I do. What is that?"

"I don't know. Something's up there."

Silver's voice came in over both their phones: "What is it, what you guys find? Report."

Horn said into his phone, "Oh, nothing much, Boss. Nothing at all. We've just been tracking, that's all."

The two men were grinning at each other. The clinking sound was growing louder, the clicking was getting faster.

Horn slipped his phone into his breast pocket. He was holding the bra up to his face with both hands and letting it rub against his skin. He was moving his face back and forth against the silk and cotton and elastic. "Hmmm."

Box grabbed for the material, but Horn was keeping it high, out of his grip. He grinned broadly, and said to the little man, "Well, I guess now we get to see her tits before she dies, don't we?"

"Could be."

Box kept reaching for the bra. Horn was holding it over his head, so that Box couldn't reach. He called Box a jockey. Then he said, "You think our gal could get herself into a little bitty thing like this? It seems to me..."

He started to say something else, but he heard a wheezing sound coming from somewhere above him, and before he could look up, the black thud of the Boulder entered the back of his head.

&&&

When Ruck got there, Box was hunkered down close to the ground, squatting like a peasant, his elbows on his knee, his hands dangling loose. His Wetherby was lying on the ground beside him. He was crying, sobbing, and making mumbling sounds, not words.

Silver's voice clicked out of the speaker on Ruck's phone. "What the hell is going on? What the hell is going on down there? I demand to know, what the hell is going on?"

Ruck brought his cellphone up to his mouth and kept yelling into it, "Shut the fuck up! Shut the fuck up!" over and over until his voice went horse and then was gone completely. He started coughing.

Ruck went over to the little man and put his hand on Box's shoulder. "What happened?"

Box wiped his nose and mouth with his sleeve and stood up. His eyes weren't focused. He said, "I'm going home." He bent over, picked up his rifle, and stood up. Then he stooped back down and lay the Weatherby back on the ground. "There," he said. "There. I don't care."

Ruck said softly, "I know. I know. Pick up your gun."

Box looked at him. "I don't care who finds out. This was wrong from the start."

Ruck said, "Sure you do. You gotta care. Pick up the gun now, scout. Go ahead."

Box stood zombie-like, staring down at the rifle lying in the dirt.

Ruck's voice got stronger. "I said, pick up the God-damn gun."

Box just stood for a moment. Then he looked at Ruck.

Silver's voice on the phone said. "I'm coming down. Where are you?"

Box started yelling at Ruck, spit coming out with each sentence. "Damn you to God-damn hell, Ruck Ruckhouser, and fuck Johnnie Silver. You done told me what to do for the last God-damn time, and I'm done with it. I come out the other side of the tunnel. You belittling and snorting and laughing and taking my God-damn pants off right there in front of my wife and kids."

Ruck told him to take it easy, that Mr. Silver was coming down. Calm down.

ANNAH TORCH   Jim DeFilippi

Box's screaming went on. "I'm finished with this feeing so small I can't measure up to nothing. Less than a man. A half a man all the time. I got balls, Ruck! I got balls bigger than you do. Bigger than God-damn Horn there, lying under the damn rock, with his balls all crushed into gravy. I'm going home while I still got mine in my sack. Look at Horn's damn leg there, hanging out. What is he, some kind of wicked witch, for Christ sake? He's a man. Was a man. Look a that blackness leaking out of him. That's his blood and pus and his shit, but it ain't mine. No, sir, it sure ain't mine." Box was shaking his head violently. "No, sir, no, sir, no, sir. I'm taking mine and going home, while I still got my own balls to play with. I don't care who the hell finds out about all of this. You and Johnnie Silver can suck me five ways till Friday, and then some, you hear me?"

Ruck kept his voice calm. "Box, pick up your gun."

"You can tell Mr. Silver for me he can have his crooked money back, I don't want it no more. What the hell I need a boat for? Fishing? I just wait till the lake freezes over and use the shanty. I ain't in no damn rush. The fish are still there."

Box turned and started walking away without his rifle, crying and sniveling, sucking in snot and mumbling to himself as he went.

Ruck raised the 300 Blackout and shot off the top of Box's head.

&&&

Ruck was slushing through the high reeds, his boots heavy with water and mud. He had the Ambush 300 Blackout pressed tightly across his chest. He got to the edge of the muck and onto dry earth. He had turned his phone off.

He was studying the land as he moved forward. He paused and tensed when he heard a woman's voice calling out. "Look to your left, Ruck, oh no, I forgot, incapable of that."

He turned his head to look at the trees and bushes to the left of him.

He kept walking. The butt of the Blackout was tucked at his shoulder now, sweeping left and right as he went forward.

ANNAH TORCH — Jim DeFilippi

The woman's voice came gain. He fired off a round in the direction he thought it was coming from. He was about to fire a second round when the woman said, "What mistakes do deer make, Ruck, when you are hunting them? Do you know? They do not look up. They look all around, but they never look up. That is why deer-stands were invented."

The sky had clouded up, the air had gotten colder, but Ruck was sweating through his shirt and onto the edges of his hunting vest.

Ruck kept moving forward, sighting the rifle, with nothing to sight it on. He was aiming it up toward the sky, toward the top of the trees. He didn't see the tripwire at his feet.

The wire broke and released a white birch sapling that sprang forward. A screwdriver lashed with twine to the sapling was driven into Ruck's belly. He stood and looked down at it. He staggered, but didn't fall. He dropped his rifle and coughed and grabbed hold of the screwdriver's handle with both hands.

With no left eye, he didn't see the large arm come over his left shoulder and grab onto his chest. He did see a large right arm and hand coming over his right shoulder. It was holding a knife.

Ruck's last thought was, "That's a good looking knife."

&&&

Chapter Thirty-three

Only once before had Johnnie Silver ever ordered someone to be murdered. The mark that time was an Armenian arms and commodities dealer who had decided to branch out into blackmailing. Aga-something. Aga-*janian*? Aga-*manian*? The guy's bottom line was already impressive, not as impressive as Johnnie's, but good enough. And yet, the guy wasn't satisfied with what he had. So he had turned to blackmail, trying to put a tap on Johnnie, got a hit put on himself instead.

In the movie *Chinatown*, J. J. Gettes asks John Huston, "How much better can you eat?" Johnnie had always wondered about that question. Why wasn't all the money in the world ever enough? He had wondered about that question for the Armenian. He had wondered about that question in himself. He had never been able to find an answer that completely satisfied him. And so, Johnnie was never satisfied.

He had tried everything from reason to intimidation before ordering the greedy rug-head to be offed. One phone call. No, two—one to a middle man with clean hands, one to the interested party. But the thing was, Johnnie had turned to professionals that time, men who knew what they were doing, men who had done this type work before. So everything went as smoothly as fine crystal. A fake car-jacking over in Brooklyn, then "three in the hat," as the boys with Jersey accents would call it. Afterwards: no arrests, no legal or reputational residue, no questions asked.

Which of course was what he should have done this time. How could he have been so stupid? Did he really think Larry and Daryl and Daryl were up to the job on this? He should have just made some calls, forwarded some money, and be done with it.

Or done the job himself. Like with Dede.

He realized the importance of top employees, but Johnnie had always preferred one-on-one solutions to any confrontation. An aggressive takeover, a

ANNAH TORCH   Jim DeFilippi

lawsuit, a business negotiation—if you could clear the decks of all the lawyers and analysts and advisors and board members—you could work with efficiency and effect. Without somebody with a vine-covered MBA whispering in your ear, not allowing you a moment to think.

When he had left the stage years ago, put aside Li'l Gloopy for the world of business, he had vowed to never again take on a partner, and he had stuck to that.

One-on-one, that was his business plan. Of course, it didn't hurt if your opponent were already wounded—a CEO whose company was leaking cash like a sieve, an investor with the SEC chewing at his boot heels, a teenage girl thinking you were some kind of god. A woman stumbling through the Woods with a bullet hole in her.

One gladiator, one opponent. It was a cleaner, clearer battle when it was uncluttered and personal. Singularity. That's why Johnnie preferred *Pai Gow* to *Texas Hold 'em*. It was you against the House, or you versus a single player in a tournament. Instead of battling five different guys, all of them wearing sunglasses and smirks and what they thought passed as poker faces.

Same thing with women. No need for additives. One guy, one gal. Don't come after them using your riches or alcohol or drugs or a mickey of Rohypnol. One man-one woman. It had worked a hundred times for Johnnie. It had worked for him and Dede. It had worked for him and Amanda.

When he had heard all of the death sounds coming from the bottom of the cliff, and later all the screaming and whimpering over the cellphone, he had come out from behind the rotted log and reassessed things. Now it was just him and his Ambush 300 Blackout, working alone, looking for game. That is the way it should have been from the start. Now, that was the way it was. One-on-one.

Look there, a droplet of her blood on a flat gray stone.

He had never considered himself a tracker, never thought about it. Kit Carson, Buffalo Bill. But Johnnie was a quick study. He had taught himself to use passable Slovak just a few days after learning it was actually its own language.

ANNAH TORCH   Jim DeFilippi

He had taught himself to be a securities analyst when he took over as CEO of Burshire-Malcom. He had acquired fifty-one percent of the place when no one was looking, and then dumped it right before it withered and died.

The Wall Street Journal had named him one of the...

"I wish I could throw my voice, Johnnie, make it difficult to locate me. I wish I were more of a ventriloquist." The woman's voice, coming from somewhere out in the reeds by the corner of the pond.

He had to smile. Competition.

"I can just see you lying out there, Annah, flat on your belly. Tucked in among the stinkweed and the skunk cabbage. God, you must smell awful. You're bleeding out, girl. Try not to cough now, hear me? That'd give away your position. Hold in that cough, can you do it? Your voice sounds weak though. You've been hit."

He made his way over to the spot he thought the voice might have come from. He found a matted down patch, something a deer might make when sleeping. From there a few drops of blood led away from the swamp and up a hill. He followed.

"Annah? Annah? You're not talking to me anymore? Are you alive still, hanging on for me?"

He followed the red droplets—which in his mind he was calling blood spores—halfway up the hill and then traversing across to the left. His boots slid down the loose dirt of a gulley and up the other side. The climb made his breathing heavy, so he took a minute to just stand and breathe.

When he had taken in enough air, he called out, "You're getting weaker, girl. You're starting to lose feeling in your fingers, your arms. Careful about blacking out. Once you see those swirls of black clouds coming in from both sides of your vision, you're about to go under. Don't do that. Take a few thick breaths, try to control your breathing. In through the nose, out through the mouth. Teeth a millimeter apart. You can do it, I know you can. Sit and put your head down on your knees a few minutes, if you can, if you can afford that."

ANNAH TORCH   Jim DeFilippi

Johnnie saw a line of matted down fern plants, and he followed it until he saw another blood spore on the ground. Then, another drop on a mat of trail pebbles. Then, another blood spore on an antique, rusted-thin shovel head.

In the places where he couldn't find any blood, he used the lines where the ground cover had been stomped down, in order to follow her trail.

So damn it, maybe he *was* Kit Carson. Maybe he was Buffalo God-damn Bill after all.

The trail was leading up now, to the top of a little natural promontory that held the skeleton of an old forest-fire watch tower. It was the highest point in the area. The trees were bare—it was stick season—so Johnnie thought that he could make out some of the tops of the buildings way off in the Capital District. He felt like God.

He raised up his chin and he called out to the air, "Annah, your voice sounded so tired, so wounded. Now you're not answering at all? Come on, let me know how you're doing."

From the top of the hill, he tracked her back down, through thickening brush and the remains of dead, fallen trees. Johnnie made sure his rifle was aimed at the ground when he stepped over one of the larger fallen trees.

"God damn, Annah, are there any ticks around here? Should I be worried about them? Don't go hiding from me in those fiddleheads over there, you know? You come up with a belly full of ticks. You don't need Rocky Mountain Fever on top of your other problems at this point."

Johnnie brought the Blackout up to his shoulder and fired off a fuselage into the bushes and into the mounds of dirt, the bullets thunking into the dirt and pinging off the rocks.

"That's your biggest threat to life right now. Lead and ticks, flying lead and burrowing ticks. They'll both get under your skin with their poison. Where will it all end, huh? Too bad."

He followed her trail for another half hour. The blood spores were splattered on the leaves of the ground, in the dirt, on fallen tree trunks.

ANNAH TORCH   Jim DeFilippi

"How much blood can one girl lose, Annah? Need a transfusion maybe, do you?"

And twenty minutes after that. "By my calculations, Annah, you must have lost at least a couple pints by now. Are you still feeling woozy? Getting woozier? Drowsy yet? Can I get you some orange juice, like they do at the Red Cross? I wish. All I got here in my canteen is water. I'll take some. Gotta stay hydrated, like they always tell you. You have water?"

Johnnie took a long drink from his canteen and emptied it. He held it upside down with the cap off and shook it a few times. He tossed it on the ground. He looked around, then went behind a tree, unzipped his fly, and began urinating.

"Annah, I'm pissing now. Too much to drink. Can you see me, watch me? I'm letting it leak out behind a tree here, because I remain a gentleman. What tree is this, you know—a maple? An elm? I never learned the names. Ahh, there, that felt good. I'm gonna shake off my dick a little bit, zip up, and then come after you. Won't be long now. Can you hear me? Can you see me? I wish you'd say something. Maybe you should be thinking up some final words to say. For posterity."

Atop the hot gray surface of a large boulder, Johnnie found the biggest blood spore yet, the size of a quarter. He touched it with his fingertip. It was warm.

He called, "Annah, have you pissed your pants yet? Shit? That's what the body does when it's dying. You lose control over all of your functions. The poison from that bullet in you gets into your blood stream. It gets to your heart and lungs. The poison gets to your brain, Annah. That's when you get delirious. Are you delirious yet?"

Taking a few more steps away from the large boulder. "Annah, I'm getting worried. You know what I'm worried about? Suppose I find you, laying there perfectly still among the fiddleheads and the skunk cabbage. Is it 'laying' or 'lying'? And I find you there, and you're already dead when I get to you. So I don't get a chance to put a bullet into your sweet face from closeup range, into your lovely neck. Like my Amanda did, whatever you say happened. That's what

ANNAH TORCH   Jim DeFilippi

all this is about, Annah. Me getting you. Please don't disappoint me, don't die out on me. I've come this far, don't go denying me the pleasure. Could you say something please, just to let me know you're still alive? Are you?"

He waited.

Johnnie followed the blood-trail back down an embankment, where it came to a small, slow moving, muddy stream.

There the trail ended.

Johnnie stood, not really confused, just uncertain as to which direction he should go. Where had she gone from here? If he had brought the bloodhounds, as he had originally considered, then this stream would have meant the girl was wading into the water to throw off the scent.

But that wasn't it. She had deliriously stumbled her way into the water, which was only a few inches deep. But from there, had she gone upstream or down? Or had she just crossed over to the other side? In the water were three flat rocks with their tops sticking out above the surface, almost like they had been placed there for stepping stones. A yard to the left, someone had cut a bunch of saplings and laid them across the surface of the stream. They would be too fragile to step on. What was that for? Johnnie thought bikers maybe had done it. He had bought his Amanda one of those fat-bikes for beach and trail riding.

But what should he do? He could walk along the slowly moving water upstream and see if he could pick up the trail from there. Or maybe go across and head away from the stream, she might have done that. Or go downstream. He looked to his right and could see where the moving water emptied into the pond. He thought he could make out the spot where his ragtag army of geniuses had begun to self-destruct.

Johnnie made his decision. He would head downstream toward the pond. Nothing logical made the choice for him. It was just instinct. Instinct as much as knowledge and logic had gotten him this far in life. It had brought him all the way from being a second-generation stage buffoon with an off-key novelty song on his lips and a dummy on his lap, all the way to the top, being one of the

ANNAH TORCH Jim DeFilippi

most monied and powerful men on the planet. A man whose future outlook was limitless and glorious. A man who...

    ...whose hearing wasn't good. When Johnnie Silver felt a powerful force that he couldn't identify pull the Blackout from his hand, he turned, and she was right there in front of him, a foot away, at full strength, unharmed, telling him, "I feel fine," and burying the metal of her hammer into his forehead.

&&&

ANNAH TORCH   Jim DeFilippi

Chapter Thirty-four

Wyzell asked her, "What happened to your arm there? Did you get yourself clipped?"

"Self-inflicted."

"Oh, so you're a cutter now?"

"Only when necessary. When in need of a couple droplets of blood."

"It's blood you need? What for?"

"Sometimes. But if you mix it with water, a little bit goes a long way."

"I'll keep that in mind the next time I need...some blood."

Annah had fired up her weekly *Hacienda*. She was getting fifteen to twenty rings out of each tug, which showed her to be at ease.

Wyzell was in a flannel shirt, underdressed for the season, but he had rolled both sleeves up to the elbow anyway. Thick gray clouds were splotching the sky. Below them, in the water, the swans were cruising. Nobody was bothering them. Their six cygnets had grown and disappeared.

Annah and Wyzell were sitting on a low mound of dirt. It was lighter in color than the surrounding area, looking freshly dug.

Wyzell turned to look at Annah. He stared at her a while. She wasn't looking back at him. He said, "Baby Johnnie's disappeared."

"Really?"

"Yeah. That guy Ruckhouser too. Along with his two mutts. You know those guys, you knew them."

"Tangentially."

"They're all disappeared for now. Both Baby Johnnie Silver and the three."

"Huh. Wow."

ANNAH TORCH   Jim DeFilippi

Wyzell kept looking at her. "Amanda's begun some plea-bargaining, early stages. With Johnnie gone, seems like Goofy's getting softer, going lighter on her. I heard it'll be insanity temp, looks like. So, what's Johnny Cash call it? She got stripes. Or maybe just some healing time in a playpen."

"Not much then."

"Not much."

Annah said, "She has a lot to heal from."

Wyzell said, "Dede's father tried to kill her. At the hearing. They had to take his plastic pistol away from him."

"Jesus, Weaz, the soup just keeps getting thicker out there."

"Yeah, it does. Unless we try to stop it."

"Not me." Annah took another drag on her cigar, the tip glowed red. "Not me at all."

Wyzell said, "I've been taken off the team, I guess, so..."

"Better that way."

"You still telling me Amanda didn't do it?"

"She's not guilty of murder, Weaz, but whatever she gets, she probably deserves it."

"Yeah? Yeah? I don't...anyway, the cops are out looking for them, Daddy and the mutts."

"Wasn't that a doo-wop group? Really though, so all four are missing? And everything is related? Where is all this stuff happening?"

"Maybe related, maybe not. Well, because, the timing was the same, but Johnnie, he was over in Rome, talking to the Pope."

"Wow. *La Papa.* Hmm."

Wyzell looked out across the water. "The Papal Nuncio insists he was over there at the time."

"Hard to argue with the Pope. That boy is infallible."

"Yeah, I've been told that. And the three mutts were out in Las Vegas."

"Well, I wish them all the best of luck. Maybe they will pop up. You cannot beat those Italian police forces."

"Really?"

"Vegas too. They get their own television shows and everything."

Wyzell was looking at her again. "Well, I just wonder if the responsible party at least achieved some proper disposal."

"Of course. Of course. I am sure they did."

"How do these perpetrators do it, you have to wonder sometimes."

Now Annah was turning to him. "After you set the hook, Counselor, a couple of hooks—a call-out, some blood droplets, some random piece of underwear—then the rest is pretty easy to facilitate."

Wyzell nodded. "Yeah, I'm sure it is. I'm sure it's easy if you don't mind...you know."

"Killing someone."

"Well, yeah, there's that."

"Weaz, we both understand it. Nothing to be proud about. Or ashamed."

Annah took another tug at the cigar, blew out a mouthful of smoke rings. She watched as they disappeared into the air. Above the pond. "Living here, all I ever have to kill is black flies."

Wyzell started looking around. "Didn't there used to be a rock here?"

Annah didn't answer him.

After a few minutes, he said to her, "Annah, I just got a new client."

"No."

"Three dead women, all of them naked, their bodies painted red—a bright red."

ANNAH TORCH   Jim DeFilippi

"No."

"They found the paint can in the guy's garage."

"No."

Wyzell waited a few beats. "How are you fixed for smokes?"

                             &&&

Watch for:

ANNAH TORCH II: VERMILLION WAYS TO DIE.

ANNAH TORCH Jim DeFilippi

Other books by Jim DeFilippi:

The Stupid People's History of America (as Lune d'Plumhouse)
Pals, Punks, and Pagans
The Juice Kittens
To Suffer the Waltz: a stage play
Blood Sugar
Cop, Cop, Lawyer
Duck Alley
Jesus Burned
Blight New York 1955
The Family Farm
The Mules of Monte Cassino
The Mules of Monte Cassino (Stage Version)
Pulp Poetry
Buf
Tuf
Enuf
The Big Big Lulu Book
Fog 50
Jive Palace
Speedo
Murka: A Variant History of the United States
Descape
Of Scarecrows and Saints: a screenplay
Weak Wings and Other Stories
Hitler's New Tenants
Jim Just Went into the Kitchen
ERX: Eat Right And Exercise
Everyday Malfeasance
More Malfeasance
Limerick Malfeasance
Stuck (story by)
Jaime-Lynn's Book (Editor)

ANNAH TORCH   Jim DeFilippi

Praise for the books of Jim DeFilippi

"BLOOD SUGAR IS A SUSPENSEFUL, OFTEN HILARIOUS THRILLER." (Newsday)

"This wacky tale finger-pops its way to a perfect ending." (Publishers Weekly)

"A good one. DeFilippi serves up suburban procedures with style." (Kirkus Reviews)

"Jim DeFilippi's story of a boyhood friendship become a lifelong bond, ending in one's death and the other's death-in-life, for me is A Separate Peace in blue collar—a wonderful book." —George V. Higgins (The Friends of Eddie Coyle)

"A damn good one. The novel's emotional range is from the grimly horrific to the absurdly comic. All of it works. There's an important new voice in the field." (Mystery Scene Magazine)

"DeFilippi carefully mixes unconventional characters, bizarre plotting, and off-the-wall language...jaunty tone and unexpected twists." (Library Journal)

"Jim DeFilippi's BLOOD SUGAR is, happily, one of the few mysteries I've read that truly surprised me. And not just once. We're quickly drawn into DeFilippi's bizarre world, heavily loaded with snappy, tough dialogue. Read this book." (The Vermont Times)

"Following in the footsteps of his greatest influences, George V. Higgins and Elmore Leonard, DeFilippi has found a niche in the world of detective thrillers." (The Catholic Tribune)

"This book has a distinct quality. It works, it hooks you." (Burlington Free Press)

"BLOOD SUGAR has a great cast, fine dialogue and a plot that strikes hardest at the least likely characters—raising the stakes higher than most mystery novels would dare. DeFilippi has trashed the formula for first mystery novels." (The Valley News)

"In the gritty, street-wise tradition of Raymond Chandler, Dashiell Hammett, and Elmore Leonard, Jim DeFilippi has written a terrifically entertaining novel....Joe LaLuna is one of the best fictional detectives I've encountered in a lifetime of reading and relishing mystery novels." (Howard Frank Mosher, author of STRANGER IN THE KINGDOM)

"The story is excellently paced and imaginatively told, in a series of flashbacks, imaginary scenarios and straightforward narrative sections, all enlivened with vernacular dialogue. DeFilippi's novel is as much about emotions as it is about actions, and it delivers a jolt of a surprise ending that entirely fits the plot's milieu." —Publishers Weekly

ANNAH TORCH   Jim DeFilippi

"DeFilippi creates a surprisingly fresh novel, a meditation on communication and on silence... full of texture. The Long Island setting is evoked vividly but with admirable restraint. A sleeper that could find its natural audience among fiction devotees." —Booklist

"Recalling the happy summertime of youth in the '50s, summons Coke bottles, friendly drunks, fussy moms, baseball games on the radio and harmless pranks." —Kirkus Reviews

"A terrific tale... a superbly crafted novel." — Cleveland Plain Dealer

"Duck Alley is the moving, funny, ultimately tragic story of two buddies growing up in the 1950s. The plotting is ingenious and makes this book a page-turner, but it's the dead-on portrait of childhood that really sets this novel apart. DeFilippi captures the combination of casual cruelty, peer pressure, intense loyalty and vivid imagination of childhood. His bits of dialogue are inspired. Readers will (be) swept up in the narrative flow and the wonderful character depictions."— Philadelphia Enquirer

"A gripping tale of friendship and fate. It left me thinking for days."—Vermont Times

"Duck Alley is rich with scenes of Jones Beach, high-school culture and, of course, the old neighborhood...stitched together with threads of discrete, peppery dialogue"— Newsday

"Colorful and often hilarious anecdotes...are expertly interlaced with current events to reveal the complexity of a friendship. The unexpected aspects of the novel are a few crucial and heartbreaking plot twists, as well as the skill with which DeFilippi wrings out profound insight." —Austin Chronicle

"Inspired Long Island dialogue, often laced with humor. The dialogue is right on, and so are DeFilippi's descriptions of youthful lunacy. Duck Alley is a meditation on loyalty and betrayal. The plot reigns in the end, however, when DeFilippi delivers a more-than-satisfying twist." —The Burlington Free Press

"The book is a solid tale of friendship, lies, and loyalty without the stereotypical, sugar-coated, happily-ever-after ending." — Inside pulse.com

"Jim DeFilippi is an odds-on, smart money choice to be among the best crime novelists." -- The League of Vermont Writers

"The book contains a real sense of the scrappy, back-lot existence of these 1950s kids. The episodes have the authentic patina of cherished memory. DeFilippi's creation is strong enough to be genuinely unsettling, and to make readers grateful for the glimmer of redemption offered in its final pages." — Seven Days

"DeFilippi captures the comfort and intimacy of a lifelong friendship. Duck Alley is a page turner. With great conversation, timing, and references to the times, it is well worth the trip. A great job."-- Winooski (VT) Eagle

ANNAH TORCH — Jim DeFilippi

"A book that grabs readers quickly and doesn't let go. The writing is precise and pithy and rings true." – LIBRARY JOURNAL

"As I closed Duck Alley I breathed, 'Whoah. That was good.'" – THE BARRE-MONTPELIER TIMES ARGUS

"A male story, told from a male's point of view, yet that point of view is so sensitive it becomes universal." – CYBER OASIS

"With sensitivity and depth…every bit a thriller as (much) as a tale of innocence, trust, and loyalty. The book is thoughtful and thought-provoking." -- COLCHESTER (VT) NEWS MAGAZINE

"A must-read!" –THE OPTIMIST

"Emotional. Intense. Nostalgic. Real. The story is filled with emotion, action and has a great punch in the end, will take you at a great pace and is deftly told. An irrefutable good read!" — ABOUT.COM

Nominated for THE HAMMETT PRIZE.

"They can all go scratch, it'll always be Duck Alley."– MARY HICKS, lifelong resident.

"The tension mounts quickly, and the prose is rare, sometimes lyrical and sometimes brutally concrete." –SEVEN DAYS

"An absolute laugh-a-minute riot."---WISTFULSKIMMIE'S BOOK REVIEWS

"A Fog of Many Colors" high-lighted in "The Best American Mystery Stories," edited by SUE GRAFTON AND OTTO PENZLER

"Great read, great history. DeFilippi's book is written in a scathing, conversational style. Historically accurate…If you are looking for a kind of Catch-22 of a book about one campaign, a book to convince you of the misery and venality of war and the way it is fought, this is it." MARK PENDERGRASS (FOR GOD, COUNTRY AND COCA-COLA)

"DeFilippi is an author who can tackle any subject and can turn it into a psycho-social critique or a descriptive saga of human frailties. BUF was great. I'm humbled."---ALEX CANTON of BOOK JUNKIES

ANNAH TORCH   Jim DeFilippi

Made in the USA
Las Vegas, NV
17 July 2021